Silent Heart
The Earl Who Stole Her Thoughts

I0835443

KAELIS KNIGHT

PUBLISHED BY EVERSPELL MEDIA

www.kaelisknight.com

Publisher's Note: This is a work of fiction. Names, characters, places, and incidents are a product of the author's imagination. Locales and public names are sometimes used for atmospheric purposes. Any resemblance to actual people, living or dead, or to businesses, companies, events, institutions, or locales is completely coincidental.

Cover Design & Art: Everspell Media
ISBN: 978-1-7644694-3-2 (Paperback)
ISBN: 978-1-7644694-2-5 (Ebook)
First Edition: May 2026
9 8 7 6 5 4 3 2
Printed in the country of purchase

Content Note:

Silent Heart is a full-length gaslamp fantasy romance intended for adult audiences. It contains mature themes, including:

- Explicit sexual content
- Discrimination and classism (Fantasy racism against magic users)
- Human trafficking and forced servitude
- Captivity and imprisonment
- Physical violence, including gun violence
- Threats of sexual violence (implied, not depicted)
- Kidnapping and abduction
- Death of a villain (on page)
- References to past loss of family members, including a child
- Grief and trauma

Please note:

Silent Heart is the first full-length novel in the *Tales of Elthera* series. While the central romance concludes with a happily ever after, certain plot threads are left open for future books in the series.

For a detailed list of specific content warnings, please visit:
kaelisknight.com/content-warnings

TABLE OF CONTENTS

THE KINGDOM OF ELTHERA
NORTHERN REACHES
GREYPORT
N
W
E
S
WIDE SEA
WESTERN
PLANES
EASTERN
TERRITORIES
CAPITAL
RESIDENCE
OF THE KING
SERPENT'S PASSAGE
THE
FREE
ISLES

Chapter One

The air was unbearable. Cigar smoke and expensive perfume clogged the underground hall, thick enough to taste. Alexander loosened his cravat and forced himself to breathe as another unfortunate soul was led onto the makeshift stage.

Around him, Greyport's elite lounged in velvet chairs, sipping brandy between bids. They might have been at the opera, if not for the iron shackles on the merchandise.

"Twenty gold sovereigns for the storm caller," someone called out, voice flat with disinterest.

"Thirty," countered another.

A muscle jumped in Alexander's cheek. His stomach turned at seeing these men and women paraded across the stage like prize cattle.

His fingers found the scar on his right hand, pressing into the ridged flesh until the ache grounded him.

He had never imagined he would end up in a place like this. The auctions existed in a grey space between legal and not, tolerated by authorities who looked the other way for the right price. Partaking in the very thing he hated most—buying and selling people as though they were livestock—was the last thing he wanted to do. But sometimes getting what you wanted meant walking straight through hell.

And hell should feel familiar by now. He had spent the last eight years in some version of it.

Beside him, Damien slouched in his chair, his golden hair bright under the lamplight, collar open just enough to suggest he already had too much to drink. He looked every inch the dissolute viscount people believed him to be.

"Remind me why we're subjecting ourselves to this delightful evening?" Damien murmured, raising his glass to his lips without drinking.

"You know why."

"Ah yes. Your tireless crusade against the Marquis of Darkwater." Damien's voice dropped. "Though I confess I'm more curious about your other recent adventures. Rumours are rife since you managed to delay the fire starter's execution."

"Let it grind."

"Easy for you to say. You're not the one deflecting questions about why the Earl of Whitmore personally intervened for a woman who burned down half the harbour." Damien swirled his untouched brandy. "The ladies at tea have been relentless. I've had to be charming for hours, Alexander. Hours."

"As if you mind."

"I mind the blisters on my smile." But then Damien's expression sobered. "Seriously though. What are you going to do about that girl?"

Alexander did not look at his friend. On stage, a young stone shaper was being led away, sold to a merchant who would likely work him to death in the quarries. "I am going to talk to her. She was employed at the shelter David ran. She might know what happened to him. Or to the other magic users who have gone missing."

“And how exactly do you plan to manage that? They're not likely to grant you an audience with a convicted murderer awaiting execution. Not even the Under-Secretary of State can walk into a prison and demand a conversation.”

"I know a man."

Damien's eyebrow arched. "This man wouldn't happen to be a certain seafaring gentleman of questionable legality?"

"He is not a pirate." Alexander watched as a tide weaver was led onto the stage, a hollow-eyed woman with a vacant stare. "Just someone with... unorthodox methods."

"Unorthodox." Damien snorted. "That's one word for it." He swirled the amber liquid in his glass, watching the bidding begin on the tide weaver. "And assuming your unorthodox friend comes through, what then? Even if this fire starter knows something, it doesn't prove Delacroix is behind all of these disappearances."

"I know it is him. I can feel it in my bones. Wherever magic users vanish, his name surfaces. That is enough to warrant attention."

Damien turned to look at his friend. "Is that the real reason? Or is your judgement clouded by that old vendetta of yours?" His voice dropped lower. "Because of Marianne?"

Alexander's voice went flat. "Don't."

"I'm just saying..."

"I said don't."

The auctioneer, a thin man with yellowed teeth, banged his gavel with theatrical relish. "Sold! Now, esteemed guests, we've saved the finest for last. A true rarity. A telepath of extraordinary power."

The crowd stirred. Whispers hissed through the hall. Mentalists were uncommon among magic users, most of whom were born elementalists.

Alexander straightened.

"Bring her out," the auctioneer commanded.

The side door opened.

She walked onto the stage with her spine straight and her chin lifted, displaying the shackles as if they were jewellery. Dark hair fell past slender shoulders, warm with copper under the lamplight. Her skin was pale, her cheeks a bit too hollow, but it was her eyes that stood out most.

They were violet-blue, luminous with that soft glow common to all magic users, and despite the iron that should have dulled them, they flared bright as they moved across the room, pausing on each face.

The crowd buzzed.

"Is that the de Clare girl?"

"Heard her parents were executed. They were hiding her."

"Look at those eyes. They say she can see straight into your head..."

The auctioneer's voice rose above the murmurs. "Lady Isabel de Clare, aged twenty-four, descended from nobility rumoured to have carried magic for generations. Her abilities include surface thought reading and truth detection, which makes her a valuable asset for negotiations, interrogations, and ensuring the honesty of one's household staff and business partners."

A murmur of interest rippled through the room.

Truth detection. Alexander went still. Someone who could tell him whether Delacroix's associates were lying. Who could help him find the evidence he had been hunting for eight years.

"Bidding starts at one hundred gold sovereigns."

"Two hundred," came an immediate response.

Alexander turned, glancing over his shoulder toward the voice. There, in the shadows of a private box in the far corner, sat Delacroix. The Marquis of Darkwater leaned forward, silver-streaked hair gleaming, pale blue eyes fixed on the stage. Alexander looked away quickly, angling his body so his face remained hidden.

"Three hundred," another bidder called.

"Five hundred." Delacroix did not even glance at the competition.

On stage, Isabel's eyes flared vivid violet, and Alexander saw the exact moment her gaze landed on the marquis.

"Six hundred," someone ventured.

"One thousand." Delacroix's tone carried warning.

The room fell silent. A thousand gold sovereigns was more than most estates earned in a year.

Damien leaned close. "Alex. That look on his face..."

"I saw it."

"What does Delacroix need a telepath for that badly?"

Alexander did not answer. His mind was racing through possibilities.

I could use her.

He shoved the thought down with disgust. He was not like the men in this room, bidding on human beings as if they were objects.

But you could save her, whispered the voice in his head. *Save her from Delacroix.*

Whatever fate awaited her in the marquis's hands, it would not be a kind one, of that he was sure.

"One thousand going once," the auctioneer called.

Alexander made his decision.

He nudged Damien. "Bid."

His friend turned, eyebrows shooting up. "Alexander..."

"Delacroix cannot know I am here. Bid as my proxy. Now."

"Going twice..."

Damien studied his friend's face for a heartbeat, and whatever he saw there made him swallow his objections. He rose languidly to his feet, every movement calculated to draw attention, and pitched his voice to carry: "Fifteen hundred gold sovereigns."

The crowd turned as one.

Alexander kept his head down, watching from the corner of his eye as Delacroix's attention snapped to Damien. Even from this angle, he could see the marquis's hands tighten on the armrests of his chair.

"Two thousand," he bit out.

Damien glanced at Alexander, who gave the slightest nod.

"Twenty-five hundred." Damien examined his fingernails as if the whole affair rather bored him.

Alexander risked another glance over his shoulder. Delacroix sat motionless.

"Three thousand," he said, his voice dangerously low.

"Four thousand." Damien didn't look up.

"Five thousand!" The marquis could no longer hide the anger in his voice.

"Six thousand," Damien announced, finally looking up to meet Delacroix's gaze with a slight, mocking smile.

Around them, the crowd held its breath. This had become more than an auction. It was a battle of wills, with a young woman's fate hanging in the balance.

"Seven..." Delacroix began.

"Ten thousand gold sovereigns," Damien cut him off, his voice ringing with finality. "Unless the good marquis would like to explain to everyone here why one telepath is worth making such a spectacle of himself?"

The threat was subtle but clear. Too much desperation raised questions. Questions a man with secrets could not afford.

Silence stretched. Then, through clenched teeth: "I withdraw."

The gavel cracked down. "Sold! To Lord Daventry for the sum of ten thousand gold sovereigns!"

Delacroix rose from his seat and strode toward the exit, his silver-tipped cane ringing sharply against the floor with each step. Before he disappeared through the doorway he cast one final glance back at Isabel.

The crowd erupted in excited chatter. Alexander rose, keeping his expression calm as he moved toward the payment office, Damien at his side.

"That was rather unexpected," the viscount murmured as they entered a private chamber where clerks waited with contracts.

"It was necessary." Alexander pulled out his bank draft. "You saw how he looked at her."

"Like she was the answer to all his dark prayers?" Damien accepted a glass of brandy from a clerk and drained half of it in one swallow. "Yes, I noticed. The question is why. And more importantly, what have you gotten us into?"

Alexander signed his name with precise strokes. "That is what we need to find out."

The door opened, and Isabel was led in.

Up close, she was even more striking, though the pallor of her skin and the shadows under her eyes spoke of weeks if not months without proper rest. Her dress, once fine silk, had been worn nearly transparent in places, mended but still showing her reduced circumstances. Yet she stood straight, meeting their gaze directly.

Her eyes fixed on Damien. "Lord Daventry." She spoke with a northern accent, her voice flat and controlled. "I suppose you're my new owner."

"Actually..." Damien began.

"Your papers, my lord." The clerk interrupted, handing over the documentation. "She's yours to command, as decreed by the Protection of the Realm Act. The binding is legal and complete."

Alexander stepped forward, taking the papers from the clerk. Isabel's gaze snapped to him, her brow creasing.

"Lord Daventry was acting as my proxy," he explained. "I am Alexander Kensington, Earl of Whitmore. You will be coming with me."

Her entire body went rigid as those remarkable eyes lit up and searched his face.

Then she blinked and the glow in them faded, replaced by a surprised look.

"Lord Kensington." She measured him with her gaze. "And what use does the Earl of Whitmore have for a telepath?"

"That remains to be seen." He turned to the clerk. "Have her unchained and her belongings sent to Whitmore Hall immediately."

The man laughed as he removed the shackles. "Belongings? She came with nothing but the clothes on her back—"

Alexander cut him off. "Then we are done here." He looked at Isabel. "Come. We are leaving."

She did not move. "Where?" she asked, rubbing her wrists where the iron had left red marks on her skin.

"To my townhouse. You will be safe there."

"Safe," she huffed. "No one is ever safe, my lord."

Before he could respond, she stepped past him toward the door, her wavy hair bouncing softly as she walked.

Alexander caught Damien's raised eyebrow and ignored it, following her out.

Isabel breathed in the cold night air. It tasted of coal smoke and the earthy decay of fallen leaves, a welcome change after the suffocating warmth of the auction hall. She let it clear her head. She was going to need a clear head.

The Earl of Whitmore walked beside her, his hand hovering near her elbow without quite touching.

As if she was going to flee.

Though she had to confess she had considered it. The thought had crossed her mind the moment they had stepped outside. But she was exhausted from weeks of poor food and little sleep, her wrists still raw from the shackles, and she had nowhere to go. The auction house had handed this man her papers.

For the moment, she was his.

A black carriage waited at the curb, and a liveried driver jumped off the seat to open the door for them at their approach. Lord Daventry climbed in first, settling onto the velvet bench with the fluid grace of a cat. The earl gestured for Isabel to follow.

She hesitated.

"It is warmer inside," he said. "And you are considerably less likely to attract attention."

Isabel climbed into the carriage without a word. She chose the seat across from Lord Daventry, pressing herself into the corner, putting as much distance between herself and the men as the confined space allowed.

The earl followed, taking the seat beside his companion, and the door closed behind him. The carriage lurched into motion.

No one spoke.

Isabel used the silence to study them. Lord Daventry leaned back against the cushions, one ankle crossed over his knee, looking for all the world like a man without a care. She let her mind brush against his, feather-light, and caught the surface of his thoughts. Something about a card game he had lost last week. And a woman's name, Clara, accompanied by a spark of affection. Nothing useful.

And Lord Kensington...

Maybe it had just been the iron that had prevented her from perceiving him earlier. She reached for his thoughts again, gently, like one might test a door to see if it was locked.

Nothing.

None of the constant noise in people's heads that had plagued her since childhood. Not even the muffled resistance she encountered when someone was deliberately guarding their mind. Just... silence. As if there was nothing there at all.

It unsettled her more than she wanted to admit.

The Marquis of Darkwater had been equally strange, though in a different way. Despite the shackles preventing her from reading his mind fully, she had found fragments. Splinters of thought, sharp and jagged, like trying to see through broken glass. Whatever was in his head, it was corrupted somehow.

Lord Kensington's mind wasn't fractured or hidden. It simply wasn't there. Or rather, she couldn't sense it.

In twenty-four years, she had never encountered anyone like him.

"Far be it from me to interrupt, but you've been gazing upon my dear friend for a particularly extended amount of time now." Lord Daventry's voice cut through her thoughts, warm with amusement. "Not that I blame you. He does have a certain brooding appeal, if one enjoys that sort of thing."

"Damien." The earl's voice was sharp.

"What? I'm merely making conversation. The silence was becoming rather oppressive." He turned to Isabel, flashing a smile that probably worked wonders on other women. "You'll have to forgive my friend. He's not terribly skilled at small talk. Excellent at scowling, though. A truly masterful scowler, our Alexander."

Isabel said nothing.

Lord Daventry's smile faltered, just slightly. " Hard to please."

"She is not here to be entertained." The earl turned, his grey eyes meeting Isabel's. "I imagine you have questions."

"Several," she said flatly.

"Then ask them."

She held his gaze. "What do you want from me?"

"Your help."

"Can one be any more vague?" she asked before she could stop herself. Suddenly realising she had been out of line, she cleared her throat and continued in a more measured tone. "What manner of help, my lord?"

If he was offended by her impertinence, he was too much of a gentleman to let it show. "I am investigating someone," he said. "A man I believe to be involved in criminal activities. Your abilities could help me find the evidence I need to bring him to justice."

"Criminal activities?" Isabel let the words hang.

"I would not have bought you otherwise."

"Bought me", she said bitterly. "Yes. You did do that, didn't you."

Lord Daventry shifted uncomfortably. "To be fair, the alternative was considerably worse. The marquis—"

"Is that supposed to make me feel better?" Isabel cut him off. "That my new owner is somehow preferable to the other man who wanted to own me?"

Silence. Lord Daventry's eyebrows rose toward his hairline, and beside him, the earl's expression went blank. The two men exchanged a glance that spoke volumes.

Isabel caught herself too late. She had cut off a viscount mid-sentence, spoken to her betters as though she were still their equal. Twelve years of servitude, and still she could not bend her tongue to the shape of submission. She had been raised in a great house, taught to carry herself as a lady. That girl was supposed to be dead, buried beneath years of bowing and silence. Yet she kept resurfacing at the worst possible moments.

"Forgive me, my lords," she murmured, dropping her gaze. "I spoke out of turn."

The carriage rattled over cobblestones. Outside, the streets of Greyport slid past, gaslight and shadow chasing each other across the glass.

She had been so close.

Months of careful planning, of biding her time in Lord Bentley's household, waiting for the right moment. She had convinced the old merchant to bring her along on his next trading voyage to the capital, suggesting that a telepath might prove useful when negotiating prices. From there, she could have slipped away in the crowds. Found a ship bound for the Free Isles, where magic users were said to live free, without masters.

And then the creditors had come. Lord Bentley's debts had finally caught up with him, and the magistrates had seized everything to settle his accounts: His ships, his household, along with the servants.

And her.

All her careful plans had been shattered in a single afternoon. And now here she was. Back to nothing, with no resources and no way out except through the whims of yet another master.

Unless she could find another way.

Her eyes moved to Lord Kensington again. If she couldn't read his thoughts, she would have to read his actions. His words.

"You said I'd be safe," she said quietly.

He nodded once. "You will be."

"Safe from whom? From the marquis? From the zealots?" She paused. "From you?"

His jaw tightened. "I am not going to harm you."

"I've heard that before."

"I imagine you have." He met her gaze directly. "I am not asking you to trust me. I am asking you to consider my offer."

"And what exactly are you offering?"

"A chance," he said. "Help me, and when this is done, I will grant you your freedom. Legal papers. The means to start a new life. One that does not involve being bought and sold."

Freedom.

Her breath caught at the word. Hope stirred, but she crushed it down before it could take root. She had been promised freedom before. Had learned exactly how much such promises were worth.

And yet, if there was the slightest chance that he meant what he said...

She would hear him out. That much cost her nothing. And perhaps this path would prove easier than the desperate measures she had been weighing.

"And what happens if I refuse?" she asked, her gaze steady on his.

He didn't answer, and as the silence stretched, Lord Daventry looked between them, suddenly watchful.

"That's what I thought," Isabel said softly.

The carriage slowed as it turned through a set of tall iron gates and rolled up a private drive. Through the window, Isabel watched a grand residence emerge from the darkness. For a townhouse, it looked remarkably like a mansion. It was set well back from the road, the windows glowing warm with lamplight. Whitmore Hall, she presumed. Her new home.

Her new prison.

The door swung open and Lord Kensington climbed out first, then turned to offer her his hand. Isabel ignored it. She stepped down on her own, her worn shoes finding the cobblestones without assistance.

Golden light spilled across the front steps as the townhouse door opened in front of them. A man stood at the entrance, silver-haired and impeccably dressed, his posture perfectly straight.

"My lord," he greeted them with formal politeness. If he found anything unusual about his master arriving home at such late hour accompanied by an unfamiliar woman, his expression betrayed none of it. "Welcome home."

"Hartley." Lord Whitmore nodded. "This is Miss de Clare. She will be staying with us. Have a guest chamber prepared, and in the meantime show her to the dining room. I expect she has not eaten yet. Whatever remains from tonight's supper should be set out for us. I will be joining her shortly."

"At once, my lord." The butler's gaze moved to Isabel, assessing her with perfect courtesy. "Miss de Clare. If you will follow me."

Isabel cast a glance back at the earl. He stood at the base of the steps, Lord Daventry beside him, watching her with an expression she couldn't read and a mind she couldn't touch.

Then she turned and followed the butler inside.

The entrance hall was exactly what she had expected. A flawless expanse of marble flooring and walls of dark-stained wood, watched over by the gilded portraits of stern-faced ancestors. It spoke of generations of wealth and power, condensed into one imposing display.

Hartley led her through the hall and into a dining room dominated by a long mahogany table, polished to a mirror shine. Candlelight danced across the crystal glasses and polished silverware laid out before each seat.

"If you would care to take a seat, miss." The butler pulled out a chair for her near the head of the table. "I shall have something brought out immediately."

Isabel sank into the chair. It was more comfortable than anything she had sat on in years. Or lain upon, for that matter.

Hartley withdrew, and Isabel was alone.

She looked around the room, taking in the fine china displayed in glass cabinets, the heavy velvet drapes framing the large windows, and the warm hearth beneath the portrait of a man and woman who Isabel presumed to be the earl's parents. The woman had the same intense grey eyes.

How bizarre this all was. Three hours ago she had been in a cage beneath an auction house, waiting to be sold. Now she sat at a lord's dining table, being served his leftover supper as if she were an esteemed guest.

She would not trust him. She could not, especially when her powers failed her so completely in his presence. If this man had secrets—and she was certain he did—she would have to pry them loose the old-fashioned way. With observation and wit.

And yet, despite her deep-seated distrust of nobility, or people in general for that matter, she had to admit that the earl seemed different from the masters she had served before. He had neither threatened her, nor regarded her with the revulsion she had grown accustomed to from others. Quite the opposite. He had offered her shelter, and he spoke to her in a polite manner.

Whether that was a good or a bad thing, she had yet to determine. In any case, she would have to play along, at least for now. She would listen to what he had to say and let him believe she was considering his offer.

But she would not forget what she was to him. What he was to her.

And she would not stop looking for a way out.

The door opened. A maid entered carrying a tray laden with cold meats, bread, cheese, and a steaming bowl of soup.

Isabel's stomach clenched with a hunger she had been trying to ignore for too long.

The maid set the food before her with a small curtsy. "Will there be anything else, miss?"

"No. Thank you."

The maid withdrew.

Isabel hesitated for just a moment, but her empty stomach was too much to ignore. She grabbed the spoon and began to eat.

Damien made straight for the sideboard, reaching for the crystal decanter before Alexander had even closed the door of the drawing room behind them.

"Well." He pulled the stopper free and poured a generous measure of brandy. "What in God's name have you inflicted upon us, my friend?"

Alexander crossed the room in three strides, plucked the glass from Damien's hand, and drained it in one swallow. The liquor burned a path down his throat, sharp and welcome.

The viscount raised a brow.

"Pour another."

"I intend to." Damien reached for a second glass, measuring out a pour for each of them. "You realise she's going to be an absolute nightmare to manage. That woman has a tongue like a blade and a temper to match."

Alexander reached for his glass and raised it to his lips, only taking a sip this time. "I noticed."

"Did you also notice she's rather striking? Those eyes alone could stop a man's heart at twenty paces." Damien settled into one of the leather armchairs, stretching his legs toward the fire. "Though I suspect she'd prefer to stop it with a well-aimed insult."

"Her appearance is irrelevant."

"Irrelevant as it may be, it is also a fact." Damien studied the amber liquid in his glass. "How exactly do you plan to convince her to help you? She doesn't strike me as the cooperative sort. More the sort to set your curtains ablaze while you sleep, if she had the gift for it."

Alexander moved to the window, staring out at the darkened street. A light rain had begun to fall, speckling the glass. "I will find a way."

"If you say so." He raised his glass and took a long swallow before he continued. "But she did raise a rather pointed question in the carriage. One you failed to answer. What happens if she refuses?"

Alexander pressed his lips together.

"Do you actually have a plan here?" Damien went on. "Because this is not like you, Alex. Employing a slave—"

"She is not a slave." The earl turned sharply from the window to face his friend. "Magic users have not been slaves for twelve years. The Reform Act—"

"The Reform Act." Damien laughed, though there was no humour in it. "A mere formality. In the eyes of the people, they're still property. And you know it."

Alexander could not argue that. He took a long drink of his brandy instead, letting the silence stretch.

"So what are you going to do?" Damien insisted. "Keep her forever if she doesn't agree to help? That's not who you are."

"Of course I am not going to keep her." Alexander crossed to the chair beside his friend and dropped into it, his shoulders heavy against the leather. "But I cannot simply let her go either. Not yet."

"Why not?"

"You saw how Delacroix looked at her." The memory of it tightened his chest. "Whatever he wanted her for, he wanted it badly. This is not over. If I release her now, she will be alone. Unprotected. Easy prey for a man with resources and no scruples about using them."

"How noble of you." Damien tipped back the last of his brandy. "And the fact that she also happens to be a remarkably useful asset in your quest against Delacroix had nothing whatsoever to do with your decision to obtain this most unusual acquisition?"

Alexander shot his friend a sharp look.

Damien raised his hands in mock surrender. "I shall say no more." He rose from his chair, setting his empty glass on the side table. "I'm certain you have much to discuss with your new houseguest. I'll leave you to it."

He was halfway to the door when Alexander straightened in his chair. "Damien."

The viscount paused, glancing back.

"Be here tomorrow evening. Vera arrives in the afternoon. We will dine together."

Damien's face arranged itself into an expression of exaggerated dismay. "Must I? Your little sister is hardly my most devoted admirer. Last time we dined together she called me a peacock with pretensions."

"She was not wrong."

"She also threw a bread roll at my head."

"You deserved it." Alexander allowed himself the ghost of a smile. "I insist. There is much to discuss, and I would rather not repeat myself."

Damien sighed with theatrical resignation. "As you wish. For you, I shall endure Lady Vera's withering contempt. But if she throws anything sharper than bread, I'm holding you personally accountable." He sketched an elaborate bow. "Until tomorrow, then."

The door closed behind him, and the room fell silent, save for the fire crackling in the hearth and the rain tapping against the windows.

Alexander sat motionless, staring into his glass.

How in God's name was he going to convince that stubborn woman to help him?

He drained the last of his brandy and set the glass aside. Then he rose to his feet. He had a guest waiting.

Isabel set down her spoon and reached for the linen napkin, dabbing at her lips with as much dignity as she could muster. The bowl before her was empty. So was the plate of cold meats and cheese. She had eaten everything, devoured it, really, with a haste that bordered on embarrassing. She couldn't remember the last time she had eaten so well, or so much for that matter.

The door handle turned.

Isabel hastily swallowed the last crumb of bread and rose to her feet as the earl entered.

He crossed the room with quick strides. "Please, sit." He reached her before she could step away from the table, taking the back of her chair and holding it steady to help her settle back down.

As she folded her napkin in her lap, his gaze moved from her face to the clean porcelain dishes and back again. If he noticed how thoroughly she had cleaned her plate, he had the manners not to comment on it.

"I trust everything was to your satisfaction?"

"It was most welcome," Isabel said. "Thank you for your hospitality."

He gave a sharp nod. "I apologise for keeping you waiting." Moving to the head of the table, he took the chair nearest hers. "I had to see Lord Daventry out."

Without waiting for a response, he took his seat. A moment later, the maid appeared with a second platter, setting it before him with a curtsy before retreating. The earl picked up his fork.

"I hope you do not mind the company. I have not had the chance to dine yet, either."

Isabel said nothing. She watched him as he worked through his meal, his movements efficient and unhurried.

Once more, she reached for his mind, but nothing. Just a vast emptiness where his thoughts should be.

She had spent her entire life surrounded by noise. The constant hum of other people's thoughts, their fears and their desires bleeding into her consciousness whether she wished it or not. She had learned to build walls, to reduce the chaos to a manageable level. But she had never had the experience of sitting across from someone whose presence required no effort at all. Someone whose company was almost peaceful.

Yet this peace came at a price. With her previous masters, she had always known what was coming. Had felt their intentions before they spoke them, had been able to brace herself for their cruelty and their demands. But this man gave her nothing. No insight. No warning.

She was absolutely blind, and as much as she welcomed the mental silence, she hated not knowing what he was thinking.

The earl set down his fork and took up his wine, taking a long drink. When he set the glass down, his grey eyes met hers.

"I can see you have something on your mind," he said, picking up his napkin to blot the corner of his mouth. "Please, speak freely."

Isabel folded her hands in her lap and took a deep breath. "Lord Whitmore, may I ask, what are your plans for me?"

He leaned back in his chair, seeming to consider his words before speaking.

"I did not *plan* on buying—" He paused, a muscle tightening in his jaw. "On having you accompany me home today, Miss de Clare. I can imagine you do not trust me, but please believe me when I say that I take no more pleasure in this situation than you do." He set the napkin aside. "It certainly is not my custom to employ magic users."

"Then why *did* you buy me?" Unlike him, she saw no need to cloak the ugly truth in polite phrasing. "If you truly have no desire to use people like me, then why acquire me at all?"

"Because I know the man who wanted you." His voice was grave. "And I know he did not want you for anything good."

"You said as much in the carriage. But how can you know what his intentions were?"

She thought of the marquis's mind, those fractured shards of thought. And she had to admit that what she had glimpsed there had not been reassuring.

"Because I have witnessed what he has done in the past," the earl said. "I could not, in good conscience, let him have you."

"Yet that is not the only reason you bought me, is it?" Isabel held his gaze. "You said you need my help. To expose a criminal? Is he the man you spoke of?"

"Yes." The admission came without hesitation. "Your abilities could prove invaluable in bringing him to justice."

"And in return, you will grant me my freedom," she recalled his earlier promise. "But what if this man turns out to be innocent? Or if we cannot find any evidence? How long will you keep me in your service before you decide to let me go?" Her voice hardened. "At what point will you decide that I have earned my freedom?"

The earl rose from his chair and moved to the sideboard. He lifted the stopper from a crystal decanter and poured himself a measure of amber liquid.

"Would you care for a drink, Miss de Clare?"

"No."

He gave a silent nod, raised the glass to his lips and drank.

Isabel rose as well. "You haven't answered my question," she said.

He set the glass down. "The matter is complicated."

"Then uncomplicate it." She took a step toward him. "Why can't you free me now, if I agree to help you? Does it matter whether I assist you as a servant or stand beside you as an ally?"

"Because you would not be safe on your own."

"I can take care of myself."

"You do not know what he is capable of."

"And you don't know what I am capable of." She lifted her chin. "I have defended myself against worse than a greedy lord with too much money and not enough scruples."

"Is that so?"

He moved before she could react.

One moment he stood by the sideboard, the next he was before her, and she found herself backing away instinctively until her shoulders met the wall. He followed, planting his hands on either side of her head, caging her between his arms.

Isabel's heart slammed against her ribs.

Up so close, his eyes looked even brighter than they had from afar, she thought. Then the dark, heavy scent of brandy and cedar hit her senses, a scent so intoxicatingly masculine that it made her breath catch.

He held her gaze, intent and unwavering.

"You think you can defend yourself against a monster like him?" His voice was low, and she felt the resonance of it deep in her chest, sending a shiver down her spine. "With no protection, no one looking after you?"

She met his gaze without flinching. Her pulse hammered in her ears, her breath coming faster than she would have liked, but she refused to look away. Refused to show him how much he affected her.

With anyone else, she would have shown him exactly what she was capable of. A well aimed push of her mind, a carefully planted thought, and he would have stumbled back gasping, convinced his heart was failing or his lungs were filling with water.

But her gift did not work on him. Could not work, if she had no access to his mind.

"If you mean to frighten me, my lord," she said, her voice steady despite her racing heart, "you will have to try harder than this. I have been cornered by men far more dangerous than you, and I am still standing."

He stared at her with an intensity that made her skin prickle, and for a heartbeat she thought he was going to say something in return. But then he stepped back, freeing her, and turned to face the window. She caught his reflection in the dark glass, but his expression gave nothing away.

Isabel used the reprieve to steady her breathing. She pressed her palms flat against the wall behind her, letting the cool plaster ground her.

"I am not your enemy, Miss de Clare."

His voice was quiet, the sharp edge gone.

"Forgive me if I find that difficult to believe," she said, "given that you just had me quite literally trapped."

He did not turn from the window, but she saw his shoulders rise and fall with a slow breath.

"I understand that you have no reason to trust me." He paused. "But I am asking you to consider that we may share a common cause. By helping me, you would be helping yourself. And others like you."

"Common cause? Would you be so kind as to explain what exactly you mean by that?"

He turned around, his face grave.

"I have spent eight years trying to bring the Marquis of Darkwater to justice. I have gathered information, followed leads... but he has slipped through every trap I set." He strode to the hearth, resting a hand against the mantelpiece as he stared into the flames. "Delacroix is responsible for crimes you cannot imagine, Miss de Clare. Crimes against people like you. Magic users who vanish without a trace and are never seen again. All the evidence I found points to him being behind their disappearances." He turned to face her again. "I believe he is doing terrible things to them. And I believe that you may be the key to finally stopping him."

A cold unease settled in her chest.

"Why me?"

"Because you can see into the minds of his allies, the people who help him cover his tracks. You can find the missing pieces, the evidence I have been looking for."

"And if I cannot?"

His eyes did not waver from her. "All I ask is that you try."

She studied him in the dim light of the dying fire, this unreadable man who had paid a fortune to save her from the man he believed to be a monster.

"You speak of justice," she said slowly. "But this feels personal."

His expression flickered, and just for an instant, a flash of raw emotion passed behind his eyes before he shuttered it away.

"It is," he admitted. "Delacroix took people from me. People I loved. A long time ago. But that does not make his crimes any less real, or the people he has hurt any less deserving of justice."

His honesty surprised her. She had expected deflection, not this quiet confession.

"I cannot force you to help me," he continued. "I will not pretend that your situation gives you much choice, but I want you to know that I would not compel you against your will. If you refuse, I will not punish you for it. But I am asking you to consider what I have told you."

Isabel said nothing.

"You may have the day tomorrow to think." He moved toward the door. "I will have Hartley show you to your chamber. Rest. Consider my offer. By evening, I would ask that you join me for dinner. My sister arrives tomorrow afternoon, and Lord Daventry will be dining with us as well. You may give me your answer then."

He paused at the door, his hand on the frame.

"Whatever you decide, Miss de Clare, know this: while you are under my roof, no harm will come to you. That much I can promise."

Without another glance in her direction, he stepped through the doorway and was gone.

Isabel stood motionless, her gaze fixed on the empty frame.

Then, slowly, she sank into the nearest chair and pressed her hands to her face.

What in God's name had she stumbled into?

Chapter Two

The knocking came from far away, a distant sound. She was walking along a cobblestone street, darkness all around her. From behind, footsteps echoed through the mist. She turned, heart pounding, but could make out nothing between the fog and the shadows. The knocking echoed through the blackness, growing louder, closer...

Isabel's eyes fluttered open, and for a moment she couldn't remember where she was. The ceiling above her was white and high, edged with delicate plasterwork. Sunlight slanted through half-drawn curtains, painting warm stripes across an unfamiliar counterpane.

The auction. The earl. Whitmore Hall.

The memories came back in pieces. After he had made his proposal, she had been shown to this room by the silver-haired butler, where a nightgown of soft white cotton had been laid out across the bed. The sight of it had made her stomach twist. That they had thought of such a thing, that she was dependent on these strangers for even the most basic necessities, had made her cheeks burn. Her first instinct had been to ignore it, to sleep in her own worn dress. But the thought of soiling those pristine sheets with the grime of the auction house had stayed her hand. And so she had changed, slipped between the smooth linens, and sunk into the softest bed she had ever touched.

The knocking came again.

"Miss de Clare?" A woman's voice, tentative but persistent. "Miss de Clare, are you awake?"

Isabel pushed herself upright, wincing at the rawness around her wrists where the iron shackles had bitten into her skin for hours the day before. She looked around the room and her gaze fell on a dressing gown hanging from the valet stand near the wardrobe. She rose, crossed to it, and slipped her arms through the sleeves before tying the sash at her waist.

"Yes. Come in."

The door opened to reveal a young maid in a crisp black dress and white apron. She couldn't have been more than eighteen, with round cheeks and nervous eyes that darted around the room before settling on Isabel.

"Begging your pardon, miss. His lordship sent me to ask if you'd join him for luncheon."

Luncheon. Isabel blinked. "What time is it?"

"Just gone noon, miss."

Noon. She had slept for nearly twelve hours. When had she last rested so deeply?

"I'll be down shortly," she said.

The maid bobbed a curtsy but didn't leave. "If you please, miss, I've brought you something to wear. His lordship thought you might..." She hesitated. "That is, your dress from yesterday was in quite a state, so Mrs. Hartley found a gown that might serve until better arrangements can be made."

She held up a modest day dress in dove grey, plainly cut but clean and well-made. A servant's dress, Isabel realised. One a senior housemaid might wear on her day off.

It was finer than anything she had owned in years.

"Thank you," she said, and meant it.

The maid, who introduced herself as Jenny, wheeled a small serving cart into the chamber, its brass fittings catching the light as it rolled across the polished floor. Upon it sat a porcelain pitcher and a folded cloth. Jenny guided the cart toward the washstand in the corner, a modest piece of furniture with a marble top and a wide basin set into it. The young woman lifted the pitcher and poured steaming water into the basin.

Isabel followed and stood before the washstand, breathing in the lavender that rose with the steam. Beside the basin lay a small cake of soap and a silver-backed hairbrush. She picked up the brush, turning it over in her hands. The bristles were soft, the handle ornately carved with delicate scrollwork. It was beautiful. Small luxuries like these she had once taken for granted, back when she was still Lady Isabel de Clare. A lifetime ago.

She lifted the brush to her hair. It glided through the tangles without catching, and her mouth curved at the ease of it. She continued brushing, watching the motion of her arm in the mirror above the washstand, when suddenly she caught sight of her face and went still.

Her hand froze mid-stroke, the brush caught halfway down a tangled strand.

She looked dreadful. Her face was pale, her cheekbones too sharp, the hollows beneath them carved by too many missed meals. Near her hairline she spotted a small scar she had almost forgotten about. A memento from a master with a heavy hand and a ring whose gemstone had cut deep on a night when she had failed to hold her tongue and he had failed to hold his liquor. She looked, she thought, like exactly what her papers declared her to be.

"Shall I help with your hair, miss?"

Jenny's voice pulled her from her thoughts. Isabel lowered the brush and nodded, stepping aside so the maid could take over.

She let the girl work in silence, pinning and arranging. Ordinarily Isabel kept her mental walls firmly in place. It was a constant effort, but a necessity when every unguarded mind threatened to drown her in a tide of thoughts that were not her own. However, if she wanted to come to a decision whether or not to help the earl, she needed to know who she was dealing with. And there was no better window into a man's character than the unguarded thoughts of those who served him.

She lowered her defences and let the surface of Jenny's mind wash over her.

Who is this woman, and why has his lordship brought her here in the middle of the night? Poor thing, she is far too thin! Maybe I can sneak an extra roll onto her breakfast tray tomorrow...

The unexpected kindness caught Isabel off guard. She swallowed the knot in her throat, and when she listened back in, the girl was thinking of the day ahead.

I must see to the fire before luncheon is served. His lordship prefers the flames steady and warm. If I do it just right, he might even offer me one of those rare smiles of his. He has such a lovely smile when he bothers to use it...

Isabel quickly withdrew. The girl's thoughts had told her little of use, but a servant who daydreamed about her master's smile at least was not one who lived in fear of him.

When Jenny was finished with her hair, she helped Isabel into the borrowed dress. The fabric hung loose at the bodice and fell short at the hem, but it was clean and unfrayed. More than could be said for her own worn gown.

"There you are, miss." Jenny stepped back, surveying her work. "Shall I show you downstairs?"

Isabel nodded. "Lead the way."

Whitmore Hall looked different in the bright of day. Last night, shadows had swallowed most of the view, though even then she had sensed the scale of the place. But now, with sunlight streaming through tall windows, she could see just how vast it really was. Corridor after corridor stretched before her, rooms opening onto rooms, the ceilings so high one could fit an entire cottage beneath them.

She followed the maid down the main staircase, past portraits and vases filled with fresh flowers that looked as though they had been arranged that very morning.

They stopped before a set of double doors that Isabel recognised from last night. "The dining room, miss. Lord Whitmore is expecting you."

Isabel straightened her borrowed dress and lifted her chin.

Then she pushed open the doors and stepped inside.

Bright light streamed through tall windows that lined the far wall, overlooking a garden that had long since surrendered to autumn. The last of the roses clung stubbornly to their thorny stems, and the hedges had taken on the russet tones of the season. But the sky beyond was a brilliant, cloudless blue. Sunlight poured through the glass, warming the pale blue walls and catching on the polished mahogany of the long table set for two.

The Earl of Whitmore stood at the window with his back to her, hands clasped behind him, his dark silhouette framed by golden light.

Jenny slipped into the room behind Isabel, moving purposefully toward the fireplace. Isabel watched as she arranged the kindling and could not help the smile that tugged at the corner of her mouth as she remembered the maid's earlier thoughts.

Steady and warm.

"Miss de Clare."

The earl's voice drew her attention back. He had turned to face her, his bright, grey eyes calm and unreadable as ever. In the light of day, he looked less severe than he had the night before, though no less imposing. He stood with a posture accustomed to command, his dark hair neatly combed and his coat immaculate.

"Good afternoon," he said. "I trust you slept well?"

Isabel cast a glance toward Jenny, who was peeking over her shoulder at them. The earl's gaze, however, remained fixed solely on Isabel.

"Yes," she said. "Thank you."

He gestured toward the table. "Please. Sit."

The earl crossed the room and pulled out her chair, waiting until she had settled into it before taking his own seat beside her.

Jenny rose from the hearth, brushing off her apron. "My lord, shall I have luncheon served?"

"Yes," he answered, his eyes never leaving Isabel's face.

Jenny hesitated for the briefest moment, her gaze flickering between them. Then she dipped a curtsy. "I'll have it brought out at once, my lord."

She slipped from the room and pulled the door shut behind her.

"I see Mrs. Hartley found you something to wear," the earl said, his gaze travelling over her dress. "I hope it will do until we can have a proper wardrobe fitted for you."

"It serves well enough," Isabel replied. "And there is really no need for a whole wardrobe."

His eyes moved down the ill-fitting sleeves of her gown—and stopped as they landed on her wrists, exposed by the too-short fabric.

The earl's expression darkened.

"I cannot believe they still use those wretched irons," he said, his voice a low growl. "After the Reform Act, one would think things might have changed."

He leaned closer and reached for her hand.

"I will have someone sent to your room to tend to these," he said. "This should not be left untreated."

Isabel straightened in her chair, but before she could react he had already taken her hand, turning it over gently in his own—and she drew in a sharp breath.

The moment his fingers touched her skin, the strangest sensation washed over her.

The world went *quiet*.

It was as if a great weight had been lifted from her mind. The constant pressure of other people's thoughts, that ever-present hum, whether she was in a crowded room or alone in the dead of night, suddenly vanished.

For the first time in as long as she could remember, her mind was entirely her own.

Her body went rigid with shock. What was this? What had he done? She stared at him, searching his face for some sign that he understood what had just occurred, but his expression revealed nothing, his attention still lowered as he inspected her wrists.

Then he looked up and met her eyes, his gaze dropping to her mouth for the briefest moment before snapping back up. Isabel's heart hammered against her ribs.

"Forgive me," he said, clearing his throat. "That was inappropriate of me."

The earl abruptly released her hand and sat back, straightening in his chair.

The noise of the world came rushing back in an instant. Isabel blinked in confusion.

What in God's name had just happened?

Before she could gather her thoughts enough to speak, the door opened and another maid entered, wheeling a serving cart laden with covered dishes. She set out a platter of sliced cold ham, a wedge of game pie, and a bowl of pickled vegetables alongside crusty bread and a steaming pot of tea. She poured for both of them, dipped a curtsy, and withdrew without a word.

They ate in silence.

Isabel barely tasted the food as her mind turned over what had just happened.

She stole glances at the earl in between bites, studying his profile, the strong line of his jaw, the seemingly ever-present furrow between his brows. He gave no indication that anything unusual had occurred. Perhaps, for him, nothing had.

"If you do not mind me asking," he said, breaking the silence, "have you had a chance to consider my offer?"

Isabel's gaze lifted from her plate to find him watching her. She set down her fork.

"I have," she said carefully. "Though I confess I have not yet reached a conclusion."

"May I ask what gives you pause?"

The fact that I cannot read your mind. The fact that you touching me silenced every thought but my own. The fact that I have no idea who—or what—you really are.

"There are many factors to consider," she said.

"I understand," he replied, setting down his own fork. "And I would not rush you, except..." He paused. "There is some urgency to the matter. A magic user's life hangs in the balance. A woman has been accused of a crime I am not certain she committed. I could use your help in determining whether she is innocent."

Isabel's chest tightened. A life in the balance. Of course there was.

"So first I am to hunt a supposed criminal with you," she said, not bothering to soften her tone, "and now I am to save a convicted woman's life. Is there anything else on that list? You might as well say it now."

He stared at her, clearly taken aback by her outburst.

Isabel drew a breath and looked away. "Forgive me, my lord. Sometimes my temper gets the better of me."

"So I have noticed," he said dryly.

She met his eyes again, forcing herself to speak more calmly. "You gave me until dinner to decide."

"Then until dinner you shall have."

They held each other's gaze across the table, the silence between them stretching.

Then the door burst open to admit a young woman in a flurry of blue velvet and windswept dark hair, her cheeks flushed red, her eyes the same striking grey as the man's beside her. And behind her, looking considerably less enthusiastic, trailed Lord Daventry in an elegantly rumpled coat.

"Alexander, look who I found lingering at Lady Deacon's!" Vera announced, sweeping into the room. "Alone with the young widow, if you can believe it. Honestly, Damien, have you no shame—"

She stopped mid-sentence, her gaze landing on Isabel.

"Oh." Vera's eyebrows rose. "I didn't realise you had company." She shot Damien a pointed look. "You might have warned me."

"When, precisely?" The viscount strolled in behind her, entirely unruffled. "Between your lecture on propriety and your detailed critique of the baroness's wallpaper, I couldn't slip in a single word."

"You were taking tea alone with a beautiful young lady, Damien. What was I supposed to think?"

"That I was gathering intelligence, like a dutiful ally?"

"You were flirting."

"If I did any such thing, it was merely to gain her confidence."

Alexander pushed back his chair and stood, already bracing himself for what was to come. His sister had a talent for turning even the simplest situation into a theatrical production.

"Isabel, this is my sister, Lady Vera. Vera, allow me to introduce Miss Isabel de Clare. She is my—"

Before Alexander could say another word, Isabel rose from her chair, extending her hand to Vera. "I'm your brother's slave," she said with a smile. "Pleased to make your acquaintance."

Damien choked on a laugh. Alexander pinched the bridge of his nose and exhaled slowly.

Vera's mouth fell open. She stared at Isabel, then at her brother, then back at Isabel again.

"Alexander James Kensington," she said, her voice dangerously quiet. "Explain yourself. At once."

"She is not my slave," he said wearily. "She is my guest."

"Am I indeed?" Isabel's tone was deceptively light. "I wasn't aware guests were typically acquired at illegal auctions."

"To be fair," Damien cut in, "it was more of a rescue operation than a planned purchase."

"Miss de Clare was being sold at a private auction last night," Alexander clarified. "A perfectly legal auction, mind you"—he cast a glance at Isabel, who met his gaze with her chin raised—"if somewhat unofficial. The Marquis of Darkwater was bidding for her. I intervened."

The change in Vera's expression was immediate.

"Delacroix," she said quietly.

"Yes."

Brother and sister exchanged a look that needed no words.

Vera drew a breath and turned back to Isabel, taking her hand once more.

"Well then. It is a pleasure to meet you, Isabel. Truly." She stepped back, her gaze travelling critically over the grey dress. "But we are going to have to do something about that gown. Please tell me you have something else to wear."

"Actually, I..."

"I have already informed Miss de Clare that we will have a proper wardrobe fitted for her," Alexander supplied.

"Wonderful. Then you won't mind if I take the lead on that matter." It wasn't a question. "I know all the best modistes in Greyport, and I refuse to let this poor woman suffer through another meal in such ill-fitting attire."

"By all means." Alexander gestured vaguely. "You are far better suited to the task than I am."

"That goes without saying." Vera was already circling Isabel, assessing her from head to toe. "We'll need day dresses, evening gowns, proper undergarments—oh, and something for the autumn ball, of course."

"The autumn ball?" Isabel looked between them, clearly lost.

"Lady Deacon's annual affair," Damien offered. "Which is precisely the reason I paid the young widow a visit this morning, by the way."

Vera arched an eyebrow. "Of course it was."

"The ball is in a fortnight," Alexander explained, turning to Isabel. "Several of Delacroix's known associates are expected to attend. It seemed a good opportunity to gather information."

"Hence my visit to the baroness as well," Vera added. "I wanted to confirm the guest list and see if anyone of interest would be present. You can imagine my surprise when I arrived to find Damien already at her side over tea and biscuits."

Damien opened his mouth to retort—

"Enough." Alexander's voice silenced them both. "Vera, if you want to take Miss de Clare to the modiste, then by all means, go. But please try not to spend the entire month's household budget in a single afternoon. We have had some unexpected expenditures last night."

"I would hate to make promises I cannot keep."

"And take Damien with you," Alexander continued, letting the remark pass. "I will not have either of you wandering the streets un-escorted. Not after last night."

Vera's expression soured. "I don't need a chaperone, Alexander."

"You cannot seriously be subjecting me to an afternoon of holding parcels and offering opinions on ribbons," Damien said at the same moment.

"Not another word." Alexander had heard quite enough. "Damien, you will ensure the ladies' safety. Or have you forgotten why Miss de Clare needed rescuing in the first place?" He turned to his sister before she could object further. "And Vera, unless you would prefer I send you back to Whitmore Manor, you will accept the arrangement. You may have the run of our country estate, but in my house, you follow my rules."

The room fell silent.

Alexander noticed Isabel watching the exchange, her gaze moving between the three of them.

"I cannot join you," he continued, his tone softening. "I have a meeting this afternoon regarding the harbour case." He turned to Isabel. "It is about the woman I mentioned earlier."

Damien's eyebrows rose. "Going to see the smuggler?"

"He is not a smuggler."

"A pirate, then."

"He is not a—" Alexander stopped himself, recognizing the glint in Damien's eye. "Off with you. Enjoy your outing."

Vera squeaked with delight and hooked her arm through Isabel's. "Come along, Isabel. We have so much to discuss. I want to hear everything about how you met my brother."

They swept out of the room, Damien following close behind. In the doorway the viscount turned around to face Alexander, a grin tugging at his lips.

"She's even more striking in daylight, your telepath."

"She is not *my* telepath."

"If you say so." The viscount's smile turned infuriatingly smug.

"Get out, Damien."

His friend laughed and sketched an ironic bow before disappearing after the women.

Alexander stood in silence for a moment, staring at the empty chair where Isabel had been sitting only moments before. The scent of lavender still lingered faintly in the air.

He should not have taken her hand. But he could not resist the impulse when he had seen the state of her delicate skin. He thought of the moment he had touched her, the way she had looked at him. The sharp intake of breath. The confusion in her eyes.

She had felt something. He was certain of it.

Isabel watched through the carriage window as the streets of Greyport transformed around them.

The modest townhouses and corner shops of the residential district gave way to broader avenues lined with gas lamps and elegant facades. Here, the buildings stood taller. The stonework had been scrubbed clean, and the polished windows glared in the afternoon light. Fashionable couples strolled arm in arm past shop fronts where jewellers displayed gold and gemstones on velvet trays. This was the heart of Greyport, the commercial district where the wealthy came to spend their fortunes.

Isabel had rarely seen this part of the city. Lord Bentley had occasionally brought her along on business dealings, using her abilities to gauge the honesty of his trade partners. But even then, they had not ventured into these fine streets. Most of the time she had remained confined to his household, helping the maids with common tasks and screening the staff for dishonesty and thievery. Her primary purpose, however, had been to accompany him to card games in dubious company, giving him subtle signs of when to wager high based on what she gleaned from the other players' minds.

Unfortunately, he had not always heeded her warnings. Greed had a way of making men deaf, and Lord Bentley had fancied his instincts sharper than any telepath's counsel. His mounting debts and eventual bankruptcy had been the inevitable result.

"We're here!" Vera announced as the carriage rolled to a stop.

Isabel pulled her attention back to the present. Through the window she could see a graceful corner establishment with large bow windows, behind which mannequins displayed the latest fashions in rich fabrics of emerald, burgundy, and midnight blue.

Lord Daventry descended first, holding the door open for them with an exaggerated bow. "Ladies."

Vera took Isabel's arm as they crossed the cobblestones toward the shop, and the viscount fell into step close behind. Isabel couldn't help but feel hemmed in. They never let her out of their sight.

A small bell chimed as they entered Madame Fontaine's establishment. The air inside was warm and carried the rich scent of fresh linen. Bolts of fabric lined the walls in neat rows, and ribbons in every colour imaginable spilled from display cases. From the back rooms Isabel could hear the rhythmic clatter of sewing machines.

A stout woman of middle years with greying hair pinned in an elaborate chignon approached them immediately, her manner brisk but welcoming.

"Lady Vera! What a pleasure." Her gaze swept over Isabel and lingered on her eyes. "And who might this be?"

"Miss Isabel de Clare," Vera said smoothly. "An esteemed guest of my brother's. She requires a complete wardrobe." She let the words hang in the air for a moment. "Day dresses, evening gowns, undergarments, outerwear, all the necessities. And we shall need at least one ensemble she can take with her today. Spare no expense, Madame. I hope that won't be a problem?"

Madame Fontaine's guarded expression melted into a bright, obliging smile. "But of course not. This way, if you please."

Isabel found herself guided onto a small platform before a trio of mirrors, where she was measured and draped in muslin while Madame Fontaine circled her with pins between her lips. Vera settled onto a tufted settee nearby, leafing through fashion plates and issuing a steady stream of opinions.

"The forest green, definitely. And the burgundy, it will complement her colouring beautifully. Oh, and we simply must have something in that lovely slate blue."

Time slipped past in a haze of fabric swatches and murmured consultations. Isabel stood still as instructed, watching the proceedings in the mirror, slowly feeling herself begin to relax.

When had anyone last fussed over her like this? When had anyone cared what colours suited her, or whether a neckline was flattering? The attention was foreign to her now, but once, long ago, it had been familiar. Her mother had delighted in choosing fabrics for her, had brushed her hair each night before bed. Her father had taught her to ride in the meadows behind their country house, laughing when she outpaced him.

With the memories surfaced the old pain. A pain she had buried so deep that she had almost forgotten about it. Grief was a luxury she couldn't afford. Not when survival demanded every scrap of her strength.

She forced it back down, locking it away once more.

"Isabel? Are you quite all right?"

She looked up to find Vera watching her with concern.

"Forgive me." Isabel managed a smile. "I am simply overwhelmed. It has been a very long time since anyone has shown me such kindness."

Vera rose from the settee and crossed to stand beside her, taking her hand gently.

"Well," she said softly, "you had better grow accustomed to it. As our guest, you shall want for nothing."

Isabel's throat tightened. "Thank you. For everything."

Across the shop, the viscount had abandoned all pretense of usefulness and was leaning against the counter, deep in conversation with a pretty shop assistant who giggled at something he said. He caught Isabel's eye in the mirror and offered a small wink.

"Don't mind him," Vera said, following her gaze. "He flirts like other men breathe. It means nothing."

"I wasn't concerned."

"Good. Because if you were entertaining any notions in that direction, I would counsel you to abandon them. Damien is loyal to the bone, but he makes for poor husband material."

Isabel felt heat rise to her cheeks. "I certainly wasn't... I had no intention of—"

"Are we quite finished yet?" Lord Daventry appeared at Vera's side. "If I continue to engage the young lady at the counter any longer, she may begin to form expectations."

"Another few minutes," Vera said. "They're just finishing the hem on the day dress."

The viscount sighed theatrically but retreated to wait by the door.

Shortly after, they emerged from Madame Fontaine's laden with parcels. Lord Daventry carried the bulk of them, having been firmly informed by Vera that this was his penance for spending the entire fitting flirting with the staff.

"These weigh an absolute ton," he said, shifting the boxes in his arms. "Remind me again why I'm carrying them when they could have been delivered with the rest?"

"Because Isabel can hardly attend dinner with nothing to wear," Vera replied.

"Fair point." The viscount glanced at Isabel with a grin. "Though I confess I would have been perfectly content to see Miss de Clare attend dinner in nothing at all. Her natural beauty needs no adornment."

Isabel bit back a laugh. The man was utterly incorrigible.

"Damien!" Vera's voice could have cut glass. "That was most inappropriate."

"What? I was paying her a compliment."

"You were being insufferable. As usual."

Isabel found herself smiling at the familiar rhythm of their bickering. It was almost soothing. In the shop she had changed into one of the new ensembles, a soft grey wool day dress with a fitted bodice. Over this, she wore a warm coat in deep blue, and a shawl of fine cashmere. Now, as they crossed the cobblestone street, she pulled the shawl tighter. The afternoon had turned while they were inside, the earlier sunshine swallowed by clouds rolling in from the harbour. An icy wind swept down the avenue, carrying with it the promise of rain.

She felt him before she saw him.

A presence at the edge of her awareness, cold and sharp, like a splinter of ice lodged in her mind. She reached instinctively for his thoughts and found only chaos, a fractured tangle of impressions that resisted her touch and made her head hurt.

Then his tall, lean figure stepped out of a doorway directly into their path, blocking the way forward. Silver laced through his dark hair at the temples, yet his face bore few lines. He wore a dark coat buttoned high, one gloved hand resting on the head of a walking cane. A handsome man by any measure, though his pale, watchful gaze was unsettling.

"Lady Vera." He smiled, though it did not reach his eyes. "What a delightful surprise. And Miss de Clare." His gaze travelled over her new attire. "How fascinating. You have made quite the transformation since the auction."

Vera's hand tightened on Isabel's arm, pulling her back half a step. Beside them, Lord Daventry shifted his weight, angling his body between the women and Delacroix.

"Lord Darkwater," the viscount said, his tone deceptively light. "What an unexpected pleasure."

"Indeed." The marquis's eyes moved between them, lingering on the parcels in the viscount's arms. "How generous of you, Lord Daventry, to lavish such attention on your newest acquisition." His smile sharpened. "Are you hoping to pass her off as your new mistress? It seems a waste of her talents, but I suppose you must have exhausted all other possibilities in your usual circles by now."

Lord Daventry set the parcels down carefully. When he straightened, he squared his shoulders and drew himself to his full height, forming a wall between Delacroix and the women behind him.

"My affairs are none of your concern, my lord."

"Evidently not." His gaze slid past the viscount to fix on Isabel. "Miss de Clare. I do hope you are enjoying your new circumstances, whatever they may be. Though I confess, I find myself curious. Does Lord Daventry know the full extent of what he purchased? Or is he content to let such a rare gift go to waste?"

"That's quite enough." Lord Daventry's voice had lost all pretense of warmth. "If you'll excuse us, we have an engagement to keep. Ladies?"

He moved to usher them past, but the marquis did not step aside.

"I look forward to continuing our acquaintance, Miss de Clare," Delacroix said softly, his eyes never leaving hers. "I have a feeling our paths will cross again. Very soon."

"You will do no such thing." The viscount's words were quiet, but the threat in them was unmistakable.

For a moment, the two men just stood, staring at one another. Then Delacroix smiled and stepped aside with an elaborate bow.

"Good day, Lady Vera. Lord Daventry." His gaze found Isabel one last time. "Miss de Clare. Until we meet again."

Vera gripped Isabel's arm and steered her firmly toward the carriage. Lord Daventry scooped up the parcels and followed close behind, keeping himself between the women and the marquis until they were safely inside.

"Home," he called to the driver as he pulled the door shut.

The coach jerked forward. Outside, a light rain had begun to fall, tapping softly against the roof and streaking the windows with grey.

Inside, there was only silence.

Vera sat beside Isabel, turned toward the window, her reflection pale and troubled in the rain-spotted glass. Across from them, the viscount's easy charm had vanished altogether. He sat with one ankle crossed over his knee, elbow braced on his thigh, chin resting on his fist. His gaze was distant, his brows furrowed.

The encounter had stripped away the last of Isabel's doubts. The marquis was every bit as dangerous as they had warned her.

And yet Vera and Lord Daventry had protected her. Without hesitation.

For twelve years she had relied on no one but herself. The idea of trusting others, of allowing herself to depend on their goodwill, terrified her.

Still...

Isabel knew she shouldn't. But she had to know.

...that was too close. If Alexander finds out I let him get that near to her...

That was the viscount. And Vera—

...we have to find a way to bring him to justice. He cannot be allowed to continue...

Isabel pulled back and sealed herself off. She had heard enough to make her decision. Perhaps she had known all along what her answer would be.

She would help the earl.

But she would do it on her own terms.

Dark clouds had rolled in from the sea, heavy and low, turning the afternoon sky a leaden grey. The wind cut sharp and cold as Alexander made his way along the southern docks, past merchant vessels and fishing boats that rocked and strained against their moorings. The air was thick with the smell of brine and the metallic tang of approaching rain.

He found the *Sea Witch* at the far end of the quay, moored apart from the larger trading ships. She sat low in the water, her dark hull freshly tarred, her rigging taut and singing in the rising wind.

A burly man with a shaved head intercepted him before he could reach the gangplank, arms folded across his broad chest.

"State your business."

"I am here to see Captain Raines. He is expecting me."

The man's eyes narrowed, but then he jerked his head toward the ship and turned around. "This way, then. Captain's in his cabin."

Alexander followed him up the gangplank and across the deck, where sailors paused in their work to watch him pass. The ship swayed beneath his feet, timbers groaning, and somewhere above them a loose halyard clanged against the mast. The sailor led him to a door at the stern and rapped twice before pushing it open.

"Visitor for you, Captain."

The cabin was larger than Alexander had expected, and surprisingly well-appointed. Lanterns hung from brass hooks, their flames illuminating the polished mahogany floors and the deep green velvet of the settee against the wall. Charts covered one side of the room, and an oversized bed dominated the other, while at the centre stood a desk, laden with a bowl full of exotic looking fruit. Behind it sat a man who seemed as much a part of the sea as the ship itself.

Dominic Raines was broad-shouldered with bronzed skin, his dark hair worn longer than fashion dictated, a few wayward curls falling across his brow, his bright green eyes the colour of sun through shallow water. He sat tilted back in his chair, boots propped on the corner of the desk, a small knife in his hand, methodically peeling an apple.

"Lord Whitmore." A slow smile spread across his face as he swung his feet down and leaned forward, resting his forearms on the desk. "I must admit, your request for a meeting had me intrigued. What brings you aboard?"

The sailor behind Alexander withdrew, pulling the door shut behind him.

"I need a favour," the earl said without preamble.

Raines laughed, a low, rich sound. "Straight to business." He carved a slice from the apple and ate it off the blade. "Please, sit. Have something to eat."

"I will stand."

"Suit yourself." Raines shrugged and leaned back in his chair. "What sort of favour are we discussing?"

"Access to Greyport Prison."

The captain's expression sobered. "That's no small task."

"Which is why I am coming to you."

"Flattery." Raines pressed the hand holding the knife to his chest. "How refreshing." He turned the apple over in his fingers. "Who are you trying to reach?"

"A woman. A magic user, accused of murder. She is scheduled to hang within the fortnight."

"Ah." A smile tugged at the corner of his mouth. "You want to see the fire lady." He carved another slice. "Tell me, Lord Whitmore, how did you manage to delay her execution? Even an Under-Secretary of

State would struggle to stay a hanging once the magistrate has signed the warrant."

"With friends in the right places, a great many things can be accomplished."

"So it would seem." Raines studied him for a moment. "Well. This is going to cost you."

"How much?"

"The currency I'm after isn't gold, Lord Whitmore. It's company." He set down the apple and the knife, meeting Alexander's gaze directly. "A favour for a favour."

"Whose company?"

"I hear you've recently acquired a rather extraordinary new asset. A telepath, if my sources are to be believed."

Alexander did not bother asking how the captain had learned of Isabel's true whereabouts. The man had eyes and ears everywhere. "She is not for sale," he snapped.

Raines lifted his hands in mock surrender. "Easy, my lord. I have no intention of taking her from you. I merely wish to borrow her talents for an afternoon."

"Out of the question. There must be something else I can give you."

"I'm afraid not." The captain folded his arms across his chest. "This is my price."

Alexander considered his request. He knew the Raines family well enough. They came from a long line of distinguished seafarers, with deep ties to both the merchant guilds and the Royal Navy. Dominic's elder brother James had been one of the most decorated captains in the naval fleet before he and his ship had been lost at sea three months past. And Dominic himself, for all the rumours that swirled around him, had always struck Alexander as an honourable man, though he clearly operated in the grey spaces between law and lawlessness.

The thought of leaving Isabel in this man's company, even for an hour, sat poorly with him.

But he needed to speak with the fire starter. And Raines was his only way in.

"Can I trust that your intentions are decent?"

The captain schooled his features into an expression of wounded innocence. "I can assure you, Lord Whitmore, my intentions are perfectly decent."

Alexander held his gaze. "Under two conditions," he said at last. "First, Miss de Clare must agree to this herself. I cannot speak on her behalf. Second, I will accompany you on whatever outing you have planned with her."

"Agreed." Raines extended his hand, but as Alexander reached to clasp it, the captain pulled back. "But you will remain in the background. I cannot have you interfering in my affairs."

"Very well." Alexander kept his hand extended.

"Then we have a deal." Raines grasped it and shook firmly.

"Now." Alexander withdrew his arm. "As for the fire starter."

Raines rose from his chair and crossed to a cabinet, producing a bottle of amber liquid and two glasses. "Drink?"

"No."

"Pity. You're missing out on the finest whiskey this side of the Serpent's Passage. I acquired it myself on my last voyage to the Free Isles." He poured one for himself anyway and took a slow sip. "I can arrange a private audience. No guards." He swirled the liquid in his glass. "Is it just a conversation you're after, or should I prepare for something more dramatic?"

"That depends on what we learn. Can it be arranged on short notice?"

"At a price."

"I assume this time you actually mean gold?"

Raines grinned, lifting his glass in a small salute. "I knew I was going to enjoy doing business with you, Lord Whitmore. You understand how these things work."

Chapter Three

The rain had begun an hour ago and showed no sign of relenting.

Alexander's carriage rolled through the iron gates of Whitmore Hall, water drumming against the roof and streaming down the windows in sheets. The afternoon had stretched into evening while he sat in Dominic Raines's cabin, negotiating terms he was hardly comfortable with, and now the last grey light was fading behind dark clouds.

The carriage had barely stopped before Alexander pushed open the door and descended, crossing the short distance to the front steps at a brisk pace. The door swung open before he could reach for the handle. Hartley stood in the entrance, ever vigilant, already waiting with a towel.

"My lord."

"Thank you, Hartley." Alexander took the offered cloth and blotted the rain from his face, then handed off his damp coat and hat to the butler. "Is everyone home?"

"Yes, my lord. Lady Vera and Miss de Clare are upstairs preparing for dinner. Lord Daventry is in the drawing room. I believe he wishes to speak with you, my lord. Before dinner."

Alexander frowned but said nothing more. He crossed the entrance hall, his boots leaving wet prints on the marble, and pushed open the drawing room door.

Damien stood before the hearth, one hand braced against the mantelpiece, a glass of brandy clutched in the other. His gaze was fixed on the flames, his posture rigid.

He did not turn at the sound of the door.

"Damien."

The viscount startled, nearly sloshing brandy over his fingers.

"Alexander." He straightened and turned, his face pale. "You're back. Good."

Alexander crossed the room in quick strides. "What happened? You look as though you have seen a ghost."

Damien let out a breath that might have been a laugh in different circumstances. "Something like that."

"Is it about Isabel? Or Vera? Are they alright?"

"They're fine." Damien raised his free hand in a placating gesture. "They're upstairs, I believe." He took a long drink from his glass. "They're safe, Alex. I promise you."

The knot in Alexander's chest loosened, but only slightly. He studied his friend, noting the way his fingers had tightened around the crystal tumbler.

"What are you not telling me?"

Damien was silent for a moment. Then he moved to the sideboard and poured a second glass, holding it out to Alexander without meeting his eyes.

"We encountered Delacroix."

Alexander felt the blood drain from his face.

"Where?"

"In the commercial district. Outside the modiste's shop." Damien finally looked at him, his expression grim. "He appeared out of nowhere. One moment the street was clear, the next he was standing directly in our path."

Alexander took the offered glass but did not drink. "Did he touch her? Did he threaten her?"

"He didn't lay a hand on anyone. But he made his intentions clear enough." Damien's mouth pressed into a thin line. "He told Isabel he looked forward to continuing their acquaintance. Said he had a feeling their paths would cross again. Very soon."

Alexander went rigid. He turned away, moving to the window where rain lashed against the darkened panes.

"From now on, she does not leave this house without me. I will not let her out of my sight. Not until Delacroix is dealt with."

Damien raised an eyebrow. "And how exactly do you intend to manage that? Do you intend to follow her to her dressing room? Stand guard while she takes her morning tea? From what I have observed so far, she does not strike me as a woman who would accept such restrictions without objection."

"I do not care whether she objects. She is under my protection." Alexander turned back from the window to face his friend, his voice sharp. "Delacroix was within arm's reach of her today, Damien! After everything that man has done—" He broke off, balling his free hand into a fist, his gaze dropping to the ridged scar that ran across his knuckles.

Damien set down his glass and crossed to his friend, placing a hand on his shoulder.

"Alex," he said quietly. "Believe me, when I saw him standing there, smiling at her like she was already his... it took everything I had not to put my fist through his face."

"That was too close, Damien."

"I know."

"If anything had happened to her—"

"It didn't." Damien's grip tightened. "I got them away. He didn't follow. Whatever game he's playing, he's not ready to make his move yet."

Alexander forced himself to take a deep breath. "Forgive me," he said after a moment. "I know none of this was your fault."

Damien released his shoulder and stepped back, retrieving his abandoned glass. "You're right though. We need to be more careful. I don't know how he knew we would be there today, but that was no chance encounter. He was waiting for us."

The implication hung in the air between them.

"Speaking of encounters," Damien said eventually, his tone a bit lighter. "How did your meeting go? Did the pirate agree to help?"

Alexander shot him a look, but then went on to say: "Raines has agreed to help me get into the prison. But he wants something in return."

"Of course he does. And that would be?" he asked, raising his glass to drink.

"Isabel."

Damien choked on his brandy. "I beg your pardon?"

"Not like that." Alexander moved to the fireplace, taking up the position Damien had vacated, staring into the flames. "He wants to borrow her abilities for an afternoon. Some business of his that requires the services of a telepath."

"And you agreed to this?"

"I agreed to ask her. The choice is ultimately hers to make." He paused. "I also insisted on accompanying them. Whatever Raines has planned, I intend to be present for it."

"How reassuring." Damien lifted his glass in a mocking salute. "You're going to let a smuggler borrow your telepath for dubious purposes, and your safeguard is to tag along and watch?"

"He is not a smuggler. And she is not *my* telepath."

"If you say so."

A knock interrupted them, and Hartley appeared in the doorway, sparing Alexander from further protest.

"My lord, dinner is ready to be served. Lady Vera and Miss de Clare are awaiting you in the dining room."

Alexander drained the brandy he had been holding untouched in one swallow and set the glass aside. "Thank you, Hartley. We will be there directly."

The butler inclined his head and withdrew.

Damien straightened his cravat and ran a hand through his hair, some of his usual insouciance returning to his features. "Well then. Shall we? I confess I'm curious to see how our guest presents herself in her new finery."

Alexander ignored the comment, though he could not ignore the flicker of irritation it sparked in his chest. Damien had always had an eye for beautiful women, and Isabel was undeniably striking. The thought of his friend turning his charm in her direction left a sour taste in his mouth.

He pushed the feeling aside and followed Damien to the dining room.

Isabel barely recognised the woman staring back at her from the mirror.

The gown she was wearing was a soft blue-grey silk, with a fitted bodice and sleeves that tapered elegantly to her wrists. The colour brought out the violet in her eyes, or so Vera had insisted while directing Jenny to fasten the row of tiny buttons down Isabel's back. A borrowed pendant of sapphire and silver rested against Isabel's collarbone, and matching drops hung from her ears. Her hair had been pinned up in an elaborate arrangement of curls that Jenny had spent the better part of an hour perfecting, with a few loose tendrils framing her face.

A lady. That was what she looked like. The person she used to be, before the fever and the doctor and the cold iron of shackles.

"Stop frowning," Vera said, appearing at her shoulder in the mirror. "You look absolutely stunning. You shall turn every head in the room."

Isabel's cheeks warmed. "I hardly think—"

"Come along. They'll be waiting for us."

They made their way downstairs to the dining room, where Isabel now stood beside Vera, a crystal glass of sherry in her hand. The table had been set for four with polished silver, delicate china, and candles flickering softly across the white linen. Rain tapped against the windows, the fire crackled low in the hearth, and Vera's cheerful chatter filled the spaces in between. Isabel was only half listening.

She took a small sip of her drink and tried to calm the flutter of nerves in her stomach. The encounter with Delacroix had shaken her.

She had dealt with dangerous men before. But something about the marquis was different.

"I hope you don't mind that we started without you," Vera called out as the door opened.

Isabel turned.

Lord Daventry entered first, his familiar smile firmly back in place after the sombre silence that had accompanied their carriage ride home.

Lord Whitmore followed close behind. He looked troubled, his brows drawn together, his dark hair slightly dishevelled and damp.

His gaze found hers across the room, just as Lord Daventry stepped between them, flourishing his hand with theatrical flair.

"Ladies. I must say, the transformation is remarkable." His eyes swept appreciatively over Isabel. "Miss de Clare, you are a vision. That colour suits you beautifully. Yet I admit, part of me had hoped you might embrace my earlier suggestion and let your natural beauty speak for itself. Alas, Vera has conspired against me."

Isabel pressed her lips together, fighting to contain the laugh that threatened to escape. "I thank you for your confidence in my judgement, Lord Daventry."

Behind the viscount, the earl cleared his throat and stepped to his friend's side, casting him a scolding glance before turning to Isabel.

"You look lovely, Miss de Clare," he said.

"Thank you, my lord." Isabel inclined her head. "And thank you for the new attire," she continued. "It was not necessary to furnish me with an entire wardrobe. Nevertheless, I want you to know that I appreciate the gesture."

She meant it. In her twelve years of servitude, she had grown accustomed to hand-me-downs and servants' castoffs. If she was lucky, a master provided plain work dresses. If she was unlucky, she scraped together what she could from the other staff's discarded garments. Never once had anyone thought to clothe her in silk.

"You are most welcome." The earl gave a curt nod.

She wished, absurdly, that he had looked at her the way Lord Daventry had, with open admiration. The viscount's flattery meant nothing. She knew by now that it was just performance, part of his natural charm. But the earl...

She couldn't read the earl. What he thought when he looked at her remained a mystery. And that increasingly bothered her.

"Shall we?" Lord Whitmore gestured toward the table.

He pulled out a chair for Isabel and waited as she set her glass aside and settled into the seat. Across the table, Lord Daventry performed the same courtesy for Vera, murmuring something that made her swat his arm.

Hartley announced the first course, and a footman appeared with a delicate soup that smelled of herbs and cream. For a few minutes there was only the soft clink of spoons against porcelain.

"You should have seen the modiste's face when we walked in," Vera said, breaking the silence after they'd finished. "Madame Fontaine seemed rather taken aback at having to serve a magic user. But the moment I mentioned we required a complete new wardrobe, her whole demeanour changed. Remarkable how gold can shift one's principles."

"Remarkable indeed," Lord Daventry agreed dryly.

"Lady Vera has been far too generous," Isabel said, glancing at her hostess. "I fear I shall never be able to repay such kindness."

"There is nothing to repay," Vera said firmly. "Consider it a welcome gift. Besides, I have not enjoyed an afternoon of shopping so thoroughly in a very long while."

"And it was well worth the effort," Lord Daventry added, leaning back in his chair. "If you ever grow tired of my friend's hospitality, Miss de Clare, I would be happy to offer you refuge at my own estate. I could use a dining companion with such—"

"Damien." The earl's voice cut him off. "Enough."

Lord Daventry raised an eyebrow, and Vera pressed her lips together. Isabel glanced between the two men, but before anyone could speak, the door opened to admit Hartley.

"The second course, my lord."

Two footmen followed with platters of roasted pheasant and glazed vegetables. Conversation turned to other matters as Vera recounted their afternoon's adventures, from the modiste's recommendations to the ribbons they had debated over to the hat that Lord Daventry had declared utterly absurd.

"Speaking of this afternoon's events," the earl said after they had finished and the servants had cleared the main course away, "Damien told me about your encounter with Delacroix."

The lightness evaporated from the room.

Vera's smile faded. Isabel straightened in her chair.

"From now on," the earl continued, his gaze settling on his sister, "you will not leave this house without proper escort." He turned his head to meet Isabel's eyes. "And you, Miss de Clare, are not to go anywhere without myself or Lord Daventry present."

Isabel bit back the sharp retort that immediately rose to her tongue. She had to learn to pick her battles.

And if she was honest, the memory of Delacroix's fractured mind and his ominous promise made the earl's restrictions feel less like imprisonment and more like protection.

"I understand the necessity, my lord," she said quietly. "Though I hope this arrangement will not be permanent."

The earl's expression softened ever so slightly. "Neither do I."

Dessert was served, a rich chocolate torte, and the mood gradually eased. Vera mentioned the upcoming autumn ball, and Lord Daventry offered his opinions on which guests were likely to attend. Isabel ate slowly, savoring each bite. She couldn't remember the last time she had tasted something so decadent. Not since childhood, certainly. The sweetness melted on her tongue, rich and dark, and for a moment she forgot everything else.

As the servants cleared the dessert plates, the earl set down his napkin and turned to Isabel.

"Miss de Clare. Have you come to a decision regarding my proposal?"

Isabel met his gaze steadily. "I have, my lord. But I wonder if we might discuss the particulars in private. After dinner."

"Very well," he agreed. "As it happens, there is a matter I need to discuss with you as well."

"Well then," Vera announced, rising from her chair with a delicate yawn. "I believe I shall retire early. It has been quite an exhausting day."

She moved around the table and took Lord Daventry's arm, tugging him to his feet. "Come along, Damien. Walk me to the stairs. I want to hear more about that card game you mentioned earlier."

Lord Daventry cast a glance at the earl and shrugged, allowing Vera to steer him toward the door.

"As the lady commands," he said lightly. "Good evening, Miss de Clare. Alexander."

"Good night, Isabel," Vera added, pausing at the threshold to look back. "Do try not to be too harsh with her, Alexander. Not everyone is accustomed to your dry manner."

"I rather suspect," Lord Daventry remarked, glancing back over his shoulder, "that his manner has met its match."

The door closed behind them, and a taut silence descended upon the dining room.

The earl rose from his chair.

"Miss de Clare, if you will follow me to the drawing room?"

Isabel stood up, smoothing the silk of her skirt. "Of course, my lord."

Alexander closed the door behind them and moved to the sideboard where crystal decanters caught the amber glow of the fire.

"Would you care for a drink, Miss de Clare? I find that difficult conversations are often easier with brandy."

"Is this to be a difficult conversation, my lord?"

He paused, decanter in hand, and looked at her over his shoulder. "I suppose that depends on what you have to say."

"Then yes. I believe I would like that drink."

He poured two glasses and turned to offer her one. She lifted her hand to accept it, then hesitated. Their eyes met for the briefest moment, before she carefully took the glass.

Alexander gestured toward the large leather armchairs arranged before the hearth. "Please, sit."

She remained standing. So did he.

Alexander cleared his throat. "Miss de Clare, I should tell you that my meeting this afternoon—"

"What are you?"

The question caught him off guard.

"I beg your pardon?"

"You heard me." Isabel had not moved, but her posture had shifted. She stood straight, her chin lifted, her eyes flaring bright violet, as if to make a point. "What are you, Lord Whitmore? Because you are not like other men. I knew that from the moment I first tried to read you at the auction house."

His fingers tightened around his glass, and he could feel his pulse quicken.

"Anyone I ever met, no matter how well guarded their minds, I could always feel their presence," she continued, her voice low. "Except yours. You are completely silent. As if you don't exist. And when you touched me the other night..." She took a breath. "I will ask you once again. What are you?"

Alexander forced himself to remain still, even as his thoughts raced.

He should have known better than to think he could hide his true nature from a telepath. Then again, it had never occurred to him that his abilities might have an effect on anyone beside himself.

"Miss de Clare—"

"If I am to help you," she interrupted, "I need the truth. The whole truth. About everything. Who you really are. What your history with the marquis is." She stepped closer, and he caught the faint scent of lavender. "Why you want him destroyed so badly that you were willing to spend a fortune on me."

Alexander held her violet gaze.

The truth sat heavy on his tongue. Eight years he had kept this secret. From Damien, from Vera, from everyone. If he told her what he was, she could destroy him with one word. One whisper to the wrong person and he would lose everything: his title, his position, but most of all, the ability to hunt the man who had murdered half his family.

But she already knew something was different about him. She had sensed the silence where his thoughts should be. And if he wanted justice, he needed her help.

The risk was enormous. But the alternative was worse: letting Delacroix continue his sinister work.

Alexander looked down at the brandy in his hand and let out a heavy sigh. Then he emptied the drink in one swallow and crossed to the sideboard to set the glass aside.

"I suppose," he said, "it is only fair you knew."

He turned toward the window, staring out into the darkness.

"Eight years ago," he began, "I was engaged to be married."

In the window's reflection, he could see Isabel turn toward him.

"Her name was Marianne. She was the daughter of the Marquis of Belmore, a family friend and my political mentor. I had known Marianne since childhood." He paused. "She was kind and gentle, and I cared for her very much."

When Isabel did not speak, he continued.

"One afternoon in spring, we were to visit the venue for our wedding, a country estate half an hour's ride outside of Greyport. Vera, only a child at the time, had stayed at Whitmore Manor with her governess. My parents, Marianne, myself, and Damien, who was to be my best man, had gathered at the marquis's manor in Greyport to discuss the final details for the wedding." He drew a slow breath. "Before departing to the venue, Marianne's father pulled me aside. There was a political appointment he wished to discuss. He suggested that my parents take Marianne ahead in our carriage, and that I follow shortly with him and Damien."

He turned from the window and met her eyes.

"By the time we caught up with them, the carriage was in flames. My parents and Marianne were dead."

Isabel's face had gone pale. But she remained silent.

"Later, I found evidence that led me to believe Delacroix was behind it. Consequently my desire to bring him to justice and why I began to investigate him."

Isabel frowned. "No more omissions, my lord. If I am to help you, I need to know exactly what I am walking into. Every detail. Every piece of evidence." She set down her untouched glass and crossed her arms. "Tell me everything. From the beginning."

Alexander considered this for a moment. Then he moved to one of the armchairs and sank into the soft leather.

"Very well," he said, suddenly feeling weary. "From the beginning."

"The sunlight was warm that early spring day, and I remember the smell of tea and fresh-cut flowers filling the morning room of Belmore Manor. Marianne stood by the window. She was wearing a cream-coloured dress that day. I remember, because the sunlight that flooded the room made her look like an angel. She was laughing at something Damien had just said. He was hopeless, even then.

"I was happy. The future stretched before me like an open road. My parents were there, my mother fussing over wedding details while my father and Lord Belmore discussed politics in the corner. Damien was making Marianne laugh, and I was watching her, thinking how lucky I was.

"The marquis pulled me aside just as we were preparing to leave, asking me to discuss an opportunity with him.

"He told me about a position on the city council that had just opened up. A stepping stone that ultimately led to my current position as Under-Secretary of State for the Home Office. I was young and ambitious, and the prospect thrilled me. The Crown Prince himself had taken an interest in my career, Belmore said. It seemed my future in politics was assured.

"He suggested my parents take Marianne ahead. Damien, he, and I would follow shortly in his own carriage.

"I watched as my parents left with my bride-to-be. I never saw any of them alive again.

"The discussion lasted perhaps half an hour. I do not remember the details.

"But I remember listening to Damien and Lord Belmore discussing politics in the marquis's carriage, as I watched the countryside rolling past the windows. The forest was already in full bloom, and patches of bright flowers caught the golden sunlight under the trees. The perfect day.

"And then I saw the smoke.

"It rose above the tree line, black against the blue sky. My heart sank. Somehow I knew, even before I saw it.

"I yelled to the driver to go faster.

"We found them in a clearing just off the main road. Their carriage was overturned, engulfed in flames.

"The coachman lay nearby, motionless. The footman beside him, his throat cut.

"I was out of Belmore's carriage before it had fully stopped. I ran. I screamed their names. The heat stole my breath, but I did not stop.

"I climbed onto the overturned carriage, reaching for the side door, but it was jammed. I threw myself against it, but it would not give. I could see them through the window. Their shapes were obscured by the smoke, but even so I could see they were already gone. Yet I could not stop.

"I smashed my fist through the glass. The shards tore into my flesh, but I did not feel it. I reached inside, grasping for anything, anyone. Flames were burning my skin, still I reached out.

"Then Damien's arms closed around me from behind. He dragged me back, and I fought him, cursed him. I would have killed him if it meant getting back to that carriage. But he held on. He held on even as I collapsed onto the ground, even as I began to shake.

"I do not know how long we sat there like that. Lord Belmore appeared at our side. He had sent his coachman off to get help on horseback, leaving his carriage behind. His face was grey as he looked at the wreckage. Marianne had been all he had left since his wife's death in childbirth, and now his only child was gone too.

"Beside us, the coachman whom we believed to be dead stirred in the mud. I knelt beside him. The man's eyes were glassy.

"He whispered something. 'Da... water...'.

"Damien went to fetch him some water from the marquis's carriage. The man just shook his head and mumbled on, pointing his finger into the distance, where crows were already gathering in the trees. 'Da... water. Da... crow.'

"Then he was gone."

Alexander stopped. The room was silent except for the crackle of the fire.

Isabel's voice was quiet. "I'm so sorry."

He turned to look at her. At some point during his account she had settled into the armchair beside his. He had not even noticed her move.

Alexander felt the leather creak beneath his fingers where he was gripping the armrest. "It was a long time ago."

"How did you connect it to Delacroix?" she asked.

"I did not at first." He drew a breath. "The magistrates ruled it a robbery gone wrong. I tried to tell them it made no sense, but they would not listen."

"How did you know it wasn't a robbery?"

"My mother's jewels were still on her body. My father's purse was in the wreckage. Nothing had been taken."

Isabel frowned. "Then what did the thieves want?"

"I asked the same question." He rose, moved to the sideboard, poured another brandy and then set the glass back down without drinking, before crossing to the hearth. "Three days after their funeral, I received word. Someone had broken into Whitmore Manor."

"Your country estate?"

He nodded. "My father's study had been torn apart. Furniture was overturned, the desk smashed."

"What were the thieves looking for?"

"My parents' research." Alexander turned to the hearth, his gaze fixed on the glowing embers. "They had been studying magical bloodlines. Families where the gift lies dormant."

Isabel went still. "Was it stolen?"

"Not all of it. My parents kept a hidden safe for their most important findings. I was the only other person who knew of its existence, though until that day I had never known what it contained." He paused and met her eyes. "That day, I discovered the truth about our family. About myself."

"You're a magic user." Isabel's voice was flat, unsurprised.

"A Shield." He watched her carefully. "My parents knew since I was a boy. They kept it hidden. To protect me."

“That's what my parents tried to do, only they failed...”

Isabel turned to look out the window, her gaze distant. He was about to say something, when she suddenly snapped her head back to him. "That's why I can't read you."

"Yes."

Isabel's gaze sharpened. "But how do you know it was Delacroix who wanted that research?"

"There was a letter in the safe. Someone requesting access to my parents' findings. It bore the sigil of the Marquis of Darkwater."

"The dying coachman," Isabel said slowly. "He wasn't asking for water."

"No."

"Dark... water. Dela... croix." She stood and crossed her arms. "What could he want with this knowledge?"

Alexander's jaw tightened. "I do not know. But I am certain it is connected to the disappearances of magic users over the last years. Most of them could be traced back to the marquis in one way or another."

"What about Lord Belmore," she asked. "He must have known the marquis well. Did he not have any suspicions?"

"Not that I know. He was consumed by grief and died within a year after his daughter's death."

"So you've spent the last eight years hunting Delacroix." Isabel studied him. "Your position within the Home Office is not just about politics, is it?"

"I do aspire to make a difference in the political sphere. The Crown Prince and I share a vision for reforming the Protection of the Realm Act. We both believe it should be amended to achieve greater equality between the people of this kingdom and its magic users. But my office also affords me access to information, and the ability to move in circles where men like Delacroix operate."

Isabel moved closer, her eyes locked on his.

"Why does Delacroix want magic users? What is he doing with them?"

"That is what I need to find out, and why I need your help."

Isabel picked up her glass from the side table and took a swallow before setting it back down, letting the earl's story settle in her mind. She knew the kind of grief he had been through. She carried her own version of it, though she kept it buried in a place where not even she could see it most of the time.

"I never told Damien what I found in my father's study that day," Lord Whitmore said, breaking the silence. "I never told anyone. Until now."

Isabel glanced at him. He stood motionless, one hand on the mantelpiece, the sharp lines of his features cast in relief by the fading glow of the fire.

He had trusted her with the one secret that could destroy him. Just one word to the wrong person and the Earl of Whitmore would be exposed as a magic user. He would be stripped of his title, would lose everything he had spent eight years building. She could ruin him, and he knew it. He had told her anyway.

"Your secret is safe with me, Lord Whitmore."

He turned to look at her, brows furrowed. Then, a small smile touched his lips, softening the hard lines of his face, and she couldn't help dropping her gaze to his mouth.

"Thank you," he said.

Isabel looked away quickly, turning her attention to the coals.

"I'm sorry," she said after a moment. "For your loss. I know what it is to lose a parent. Though I cannot imagine the pain of losing a love." She glanced at him under her lashes and felt her cheeks warm as she continued. "I have never had that."

"Perhaps it is a blessing," he said.

She looked at him, frowning.

"Better to avoid such pain altogether," he continued and turned back to the fire, the glowing embers reflecting in his eyes.

She studied him in the dim light. The rigid set of his shoulders, the tension in his jaw. The way he drew his brows together when he was in deep thought.

"I will help you," she said. "I will help you bring that man to justice."

He turned to face her, opening his mouth, but before he could speak she continued: "But I have conditions."

"Name them."

"First, complete transparency. You will show me all the evidence you have gathered. I need to understand the complete picture if I am to be of any use to you."

"Of course."

"Second, total honesty. You hide nothing from me. If something is relevant to this investigation, I expect you to share it with me. Immediately."

"Agreed."

"Third." She paused and drew a breath, straightening in her chair. "When the threat of Delacroix has been dealt with, you will grant me my freedom. Officially and unconditionally."

The earl met her eyes. "You have my word."

She studied him, searching for any sign of deception, but his mind remained ever so closed to her. She had only his face to read. Only his voice to judge.

And she found that she believed him.

"Then we have an agreement, Lord Whitmore."

"We do, Miss de Clare."

He took a step towards her and extended his hand.

She stared at his outstretched palm. Her heart quickened. If she took it, would it happen again? That extraordinary silence, that sudden, blissful absence of every voice except her own?

The thought frightened her. And drew her forward in equal measure.

Slowly, she lifted her arm and placed her hand in his.

And the world fell away.

He felt her. Not just the warmth of her hand in his, but Isabel herself. It was as if she had entered a space that he had been alone in his whole life and had not even known. He could feel her presence with a sense that he did not know he possessed. As if they stood together in a sanctum in which no one else could enter.

He drew a sharp breath, his eyes never leaving hers, and searched her face for a sign that she might be feeling the same. Her eyes had gone wide the moment they had touched, and she seemed to hold her breath.

"Miss de Clare, are you alright?" he asked and let go of her hand, worried that his magic might have an adverse effect on her.

"I'm... I'm quite alright," she mumbled. "Did you feel something... unusual?"

He considered her question. His nature demanded he keep his thoughts private. But had they not just agreed to be honest to each other? Granted, she had asked for his honesty in regards to the investigations. But something told him that this new turn of events might not be completely irrelevant for their endeavours to overthrow the marquis.

Apart from all of that, he felt the strange urge to share with her what he had felt.

"Yes. Though I am not entirely sure what..." He paused. "What about you?"

She cleared her throat and lowered her gaze. For a moment it looked as if her cheeks had flushed, though he could not be sure with the sparse light that the glowing embers were providing.

"I felt..." she began, still avoiding his eyes. "I felt your silence."

He frowned. "Will you explain it to me?"

She picked up her glass and drained what remained of her drink.

"Would you mind pouring me another one?"

"Of course."

Alexander took the glass she held out to him and moved to the sideboard, grateful for the distraction. He poured a measure for her, and then picked up his own, half-forgotten drink.

When he returned, she had settled back into her chair. She accepted the glass with a quiet word of thanks and took a slow sip while he took the seat beside her.

"There is a constant hum," she said, her gaze drifting to the fading coals in the hearth. "People's thoughts, the minds around me. I can hear everyone in the vicinity. It never stops." She paused. "Over time, I have learned to block them out. To build a wall in my mind. But it never blocks the voices out completely and it requires constant effort to hold it up. When I am tired or unwell, the hum grows louder. Harder to ignore."

Alexander listened in silence, watching the warm glow of the fire soften her features.

"I can focus on a single mind if I choose," she continued. "Isolate one's thoughts like twisting the lens of a spyglass until the image sharpens. Most people are easy to read. Some seem to have a natural defence around their minds, but even those I can usually penetrate with some effort."

She took another sip of her brandy.

"Delacroix is different."

Alexander stiffened at the name.

"His mind is..." She hesitated, as if searching for the right words. "Twisted. Corrupted. I could not penetrate his thoughts, and honestly, I did not want to try. It was like pressing my hand against broken glass. But at least I could perceive him." Her violet eyes lifted to meet his. "I always know when someone is near. I always perceive the minds around me."

She paused, and something shifted in her expression.

"Except for yours."

Alexander said nothing.

"I cannot perceive your mind at all," she said quietly. "It is as if you are not there. Now, knowing of your shield magic, that explains it. But the interesting part is what happens when ... when we touch." She set down her glass and folded her hands in her lap. "It happened yesterday, too. When you touched my wrist. The contact seems to block everything else out. My mind goes quiet. The voices disappear and it is completely silent. Everything is gone, save for my own thoughts. It feels as if I am in a sphere, surrounded by a wall that nothing can penetrate."

She paused, her violet eyes finding his.

"It feels amazing," she admitted. "And terrifying at the same time."

Alexander was silent for a long moment, considering what he had just learned.

"For me," he confessed, "it was similar. And yet... the opposite." He frowned, struggling to articulate what he had felt. "I also felt as if I was in a sphere. But for once, I was not alone. I could sense you there with me, in a space where no one else has ever been."

Their eyes met in the dim light.

"Do you know what it means?" she asked.

"No," he admitted. "But perhaps there is more to my magic than I understood. It might be worth exploring, if it could give us an advantage against Delacroix."

The words hung in the air, and he realised belatedly how they might sound.

"By that I did not mean—" He cleared his throat. "I was not suggesting that we should... that I would ask you to... What I meant was, looking into my abilities. Seeing if I can use my magic somehow after all."

He could feel heat creeping up his neck.

"No," she said with a small smile. "You are right. We should pursue every possible advantage that might help bring down the marquis."

Their eyes held for a moment longer, then she looked away.

"You mentioned there was something else you wished to discuss with me," she said, breaking the silence.

"Yes." Alexander took a long swallow of his brandy, grateful for the change of subject. "I met a friend of mine this afternoon. Captain Dominic Raines."

"The pirate?" Isabel asked.

He snapped his head toward her. "He is not a—" And stopped when he saw her holding back a laugh, her eyes glinting with mischief.

Alexander shook his head. "I see Damien's influence is already taking hold."

"Pardon me, my lord," she said, a giggle escaping her. "If you don't mind me asking, what does this captain have to do with the investigation?"

"He has access to places I do not. Specifically, to the prison of Greyport, where a woman is being held that I need to speak to." He took another sip. "Leonora is a fire starter. She was arrested after the tragedy at the harbour several weeks ago. She is awaiting execution for arson and murder. I believe she may have information about Delacroix's operations."

Isabel frowned. "You want me to read her mind."

"I want you to accompany me when I speak with her, to verify if her answers are truthful. I need to find out what she knows about a man named Dave." He set down his glass on the side table. "Dave ran a shelter for magic users in the Warrens. A place called Haven. He disappeared shortly before Leonora was arrested. I have reason to believe Delacroix is responsible for both their fates."

"And how exactly is Captain Raines going to help us access the prison?"

"He has a way of making things possible." Alexander hesitated. "But he wants something in return."

Isabel's expression grew wary. "And what might that be?"

"Your assistance." He met her eyes steadily. "He has a matter of his own that requires the services of a telepath. He would not tell me the specifics, only that it would take an afternoon of your time." He held her gaze. "I told him I would pass on the request, but that the decision would ultimately be yours. And I made it a condition that I be present for whatever he has planned. I will not send you anywhere alone."

She was quiet for a moment.

"I accept," she said eventually.

Alexander blinked. "Just like that?"

"I have just agreed to help you bring down a suspected criminal. If assisting your smuggler friend is part of that arrangement, then so be it."

"He is not a—" He stopped and watched as Isabel pressed her lips together, fighting the grin that threatened to break free.

"Very well," he said, feeling a smile tug at his own lips. "I will let the captain know first thing tomorrow. The sooner we can gain access to that prison, the better."

Isabel rose from her chair, smoothing her skirts. Her expression sobered, and he noticed the weariness settling into her features.

"Then I suggest we both get some rest, my lord. It seems we have a great deal of work ahead of us."

Alexander stood as well. "Allow me to accompany you to your room."

"That is really not necessary," she said.

"As you wish."

He accompanied her to the door though and opened it for her. She paused at the threshold, turning to look at him.

"Good night, my lord."

"Please," he said quietly. "Call me Alexander."

She smiled, a small, almost teasing curve of her lips and repeated: "Good night, my lord."

He exhaled slowly. "Good night, Miss de Clare."

He watched her walk toward the stairs, the blue-grey silk of her skirt shimmering under the sconces along the corridor. She did not look back.

When she had disappeared from view, he stepped back into the drawing room and closed the door behind him, leaning against it.

His hand still tingled where they had touched.

Chapter Four

"Delacroix has been buying magic users for years," Alexander said, looking up from the ledger spread open before him, meeting Isabel's eyes across the desk.

They had spent the better part of a week like this, the two of them in the library from breakfast until dinner, working through eight years of evidence. Alexander had laid it all before her: the records, the witness accounts, everything he had gathered, and Isabel had absorbed every detail.

"At first, we thought it was simple exploitation," he continued. "Cheap labour for his estates."

"But the pattern does not fit," Vera said from the armchair by the fireplace, where she had settled after joining them mid-afternoon.

Isabel's brows lifted. "What pattern?"

"They disappear." Alexander met her eyes. "Within months of purchase, sometimes weeks. Yet there are no sales or deaths reported. They simply vanish from the registries."

"How many?"

"Forty-three that we have confirmed. Likely more." He turned a page in the registry. "There are ways of acquiring staff that bypass official channels. Those transactions leave no trace."

“You mean transactions such as illegal auctions in the basements of gentlemen clubs?” Isabel gave him a sharp look and raised a brow, but he saw the corner of her mouth twitching.

“Amongst others...” he conceded.

"And no one is investigating these disappearances?" Isabel continued.

Vera shifted in her seat. "Who would? Magic users are not exactly a priority for the magistrates."

"Unless they burn down buildings," Alexander added grimly. "In that case they are investigated very thoroughly indeed."

"What else do you have?" Isabel asked.

Alexander rose from behind the desk and crossed to one of the bookshelves that lined the far wall. He pulled down a heavy volume bound in dark leather. "Delacroix has connections." He flipped the book open to a marked page. "High-level political allies. Military contacts. And over the past two years, he has been acquiring properties at an unusual rate. Warehouses, mostly. Many of them near the harbour, in districts where questions are rarely asked."

The door opened and Damien swept in, his collar open at the throat, golden hair slightly dishevelled.

"Apologies for my tardiness. Alexander, I came as soon as I got your message."

"Tardiness is generous," Vera remarked from her armchair. "The sun is practically setting, Damien."

"I was detained by matters of importance," he replied smoothly, turning to the women with a bow. "Lady Vera, you are a revelation, as always. And Miss de Clare—" He crossed to where Isabel sat at the desk and lifted her hand, brushing his lips across her knuckles. "I must say, this investigation has improved immeasurably since you joined us. I used to dread these briefings. Now I find myself looking forward to them."

Isabel's face brightened at Damien's attention, and Alexander felt his stomach tighten when he saw the smile she gave his friend.

Damien straightened with a grin. "So, what have I missed?"

"We were just discussing Delacroix’s associates," Alexander said dryly.

"Ah." Damien dropped into the chair next to Vera's. "Then you will want to hear what I have learned."

Alexander closed the book in his hands. "Go on."

"Delacroix has been meeting with someone from the Admiralty. I could not get names, but my source says they have been discussing shipments."

"Shipments of what?"

"That is the question." Damien leaned back, frowning.

Shipments. Warehouses. Missing magic users. Alexander turned the pieces over in his mind, searching for the pattern that would make them fit.

A knock sounded at the door and interrupted his thoughts. Hartley entered, a folded paper on a silver tray.

"My lord. This arrived by courier. The man said it was urgent."

Alexander took the note and broke the seal. His eyes narrowed as he scanned the contents. "It is from Raines. He has arranged the meeting. Tonight. At ten o'clock."

He handed the note to Isabel. She studied it, her face giving nothing away.

"Ten o'clock?" Vera frowned. "That leaves you barely two hours to prepare before you must leave."

"Then we had best not waste them." Alexander turned to Isabel. "We should get ready. I will have supper brought up to your room. Wear something practical. Dark colours. We will be going through the Warrens to avoid attention."

"I will help you change," Vera said, already rising.

Isabel nodded and stood as well. Hartley followed the women out, closing the door behind them.

Silence settled over the library. When Alexander turned from the door, Damien was watching him.

"You are taking her with you?"

"Yes."

"Into the Warrens? At night? To meet a man of highly questionable character in one of the most dangerous places in Greyport?"

"I need her. If the fire starter knows anything about Dave or Delacroix, Isabel can tell if she is lying."

"And if it's a trap?"

"It is not."

"You trust Raines that much?"

Alexander held his friend's gaze. "I trust him to keep his word when he gives it."

Damien rose and crossed to the small cabinet beside the bookshelves where Alexander kept a decanter for long evenings of work. He poured two glasses and handed one to his friend. "Let me accompany you at least."

"Raines said to come alone. This might be the only chance we get to speak with the fire starter. We cannot risk losing it."

The viscount raised the glass to his lips and drank. "I will wait in the carriage then."

"Damien—"

"I promise I will not interfere in your business with the pirate. But I will not sit here, useless, while I might be of help should you run into trouble along the way." His voice hardened. "You can take me as far as the drop point or you can leave without me, but if you choose the latter, I will simply follow in my own carriage. Either way, I'm coming." Damien drained the last of his brandy, then set the glass down with a sharp click.

"Very well," Alexander conceded, knowing from long experience that arguing with Damien once his mind was set was an entirely pointless endeavour.

The carriage wheels rattled over cobblestones as they left the well-lit streets of Greyport's esteemed districts behind. Isabel pulled her dark woolen coat tighter against the cold seeping through the walls. Outside, fog had rolled in from the harbour, turning the gaslight into pale smudges of gold against the November dark.

She had been surprised when Lord Daventry climbed into the carriage behind them, settling himself beside the earl on the opposite bench. Lord Whitmore had frowned but said nothing, which Isabel took to mean the matter had already been argued and lost.

The journey was long. An hour at least, winding through Greyport's streets as the neighborhoods grew steadily shabbier outside the windows. The earl sat with his arms folded and his gaze fixed on the darkened glass, his mouth set in that grim line she was beginning to recognise as his version of deep thought. He had barely spoken since they left Whitmore Hall.

His friend, mercifully, had no such affliction.

"You know," the viscount said, stretching his legs out as far as the confined space would allow, "I once attended a supper at Lady Deacon's where the baroness herself spent the entire first course whispering the most appalling gossip about every other guest at her table. By the time the fish arrived, I knew enough to blackmail half the peerage."

Isabel raised a brow. "And did you?"

"Of course not. But I filed it all away for future use." He grinned. "One never knows when a well-placed secret might prove useful."

She felt the corner of her mouth twitch. Lord Daventry's thoughts drifted through her awareness, warm and unguarded. He was genuinely trying to put her at ease, and the kindness behind his performance was so transparent it was almost endearing.

That was the remarkable thing about the viscount. In twelve years of reading minds, Isabel had grown accustomed to the gap between what people said and what they thought. Most of them lied constantly, small lies and large ones, their words a careful mask over thoughts that were uglier, pettier, or simply different from what they showed the world. It was exhausting. Like listening to two conversations at once.

But Lord Daventry said precisely what he was thinking. His words and his thoughts ran so close together that being near him was almost restful. He held nothing back, filtered nothing out, and while that made him loud in her awareness, it also made him safe. There was no hidden blade beneath the charm. No second motive lurking behind the smile.

It was the same with Vera, whose thoughts matched her words so closely it was startling.

Isabel couldn't remember the last time she had felt so at ease around other people.

She had never had friends. Even as a child, her parents had kept her isolated, fearing that too much contact with others would expose what she was. They had lived far out in the northern countryside, where villages were sparse and neighbors distant, and visitors rarely came. Isabel's only companions had been her mother's books and the wide, empty moors beyond their garden wall. The first time she had ever seen a crowd was the day her parents brought her to Greyport, desperately seeking a doctor after they had failed to cure her pneumonia.

She pushed that thought back down before it could go further.

But if she had known what friendship looked like, she suspected it might look something like this. People who asked questions and listened to the answers. Who treated her as a person, not a thing to be used.

"You've gone quiet, Miss de Clare," Lord Daventry observed, watching her. "Should I be concerned?"

"I was thinking."

"A dangerous pastime. What about?"

Isabel hesitated. The truth was too heavy for a carriage ride, and too private for present company. She settled on a half-truth instead. "About how different it is here," she said. "At Whitmore Hall. From what I am accustomed to."

The viscount's expression lost some of its playfulness. "Different how?"

"People speak to me politely. Consider my needs. Offer me tea instead of ordering me to fetch it." She paused. "It takes some getting used to."

Across the carriage, the earl turned his head from the window, and his grey eyes found hers in the dim light.

She looked away first.

"Well," Lord Daventry said, his voice light, though she could hear the sincerity beneath it, "you had better grow accustomed to it. Lady Vera has already declared you her new favourite person, and once Vera claims someone, there is no escape. Trust me. I have been trying for years."

Isabel's lips curved. "She does seem rather determined."

"Determined is putting it mildly. The woman is a force of nature." Lord Daventry glanced sideways at his friend. "Speaking of determination, Alexander, I have been meaning to ask. Lady Deacon demanded to know whether you intend to appear at her autumn ball with a companion or whether she must endure the indignity of seating an unaccompanied earl at her table for the eighth year running."

The earl's jaw tightened. He shifted in his seat and turned to the window. "We are here," he said.

The carriage came to a halt.

Isabel looked out the window. They had stopped on the corner of a deserted street from which several alleys branched off into the dark. Fog curled between the buildings, thick and grey, and beyond it in the distance she could make out the dark silhouette of the prison rising against the night sky.

Lord Whitmore was already reaching for the door, his expression closed. "Stay with the carriage," he told his friend as he stepped out. "We should not be long."

"And if you are?"

"Then wait longer."

Damp autumn air rushed in, carrying the smell of coal smoke. The earl turned and offered Isabel his gloved hand.

She took it and stepped down into the cold.

They walked a short distance down the street, past shuttered shop fronts and darkened windows, until they reached an alley that ended in fog and darkness.

Alexander stopped at the entry where the cobblestones gave way to bare earth, one hand resting on the pistol concealed beneath his coat. Beside him, Isabel pulled her dark shawl tighter against the November chill, her breath forming pale clouds in the lantern light.

They entered the narrow lane, and as they drew closer to its end, a figure took shape in the mist. Dominic Raines was leaning against the damp brick wall with his arms folded across his broad chest, his dark coat open at the collar despite the cold, looking for all the world as if he had been waiting there for hours and hadn't minded a minute of it. His green eyes found Isabel first, and a slow, appreciative smile spread across his face.

"Well, hello, darling." His gaze swept over her with open admiration. "You must be the remarkable Miss de Clare."

Isabel's lips curved. "And you must be the captain I've heard so much about."

"All good things, I hope." Raines pushed off the wall and took Isabel's hand, bowing over it with a flourish that would have been more suited to a ballroom than a filthy alleyway. "Captain Dominic Raines, at your service. Though I insist you call me Nic. All my friends do."

"And are we friends, Captain?" Isabel asked.

"I certainly hope so."

Alexander stepped forward. "Now that we have dispensed with the pleasantries, perhaps we might get on with the reason we are here."

He heard the edge in his own voice and clenched his jaw. He did not like the way Raines was looking at her. The man had a reputation with women that rivaled Damien's, and while Alexander could trust his best friend to keep his charm well clear of anyone under Alexander's protection, Raines operated under no such restraints.

The captain squared his shoulders, his grin undiminished. "Straight to the point, as always, Lord Whitmore. To business, then." He turned and gestured toward the dead end of the alley, where a rusted iron grate sat half-hidden behind a pile of broken crates. "If you will follow me."

He crouched, pulled the grate aside, and revealed a narrow opening cut into the brickwork. A set of rough stone steps descended into blackness.

"Ladies first?" Raines offered, extending his hand toward Isabel.

"I will go first," Alexander said flatly. He ducked through the opening and descended the slick steps, but after only a few paces the darkness swallowed him whole. He stopped, unable to see more than an inch ahead.

Behind him he heard the scrape of a flint. A spark caught, flared, and warm light flooded the passage as Raines lit a torch he had pulled from a bracket on the wall. He held it out to Alexander with a smirk.

"You'll be needing this."

Alexander took the torch without comment. Raines closed the grate behind them, pulled a second torch from the wall, and lit it off Alexander's flame. Then he slipped past him and took the lead.

The tunnel was old. The walls were rough-hewn stone, and the ceiling hung low enough that Alexander had to watch his head. Water dripped from above, a persistent tap against the flagstones that echoed in the enclosed space. The air smelled of damp earth and stagnant water, and somewhere ahead Alexander could hear the faint trickle of a stream running through cracks in the rock.

"Smuggler's tunnels," Raines explained. "Built during the Fae border wars, back when the Crown needed to move soldiers and supplies without being seen. Half the Warrens sits on top of them. Very useful if one wants to avoid attracting attention."

"I imagine they are," Isabel said. Alexander glanced back and saw her eyes glowing faintly violet in the torchlight, scanning the passage around them. She moved with cautious steps, one hand trailing the wall for balance. The tunnel was high enough for her to walk upright without difficulty, while he and Raines had to stoop at intervals where the ceiling dipped.

"How far to the prison?" Alexander asked.

"Not far. A quarter of an hour, perhaps, depending on how quickly our lovely companion can manage the terrain." Raines cast a grin over his shoulder at Isabel. "The footing is treacherous in places, I'm afraid. Do let me know if you need a steadying arm, Miss de Clare."

"I shall manage, Captain. Thank you."

Alexander set his jaw and pressed forward.

They walked in near silence after that, the only sounds their footsteps and the incessant dripping of water. The tunnel branched several times, dark corridors splitting off into deeper blackness, but Raines navigated each junction without hesitation, guiding them left, then right, then down a narrow flight of steps that brought them deeper underground.

At one such junction, where the ground was particularly uneven, Isabel's foot caught on a raised flagstone. She stumbled forward with a sharp intake of breath, and Alexander turned and caught her by the arm before she could fall.

Isabel's eyes flew to his, wide and luminous in the torchlight, her lips parted.

"Careful," he whispered, and released her arm.

She straightened, brushing a loose strand of hair from her face. "Thank you."

Behind them, Raines had watched the exchange.

"This way," he said, and led them onward.

The tunnel began to climb. Gradually the descent reversed, the passage angling upward through the rock, the steps growing rougher and steeper until they emerged into a wider section that ran level again.

The corridor ended at a heavy oak door reinforced with iron bands. Raines slipped his torch into an empty iron bracket beside the frame and gestured for Alexander to do the same.

Then the captain produced a key, worked it in the lock, and the door swung inward with a groan of old hinges.

Beyond lay a narrow corridor, lit only by a guttering torch. The smell hit Alexander first. Damp straw and unwashed skin.

"The guards?" he asked.

"Having a very restful evening, courtesy of a bottle of excellent whiskey." Raines tucked the key ring back into his coat. "We have perhaps an hour before the next patrol. Less if they drink faster than expected."

Alexander turned to Isabel. Her face was composed, her shoulders straight, though the faint glow in her eyes had brightened. "Are you ready?"

"I am."

"I will ask the questions. Watch her thoughts. If she is hiding anything, or if you sense anything I should know, signal me."

Isabel gave a short nod.

Raines moved to the second door to their left and unlocked it. "In here."

The cell was barely six feet across. In it stood a narrow cot and a bucket sat in one corner. A barred window was set high in the wall, admitting a thin draught of cold air.

On the cot sat a woman.

She was younger than Alexander had expected, in her early twenties maybe, with dark hair that fell tangled past her shoulders and amber-golden eyes that flared faintly as they entered. Her cheeks looked a touch more hollow than they probably should have been, but there was strength in her frame, and when she lifted her head and met his gaze, there was no defeat in her expression. Only a fierce, simmering defiance that reminded him of Isabel.

"Leonora," Alexander said.

“I prefer Lena,” she said, narrowing her eyes.

She looked wary, her gaze moving from his face to Raines, then to Isabel, and back again.

"Who are you?"

"Alexander Kensington, Earl of Whitmore."

The wariness did not leave her face, but her posture shifted as she straightened her spine and lifted her chin. "Lord Whitmore." She held his gaze, and focusing on his eyes her expression suddenly shifted. "So we finally meet."

Alexander went still. "You know who I am."

"Dave never gave me your name. But he let a description slip once." She held his eyes. "He said you refused to accept his reports by letter and insisted on delivering the funds for the shelter in person every month, even though it put you at risk."

Alexander felt his throat tighten. "He was not wrong."

Beside him, he noticed Isabel's gaze sharpen. He had not told her about his connection to Haven.

"I have arranged to delay your execution," Alexander continued, "but I cannot hold it off indefinitely. My influence has limits."

"Yes." Lena's jaw tightened. "The guards enjoy reminding me how many days I have left."

"Then you understand why I need your help. And why there is little time."

Raines leaned against the doorframe, arms folded, keeping watch on the corridor behind them. Alexander stepped closer, and Isabel followed, her eyes never leaving Lena's face.

"This is Miss de Clare," Alexander said. "She is a telepath, and she is helping me with my investigation. I need to ask you some questions about Dave. About his disappearance and about what happened at the harbour."

Lena's gaze moved to Isabel. The two women regarded each other in silence, and Lena's amber eyes flickered briefly to the faint violet glow in Isabel's.

"A telepath." Lena's voice was flat. "So you'll know if I lie."

"Yes," Isabel said quietly.

"Good." Lena sat straighter, her hands gripping the edge of the cot. "Ask your questions, Lord Whitmore. I have nothing to hide."

Alexander drew a breath. "Tell me about Dave. When did you last see him?"

The defiance in Lena's expression cracked, just slightly, and underneath it Alexander glimpsed the raw edge of grief. She pressed her lips together and stared at a point on the wall above his shoulder.

"The day he disappeared. A day before that, a man had come to Haven. A lord, in a black carriage. He spoke with Dave in private and made him an offer. A fortune in exchange for exclusive service. Dave refused." Her voice hardened. "But I saw the man's face when he left. Dave's refusal meant nothing to him."

"Did Dave tell you anything more about the visit? Or the man?"

"Only what I already told you. I confronted him about it that evening. He was evasive. Said the man was just another wealthy lord looking to buy a magic user. Told me not to worry." Bitterness crept into her words. "The next day, Dave went out for his usual meetings and never came back, although he was supposed to meet me and..."

She paused. Her jaw worked, and she stared down at her hands.

"I waited for him at our spot in the park until dusk. When he didn't come, I went back to Haven. He wasn't there either. No one had seen him since the morning." She drew a breath. "I searched his chamber and found a calling card. On it was the name and sigil of the Marquis of Darkwater."

"Delacroix," Alexander said.

"I didn't know the name then. But I knew in my gut that it was the same man who had come to see Dave. I went to his town residence the next day, demanding an audience." Her lips curled. "His servants turned me away at the door. Told me the marquis was not receiving visitors, least of all my kind."

"How did you end up at the warehouse?"

Lena's expression went rigid.

"Days passed without any word or trace from Dave. Then someone on the street, a dock worker I had asked about him before, told me he'd seen a young man matching his description at a warehouse near the southern docks. I knew it could be a trap." She looked down at her hands. "I went anyway."

"Because you love him."

"Yes." The admission was fierce and unapologetic. "When I arrived, the warehouse was dark. Empty, or so I thought. I stepped inside and the doors slammed shut behind me. There were men, four, perhaps five. They were armed with rifles and iron chains. They knew what I was. They were prepared."

"What happened then?"

"I defended myself." Lena's amber eyes blazed despite the iron shackles, the glow of her fire stirring. "What would you have done, Lord Whitmore? Surrendered meekly and let them chain me like an animal? I burned the crossbow bolts out of the air. I threw fire at anyone who came close. And then—"

She broke off, her jaw working.

"Then there were explosions. One after another, so loud it made my ears ring. The whole warehouse went up in flames. I didn't know there were barrels in there, filled with gunpowder, I think, packed in by the dozen. The fire fed on them and spread faster than anything I could control."

"You survived because fire cannot burn you," Alexander said.

"Yes." Her voice was flat. "I walked out of that inferno without a scratch on me. And I walked straight into a young woman who was running toward the flames."

"A storm caller."

Lena looked up in surprise and nodded. "She was trying to help. Called the rain down, but the wind came with it, a gale that fanned the fire outward before the rain could smother it."

At the doorframe, Raines turned his head sharply, his gaze fixing on Lena.

"The flames reached the harbour," she continued. "The ships—" Her voice faltered. "The ships were already burning by the time either of us understood what was happening."

"And then?" Alexander asked.

"We ran. Both of us. She went one way, I went another." Lena stared at the stone floor. "I didn't get far."

"The storm caller managed to escape," Alexander explained. "She is still on the run."

Relief softened Lena's features for the briefest instant. "Good." Then worry hardened her expression. "She was trying to save people. If they catch her—"

"I know."

Silence settled over the small cell. Alexander looked at Isabel.

She met his gaze and gave a firm nod.

Alexander turned back to Lena. "The dock worker who told you about the warehouse. Do you have any idea who he was?"

"No. But I'm sure he was working for the marquis." Her voice dropped. "It was all planned. The men that were waiting for me in the warehouse, the gunpowder. Someone wanted that warehouse to burn, and they wanted me to take the blame for it."

The words confirmed what Alexander had long suspected. The harbour fire was not an accident. It was orchestrated. A political weapon designed to fuel the growing sentiment against magic users and justify tighter restrictions under the Protection of the Realm Act.

And Delacroix's fingerprints were all over it.

Alexander looked at Raines, who had been listening from the doorway without a word. The captain met his gaze and raised an eyebrow.

Alexander gave a short nod.

Raines smiled and stepped into the cell, producing the ring of keys from inside his coat. He crouched before the iron shackle around Lena's ankle and fitted a key to the lock.

Lena stared at him. "What are you doing?"

"Getting you out of here, darling." The shackle fell open with a dull clank. Raines straightened and offered her his hand with the same courtly grace he had shown Isabel in the alley. "You'll be coming with me."

Lena did not take his hand. She looked past him to Alexander.

"It is alright," he said. "Captain Raines will keep you safe until we can prove your innocence. You have my word."

Her gaze drifted to Isabel, who gave a small nod, a warm smile softening her features.

Lena turned back to Alexander. "Dave trusted you. And you seem to have earned the trust of another one of my kind. That is no small thing." She straightened her shoulders. "I will take your word, Lord Whitmore."

She took Raines's offered hand and rose to her feet. She swayed, and Raines reached to steady her with a hand at her elbow, but Lena shook him off and squared her shoulders.

"I can walk on my own, Captain."

Raines's grin widened. "I have no doubt of it." He stepped back and swept a hand toward the door. "After you."

Lena and Raines stepped out of the cell, Isabel close behind. Alexander followed, briefly pausing to pull the cell door shut. As they stepped back into the smuggler's tunnel, the captain retrieved their torches from the wall brackets, handing one to Alexander.

They started walking, Raines leading the way, Alexander falling into step beside Isabel. In the dim light, her expression was difficult to read, but her eyes still glowed faintly, and he could tell her mind was working through everything she had heard.

"You funded a shelter for magic users," she said, her voice low enough that only he could hear. "You visited every month. In person. In the Warrens."

"Yes. It was the only way to ensure the money reached the people who needed it."

She held his gaze for several paces, searching his face. Then a small smile touched her lips, and she gave a barely perceptible nod before looking ahead again.

Alexander did not know why such a small gesture should settle so warmly in his chest. Lena's words echoed in his head. Could it be true? Did Isabel trust him? And why did the thought make his pulse quicken?

At a junction where three corridors branched off into darkness, Raines stopped.

“Here we part ways, my friend." He pointed down the left-hand passage. "Follow that tunnel to the end. Do not take any of the side passages. It will bring you back to the grate where we entered."

Alexander nodded. "And you?"

"My lovely companion and I have a ship to catch." Raines glanced at Lena, and the warmth in his smile was surprisingly genuine. "The *Sea Witch* sails with the tide, and I prefer not to keep my crew waiting."

"Where will you take her?"

"Somewhere beyond the reach of magistrates and hangmen." Raines clapped Alexander on the shoulder. "Don't worry, Lord Whitmore. I'll send word once she's settled. You have my promise." He turned to Isabel and bowed with an exaggerated courtesy. "Miss de Clare, it has been an absolute pleasure. I look forward to our afternoon together. Do remind your companion that he owes me a favour."

"He is not my—" Isabel began.

"Until next time." Raines tossed them a final grin, then turned and strode down the right-hand corridor. Lena followed, but paused at the edge of the torchlight and looked back.

"Lord Whitmore."

"Yes?"

"Find him." Her voice was raw. "Find Dave. Please."

Alexander held her gaze. "I will."

Lena pressed her lips together, nodded once, and disappeared into the darkness after Raines.

The sound of their footsteps faded, until all that remained was the steady drip of water from the ceiling. Alexander stood at the junction, his torch throwing a circle of wavering light against the walls while darkness surrounded them beyond its reach.

Then he turned to Isabel. The torchlight painted her features in gold and shadow, and her violet eyes held his with an expression he could not decipher.

"Shall we?" he said, offering his arm.

She looked at it for a mere second. Then she took it, her hand settling lightly in the crook of his elbow, and together they walked into the dark.

Isabel's mind was racing.

She walked beside the earl through the tunnel, her hand resting lightly on his arm, her thoughts churning through everything she had just witnessed. The Earl of Whitmore, Under-Secretary of State, had been funding a shelter for magic users in the Warrens, at considerable risk to his reputation and his safety.

She didn't know what to do with that information.

The ground beneath her feet was uneven, the flagstones slick and treacherous, and she kept her eyes lowered, watching for the raised edges and cracks that had nearly sent her sprawling earlier.

She was acutely aware of the man beside her. The solid warmth of his arm beneath her fingers. The faint scent of cedar and wool that clung to his coat, cutting through the damp underground air. Every few steps his shoulder brushed hers, and each time it happened she felt the pull of his silence, that intoxicating absence of noise that surrounded him.

She wanted to let go of his arm. She also very much did not want to let go of his arm.

The tunnel began to climb, the passage narrowing, and she concentrated on her footing as the steps grew steeper. The earl adjusted the torch in his free hand, angling it to cast light on the ground ahead of her.

At last the passage leveled out and ended at the iron grate through which they had come in. Lord Whitmore reached up and pushed it aside, then climbed through first, turning to offer her his hand. She took it, his gloved fingers closing firmly around hers, and he pulled her up and out into the open.

Isabel drew a deep breath as they emerged from the tunnel. Cold November air filled her lungs, sharp and clean after the stale closeness of the tunnel. Lord Whitmore pulled the grate back into place behind them, and together they walked back down the narrow path toward the street where the carriage waited.

They were a few paces from the alley's mouth when Isabel suddenly froze.

A mind. Close and approaching fast, moving along the street just ahead of them. Male. Armed.

She caught the earl's arm and held him back. "Someone is coming," she whispered.

His gaze swept the alley. There was nothing but bare walls on both sides. No doorways or recesses... nowhere to step out of sight.

"Trust me," he said.

Before she could respond, he seized her by the waist and turned her, pressing her back against the rough brick wall. His body covered hers, one arm bracing against the wall above her head, the other settling at her hip. He leaned in close, his head dipping beside hers, his dark hair brushing her temple.

"No one will look twice at a man seeking a woman's company at this hour, not in this part of town," he murmured, and his breath, warm against her ear, sent a shiver down her spine.

She wasn't sure what shook her more: his closeness, the scent of him surrounding her, or the fact that he had just suggested she pretend to be his mistress. Her heart hammered so loudly she was certain he could hear it. His chest was pressed against hers, and through the layers of wool and cotton she could feel the rise and fall of his breathing, steady where hers was ragged.

So close to him, she could feel the silence radiating from him, pulling at her like the draw of a magnet, muffling the distant noise of the city until she had to strain to hear anything beyond his stillness. She could still sense the approaching mind, but it took effort, her concentration slipping each time his breath grazed her skin.

The footsteps drew closer along the street ahead. A night watchman, lantern in one hand, truncheon in the other. She held her breath as his thoughts hit her.

Look at that lucky bastard. Wish I had the night off instead of trudging through this godforsaken cesspit...

His gaze lingered on them as he passed, and Isabel felt her cheeks burn, grateful for the darkness. The watchman's thoughts turned envious, then indifferent, and his footsteps continued down the street without slowing.

"It's working," she whispered, her lips close to Alexander's ear. "He's moving on."

Alexander remained still until the footsteps faded. Then, slowly, he drew his head back from beside hers.

He didn't step away.

His face hovered inches from her own. In the faint light that reached them from a distant street lamp, she could see the dark sweep of his lashes, the grey of his eyes fixed on hers with an intensity that made her stomach tighten.

His gaze dropped to her mouth.

The breath left her lungs. Her heart was beating so hard it ached. She could feel the warmth of him through every layer of clothing between them, could feel his hand still resting at her hip, his thumb pressing gently against the curve of her waist.

All she would have to do was tilt her chin up. One inch. Less than an inch.

She wanted to. The wanting was so sharp it frightened her. This man, whose mind she could not read, whose silence drew her in, whose actions kept contradicting everything she had learned to expect from the men who held power over her, made her want to tear down every wall she had ever built just to close the distance and find out what his mouth tasted like.

She tilted her head up, her eyes drifting shut.

"There you are! I was beginning to think the smuggler had fed you to the rats."

Lord Daventry's voice shattered the silence.

The earl pulled back from her so fast that cold air rushed into the space between them. He cleared his throat and turned, straightening his coat with a sharp tug.

Isabel pressed herself against the wall, heart racing. Lord Daventry was striding toward them, his golden hair bright even in the dim light, his coat flapping behind him. His steps slowed as he drew close enough to make out the scene in front of him.

Well, well, well. Isn't this interesting.

"Damien," Alexander said, his voice admirably composed. "I thought I told you to wait in the carriage."

"Forgive me for wanting to confirm that my dearest friend was still among the living. You were gone well over an hour, and I was growing concerned." The viscount's gaze moved from Lord Whitmore to Isabel, and then back again, and the concern on his face gave way to a grin that could only be described as insufferable. "But I can see that no assistance was required. You appear to have the situation well in hand."

"We ran into a night patrol," Alexander said stiffly. "I was shielding Miss de Clare from view."

"Shielding. Yes, of course." Damien nodded, his expression grave.

"Damien—"

"Not a word, my friend. Not a single word." He raised his hands in surrender, still grinning. "Shall we? The carriage awaits, and I suspect you have had quite enough excitement for one evening."

Alexander shot him a look that would have felled a lesser man, then turned back to Isabel and offered his arm once more, his expression giving nothing away. "Miss de Clare."

Isabel took his arm. She did not trust her voice, so she said nothing.

They followed Lord Daventry back to the carriage where the driver sat huddled on his seat with his collar turned up against the cold. The viscount held the door open and handed Isabel up with exaggerated gallantry, his eyes dancing with amusement.

Inside, Isabel turned her face toward the window, watching the dark streets of the Warrens slide past. Her reflection stared back at her from the glass, violet eyes wide, cheeks flushed. She did not look at the Earl of Whitmore for the entire ride home.

Chapter Five

The front door of Whitmore Hall had barely closed behind them before Isabel slipped away.

"If you will excuse me, my lord. It has been a long evening."

She was halfway up the staircase before Alexander could even form a reply. He watched her go, her dark shawl trailing behind her, her hand gripping the banister as she ascended without looking back. The door to her chamber closed with a soft but definitive click.

Alexander stood in the entrance hall, staring at the empty stairs.

"Well," Damien said from behind him. "That was rather abrupt."

Alexander said nothing. He turned on his heel and walked to the drawing room, his stride sharp enough that his boots rang against the marble. Damien followed, pulling the door shut behind them.

Alexander went straight for the sideboard. He pulled the stopper from the brandy decanter, poured a generous measure, and drained it in one swallow. The burn did nothing to settle the knot in his chest. He poured another.

"Are you going to share, or is this a private affair between you and the bottle?"

Alexander ignored him. Damien crossed to the sideboard, reached past him for a second glass, and poured his own measure.

"I almost kissed her, Damien."

The words came out rough, scraped from somewhere he had been trying to keep locked shut for the duration of the carriage ride home. He lifted the glass and took a slower drink, the faint tremor in his hand betraying his inner turmoil.

Behind him, he heard Damien settle into one of the armchairs. "Yes, I gathered as much."

"This is not amusing."

"I didn't say it was. Though I confess I am struggling to understand the crisis. You are an unmarried man. She is an unmarried woman. You are clearly drawn to each other. Where, precisely, is the catastrophe?"

Alexander turned from the sideboard. "She is under my protection, Damien. She lives beneath my roof, and her legal papers sit in my desk drawer. I hold power over every aspect of her life. What kind of man takes advantage of that?"

"The kind of man who has spent eight years punishing himself for being alive?" Damien's tone was light, but his blue eyes were serious. "Because that is what this is really about, is it not?"

Alexander's grip tightened on the glass. "Don't."

"You cannot mourn Marianne forever, Alex."

The name landed between them, and Alexander felt the old familiar ache spread through his ribs. He turned back to the window, where the dark panes reflected the firelight and nothing of the street beyond.

"It is not about Marianne. Not solely." He pressed his thumb into the scar on his right hand. "But I have been through this before. I know what it costs to care for someone and then lose them. I will not put myself through that again, and I will not drag Isabel into it."

"So you intend to do what, exactly? Spend the rest of your days alone in this house, drinking brandy and brooding at windows?"

"If necessary."

Damien let out a long breath. "Alex, listen to me. You are twenty-eight years old. You are an earl. At some point, whether you like it or not, you will need a wife. An heir. A future that extends beyond your obsession with Delacroix." He paused. "Life does not stop simply because you are afraid of it."

"It is not fear." Alexander's jaw tightened. "It is reality. Even if I were inclined to pursue this, which I am not, it could never lead anywhere.

Not in the world we live in. She is a magic user, Damien. A registered telepath. The ton would never accept her. The council would have my head." He set the glass down, the crystal striking the wood with a sharp crack. "I would be offering her something I could never deliver. A false hope. And that is more cruel than keeping my distance."

Damien was quiet for a moment. Then he shifted in his chair, crossing one ankle over his knee.

"Perhaps she does not want what you think she wants. Perhaps she is not looking for a proposal and a country estate. Perhaps she simply wants—"

"No." Alexander cut him off. "I am not the kind of man who takes what he wants and walks away. And she is not the kind of woman who deserves to be treated that way. She has spent twelve years being used by men who held power over her. I refuse to become another one of them."

Damien studied his friend, then sighed and theatrically raised his glass.

"By all means, I concede. You are determined to be noble and miserable, and far be it from me to stand in the way of such a committed endeavour." He took a drink. "Shall we discuss something less agonizing? How did the rest of your evening go, aside from the part where you did not kiss your telepath?"

"She is not *my* telepath."

"If you say so."

Alexander moved to the mantelpiece, forcing himself to set aside the tangle in his chest and focus on what mattered. "Lena confirmed our suspicions. Delacroix visited the shelter before Dave disappeared. He made him an offer, was refused, and most likely took him by force shortly after. The harbour fire was a trap. Lena was lured to a warehouse and ambushed. There was gunpowder, stored in barrels. The whole thing was staged."

Damien's expression sobered. "Staged. To what end?"

"To give the council the excuse they need to tighten restrictions on magic users, I imagine. The people will practically beg for it, with forty-three people dead, a dozen ships destroyed, and a fire starter to blame for all of it." Alexander stared into the flames, his jaw tightening.

"This is Delacroix's doing, without a doubt. It is evident the man harbours a deep-seated hatred for magic users, the way he is taking them out one by one." He turned back to Damien. "And this fire is precisely the kind of incident that would turn public opinion against the Reform Act."

"And what will happen to Leonora now?"

"She is safe for the time being. Raines has her. He will send word once she is settled."

Damien nodded slowly, turning his glass between his fingers. "And the storm caller? Could she tell you anything more about who that was?"

"No. It seems they did not know each other. From what Lena described, the woman arrived by chance, trying to help put out the fire. Only her storm just made things worse."

"So we have confirmation of Delacroix's involvement, but nothing concrete enough to bring before a magistrate."

"No. Not yet."

A silence settled over the room, broken only by the crackle of the fire.

"The autumn ball," Damien said eventually. "Lady Deacon has invited me to call on her tomorrow for afternoon tea. And for gossip, I suspect. Her two great passions. I will see what I can learn about Delacroix's associates and whether any of them are expected to attend the ball."

"Good. Do that." Alexander pushed away from the mantelpiece and sank into the armchair opposite Damien's, suddenly feeling the weight of the evening in every muscle. He let his head fall back against the leather and closed his eyes.

Damien watched him for a moment. Then he drained the last of his brandy and set the empty glass on the side table. He rose, pausing beside Alexander's chair to grip his shoulder.

"Nothing happened tonight, Alex. And all will be righted in due time. Get some rest."

He made for the door. His hand was on the handle when Alexander spoke.

"Damien."

The viscount turned.

Alexander opened his eyes and met his friend's gaze. "Thank you. For being there tonight. For being there when I need you."

Damien's features softened, warming into a genuine smile. "Always," he said.

The door closed softly behind him.

Alexander sat alone in the dim room, his thoughts churning with the weight of the evening. He should go to bed. The hour was late, and there was much to be done tomorrow. Plans to make, leads to follow, a case to build against a man who had eluded him for eight years.

But his thoughts would not turn to Delacroix.

They turned instead to violet eyes and a sharp tongue. To the way she had tilted her chin up toward him in that alley, her lips parted, her lashes sweeping down. To the warmth of her waist beneath his hand and the way her breath had caught when he leaned close.

He had wanted to kiss her. God help him, he had wanted it more than he had wanted anything in a very long time.

And that was precisely why he could never let it happen.

He rose from the chair and crossed to the door, turning down the oil lamp on the side table as he passed. Leaving the dimmed room behind him, he climbed the stairs to his chamber. As he passed her door, he paused. No light showed beneath it. No sound came from within.

Alexander pressed his palm flat against the wood for the span of a single breath. Then he withdrew his hand, walked on, and did not look back.

Isabel paused outside the breakfast room door, smoothed her skirts, and told herself to stop being ridiculous.

She had faced down hostile masters, survived twelve years of servitude, and stared into the fractured mind of the Marquis of Darkwater without flinching. She could manage breakfast with the Earl of Whitmore.

She pushed open the door.

Lord Whitmore sat at the round table, a newspaper spread before him and a cup of tea at his elbow. Morning light streamed through the tall windows, catching the dark gloss of his hair and the sharp angles of his profile. He looked composed. As if the previous evening had never happened.

Isabel envied him that. She had barely slept.

At the sound of the door, he rose.

"Miss de Clare. Good morning."

"Good morning, my lord."

He moved around the table and drew out the chair beside his own. Isabel crossed the room and sat, murmuring her thanks. He returned to his seat, and a footman appeared to pour her tea and set out a plate of toast, soft-boiled eggs, and cold ham.

They ate in silence.

Isabel buttered her toast and tried not to think about the way his thumb had pressed against the curve of her waist. She took a sip of tea and tried not to think about how close his mouth had been to hers. She reached for the marmalade and tried not to think about the way he had looked at her with these grey eyes of his.

She was failing spectacularly on all counts.

The earl cleared his throat. "I expect Vera to join us shortly."

"That will be lovely."

More silence. The clock on the mantel ticked. A log shifted in the grate. Somewhere in the house, a door closed.

Isabel had never been at a loss for words in her life. Yet here she sat, staring at her eggs as if they held the answers to all her questions.

The earl set down his cup. "Miss de Clare, about last night—"

The door burst open.

"Good morning!" Vera swept into the room in a swirl of green muslin and bright energy, her dark hair pinned up in loose curls. "I do hope I am not interrupting. The most wonderful thing happened on my way down. Mrs. Hartley told me she has made her apricot preserves, the ones with the ginger, and I have been dreaming of them since—" She stopped, looking between them. "Why are you both so quiet?"

"We were waiting for you," the earl said evenly.

"How considerate." Vera dropped into the chair across from Isabel and reached for the toast rack. "Well, I am here now. Tell me everything. How did it go last night? Did you find the fire starter?"

Lord Whitmore glanced at Isabel, then began. He gave Vera a detailed account of the evening: the tunnels beneath the Warrens, the meeting with Lena, her confirmation of Delacroix's involvement in Dave's disappearance, and the truth behind the harbour fire.

Vera's face had grown pale during the telling. She set down her toast, her appetite apparently gone. "And Lena? Is she safe?"

"Captain Raines has her," her brother said. "He will see her to safety until we can prove her innocence."

Vera seemed to weigh this, then nodded. "What happens now? Surely this is enough to act on?"

"It is not," the earl said, his voice heavy with frustration. "Everything we have is the testimony of a convicted arsonist and the observations of a telepath. Neither of which would be admitted in any court in the kingdom. We need hard evidence. Something that ties Delacroix directly to the abductions and the harbour fire."

"Then we keep looking," Isabel said.

The earl met her gaze and held it across the table. "Yes. We do."

Isabel looked away first, reaching for her tea.

"Speaking of looking," Vera said, spreading a generous layer of apricot preserves on her toast, "Damien is collecting me this afternoon. We are both invited to tea at Lady Deacon's. She is finalizing the guest list for the autumn ball, and if anyone knows which of Delacroix's associates will be in attendance, it is her."

Lord Whitmore's brows rose. "I was not aware you and Damien were going together."

"We were both invited, and it is a tedious carriage ride to the outskirts of town. Why make it separately?" Vera bit into her toast. "Besides, Damien is useful. He charms the hostess while I listen to what the other guests are saying when they think no one important is paying attention."

"I thought Damien annoyed you."

"He does." Vera chewed thoughtfully. "But better annoyed than bored for an hour in a carriage with nothing but my own thoughts for company."

"Very well." The earl folded his napkin and placed it beside his plate. "I expect you both back before dark. And I want a full report when you return."

Vera caught Isabel's eye across the table and gave her a look that said, quite plainly, *You see what I endure?*

Isabel pressed her lips together and glanced down at her plate, hiding the smile that threatened to break through.

Lord Whitmore rose from his chair. "Miss de Clare, when you have finished here, would you join me in the library? There are aspects of the investigation I would like to discuss with you. If you are agreeable."

"Of course, my lord."

He gave a curt nod, collected his newspaper from the table, and left the room.

The moment the door closed, Vera leaned forward.

"Isabel."

She looked up to find Vera watching her with sharp grey eyes, so like her brother's, yet so much warmer.

"Did something happen last night that you haven't told me about?" Vera asked. "Because the air in this room just now was thick enough to cut with a knife."

Isabel opened her mouth to reply, only to snap it shut a second later as a traitorous heat crept up her neck.

"Nothing happened," she said.

Vera studied her for a moment. Then she reached for the teapot and refilled both their cups.

"If you say so," she said, and the echo of her brother's best friend in those four words was so precise that Isabel wondered, briefly, whether Vera might enjoy the viscount's company rather more than she cared to admit after all.

Alexander stood at the window of the library, watching the grey November sky and trying to decide what to say to her.

He had spent the better part of the morning composing and discarding speeches in his head. Each version sounded worse than the last.

Nothing had happened. He would do well to remember that. And if nothing had happened, then there was nothing to address.

He turned from the window when he heard her footsteps in the corridor. By the time she knocked and entered, he was standing behind the desk, his hands clasped at his back.

"Miss de Clare. Please, come in. Take a seat."

Isabel crossed the room and settled into one of the leather armchairs before the desk. She folded her hands in her lap and looked up at him, her violet eyes steady.

For an instant, as their gazes met, he thought he saw something there. Then he quickly looked away and sat down behind the desk.

"We have Lena's testimony," he began, pulling a ledger toward him, "but nothing that would hold up before a magistrate. We need physical evidence."

If Isabel was surprised by his briskness, she gave no sign of it. She straightened in her chair. "The warehouse," she said. "Where the fire started. Has anyone searched it since the night of the blaze?"

"The magistrates conducted a cursory inspection and ruled it an act of arson by a magic user. I doubt they looked much further than that."

"Then perhaps we should. If the gunpowder was stored there deliberately, there may be records of who leased the building, who arranged the shipments. And if any of the dock workers or harbour staff were involved, we can question them." She met his gaze. "I will know if they are lying."

Alexander considered this. The southern docks were busy during the day, crowded enough that two well-dressed visitors asking questions would not draw too much attention. And Isabel had a point. The warehouse was the one location where Delacroix's operation had left a physical trace. If there was evidence to be found, it would be there.

"Agreed," he said. "We will go this afternoon, while Vera and Damien are at Lady Deacon's. Less chance of drawing attention if we go quietly."

"Just the two of us?"

"Is that a problem?"

A brief silence. Then Isabel shook her head.

"Shall we leave in an hour?" he suggested.

"An hour," she agreed and rose from her chair.

She paused at the door and glanced back at him, and for a moment he thought she was going to say something more. But she simply inclined her head.

"I will see you shortly, my lord."

She left, pulling the door closed behind her.

Alexander sat motionless at the desk, staring at the closed door. He had said nothing about the alley. She had not mentioned it either. The matter, it seemed, had settled itself.

He pulled the ledger closer, opened it, and began reviewing his notes on Delacroix's known properties.

He did not think about the look in her eyes last night. Did not think about the softness of her hip beneath his palm, or the scent of lavender that had filled his senses when her lips had been a breath away from his.

No, he did not think about any of that at all.

The harbour was a wound that had not yet healed.

Isabel saw the damage long before they reached the southern docks. Charred, skeletal pilings jutted from the water where the moorings had burned away, and scorched stone streaked the quayside in broad, ugly bands. The warehouses nearest the water stood gutted, their roofs caved in. Even weeks after the fire, the smell of charred wood hung over the district, sharp enough to catch at the back of her throat.

The carriage let them off at the edge of the commercial quarter, and they continued on foot. Lord Whitmore walked beside her, his collar turned up, his hat pulled low. He wore a plain coat today, dark and unremarkable, and without the tailored finery he could almost pass for a merchant or a clerk. Almost. His posture gave him away. No clerk carried himself with such rigid, military straightness.

The docks were busy despite the destruction. Dock workers loaded cargo onto newly moored vessels, cart drivers shouted at one another over the clatter of hooves and wheels, and gulls wheeled overhead, screaming. Isabel kept her walls up, letting the noise of so many minds wash past her without engaging. The hum was loud here, dozens of thoughts tangling together, but she had long practice at keeping it at a manageable distance.

In the heart of the district's wharves, they found the warehouse. Or what little the fire had left of it.

The roof was gone. Three of the four walls still stood, though the brickwork was blackened and cracked, and the fourth had collapsed into a heap of rubble. A heavy chain had been strung across the entrance, and from it hung a wooden sign bearing the magistrate's seal: *By Order of the Crown. No Entry. Investigation Concluded.*

The earl studied the chain for a moment. Then he stepped around the side of the building, where a section of the collapsed wall had left a gap wide enough to pass through. He held out a gloved hand to help Isabel over the rubble, and they slipped inside.

The interior was a ruin. The floor was covered in debris, a mix of shattered timber and twisted iron. Broken glass littered the ground, glinting in the pale afternoon light that filtered through the open roof. Puddles of stagnant rainwater had gathered in the hollows, and weeds had already begun to push through the cracks in the flagstones. The walls were streaked with soot, and the air tasted of ash and damp.

They moved through the wreckage in silence, stepping carefully over the debris. Isabel scanned the ground, looking for anything that might have survived the blaze, while Lord Whitmore examined the walls, running his fingers along the brickwork, crouching to inspect marks on the floor.

A mind entered her awareness, close and approaching.

"Someone is coming," she murmured.

The earl straightened. A moment later, a stocky man in a watchman's uniform appeared in the gap in the wall, one hand on the truncheon at his belt.

"Oi. What do you think you're doing in here? Can you not read? The site is closed."

Lord Whitmore turned to face him, unhurried. He reached into his coat and produced a folded document, holding it up so the watchman could see the seal. "Alexander Kensington, Under-Secretary of State for the Home Office. We are here to conduct a further inspection of the premises. New evidence has come to light that warrants additional investigation."

The watchman squinted at the document, then at the earl, then at Isabel. His jaw worked as he weighed his options.

A lie, Isabel thought. Or close enough to one. But she held her tongue and reached for the man's thoughts instead.

Kensington. Sound familiar. One of them lords from the council? Looks the part, I suppose. But nobody told me about no new investigation. Boss won't like this one bit...

"I wasn't informed of any further inspection, my lord," the watchman said carefully.

"You would not have been. The matter is sensitive." The earl's tone left no room for argument. "You may continue your rounds. We will not be long."

The watchman hesitated another moment, then touched his cap and retreated through the gap in the wall.

Isabel waited until his footsteps had faded before she turned to the earl. "We don't have much time. He didn't believe you. He's on his way to find his boss."

Alexander's expression sharpened. "Then we had better be quick."

They split apart, working faster. Isabel picked through the wreckage near the centre of the building, where the blast had been strongest. Little remained here beyond charred wood and twisted metal.

Lord Whitmore had moved to the far wall, where the remains of several large barrels lay scattered.

"That is odd," he said.

Isabel crossed to him. "What is it?"

He held up a splinter. Burned into the wood, partially obscured by soot but still legible, was a stamped mark: an anchor crossed with a sword, surrounded by a crown of laurels.

"This is a Royal Navy insignia," the earl said, his brows drawn together. "These barrels were military issue. Standard naval gunpowder stores."

"What would naval gunpowder be doing in a private warehouse?"

"Precisely." He turned the fragment over, examining it. "Naval ordnance is strictly accounted for. Every barrel is logged by the Crown arsenals. For this quantity to end up in a civilian warehouse near the docks..." He slipped the piece into his coat. "Either someone in the Admiralty is smuggling military supplies, or they were stolen. Neither explanation is reassuring."

Isabel opened her mouth to respond, then stopped. Two minds, approaching fast. The watchman, and another, this one irritated and suspicious.

"Two men coming," she said. "The watchman and his sergeant."

Lord Whitmore was already moving. "We have what we came for. Follow me."

They crossed the ruined floor quickly, stepping through the gap on the far side of the building, away from the approaching men. The earl took Isabel's arm and guided her around the corner, through a narrow passage between two adjoining warehouses, and out onto a side street that led away from the docks.

They did not run, but the earl kept their pace brisk. Isabel matched his stride, her hand tucked into the crook of his elbow, her heart beating fast.

They reached the carriage without incident. Lord Whitmore handed her up and climbed in after her, pulling the door shut.

"Home," he called to the driver.

The carriage lurched forward, and Isabel let out a breath. The earl sat across from her. He pulled out the charred barrel fragment from his coat and turned it over in his hands, his thumb tracing the edge of the navy insignia.

"Royal Navy gunpowder," Isabel said. "In a warehouse linked to Delacroix."

The earl looked up, his grey eyes sharp. "We have to find out how it got there."

They heard the quarrelling before they reached the drawing room door.

"I am merely saying," Vera's voice carried into the corridor, sharp with exasperation, "that one does not need to compliment every woman in the room on her complexion in order to gather intelligence."

"And I am merely saying," Damien replied, his tone maddeningly serene, "that a well-placed compliment opens doors that blunt questions never could. It is a skill, Vera. An art form, if you will."

"It is a spectacle."

Alexander pushed open the door. Vera stood by the fireplace, her arms crossed, colour high in her cheeks. Damien occupied his usual armchair, one leg crossed over the other, a glass of sherry dangling from his fingers, looking thoroughly unrepentant.

Both turned at the sound of the door. Vera's irritation dissolved into curiosity the moment she saw the state of them. Alexander was aware that he and Isabel made quite a picture. Their coats were smudged with soot, the hems grey with ash, and something that appeared to be a cobweb was caught in Isabel's hair.

"Good heavens." Vera's eyes widened. "Where on earth have you two been?"

"The southern docks," Alexander said, crossing to the sideboard. "We paid a visit to the warehouse where the harbour fire started."

"You went to the docks?" Vera looked between them. "Just the two of you?"

From the armchair, Damien raised an eyebrow but said nothing. He took a slow sip of his sherry, his expression studiously innocent, and Alexander chose to ignore him.

"We cannot afford to waste time, not if we want to stay ahead of Delacroix." Alexander poured himself a brandy and turned to face the room. "And it was worth the trip."

He reached into his coat and produced the charred barrel fragment, setting it on the side table where the firelight threw the stamped insignia into sharp relief. Damien leaned forward. Vera moved closer.

"What is that?" she asked.

"A piece of one of the gunpowder barrels that caused the explosions." Alexander tapped the mark with his finger. "And that is the insignia of the Royal Navy."

Damien set down his sherry. "The navy. That raises rather more questions than it answers."

"It does," Alexander agreed. "And none of them are comfortable."

Vera frowned. "Could Delacroix be working with someone within the navy?"

"That is what we need to find out." Alexander looked at Damien. "I need you to ask around. Your circles, the clubs, the card tables. See if anyone has heard rumours about Delacroix and the Admiralty. Any connection, however tenuous."

Damien nodded. "I will see what I can turn up."

"Good. Now." Alexander settled into the armchair opposite his friend. "What did you learn at Lady Deacon's?"

Isabel moved to the settee near the fire and sat down, Vera claiming the seat beside her, her earlier pique with Damien apparently set aside in favour of business.

"The guest list for the autumn ball is nearly finalized. Delacroix has been invited but has not yet confirmed his attendance," his sister explained.

"However," Damien added, "several of his known associates are expected, amongst them the Harlow brothers."

"The Harlow brothers." Alexander filed the information away. "What else?"

"Lady Deacon mentioned that Delacroix has been uncharacteristically social of late," Vera said. "Attending salons, accepting invitations he would normally decline. She found it curious. So do I."

"He is positioning himself," Isabel said quietly from the chair beside Vera. "Building alliances. If the harbour fire is meant to shift opinion against magic users, he will want influential people on his side when the council debates new restrictions."

Alexander met her eyes. She had a point. The political dimension of Delacroix's scheme seemed to become clearer by the day.

"All the more reason to be at the ball," he said. "If Delacroix's associates are attending, Isabel can read them. We may learn more in one evening than weeks of searching warehouses."

Damien reached for his sherry and drained the last of it. "Well, on that cheerful note." He rose and straightened his coat. "I should be on my way."

"You are not staying for dinner?" Alexander asked.

Before Damien could answer, Vera spoke. "He cannot. He has a prior engagement." Her tone was clipped, her gaze fixed on the fire. "Miss Jenson and her family were kind enough to invite him to dine with them this evening. An invitation he accepted with remarkable enthusiasm, considering he had known the girl for all of twenty minutes."

Damien turned to Vera with a look of wounded innocence. "It would have been ungracious to refuse. Her father is a baronet. One does not slight a baronet's hospitality."

"You accepted because she has blonde curls and a pretty smile."

"Those are also valid considerations."

Vera pressed her lips together and said nothing more, though her jaw was set in a way that Alexander recognised. He glanced at Damien, who seemed entirely oblivious, and decided this was not a matter worth stirring. Not tonight.

"Very well," Alexander said. "Go. But I want you here tomorrow morning. Early. We have a great deal to discuss."

"Define early."

"Before noon, Damien."

"I shall do my utmost." The viscount sketched a bow. "Lady Vera, Miss de Clare, a pleasure as always."

Vera did not look at him.

Isabel rose from the settee. "If you will excuse me as well, my lord. I should like to change before dinner. I am hardly presentable in my current state."

"Of course." Alexander stood up and nodded.

Vera stood as well. "I will join you, Isabel. I want to hear all about your recent adventures." She hooked her arm through Isabel's and steered her toward the door, already peppering her with questions.

The women disappeared into the corridor, and Damien, who had been shrugging into his coat, paused at the door. He glanced back at Alexander with a familiar half-smile.

"The two of you, alone at the docks all afternoon." He adjusted his cuffs. "Investigating."

"Yes, Damien. Investigating."

"Of course. How very industrious." He pulled on his gloves, grin widening. "Until tomorrow, then."

He was gone before Alexander could respond. Alone in the drawing room, he sank back into his armchair with a slow exhale and picked up the charred fragment from the table beside him, frowning as he turned it over in his hands.

Isabel closed the door and leaned against it, letting out a slow breath. The silence of her chamber was a relief after Vera's relentless questioning.

Though she did not mind the company. Quite the opposite. The younger woman was refreshingly direct, her words matching her thoughts with a candor that Isabel found almost disarming. In that respect, she was remarkably similar to Damien, though Isabel suspected neither of them would appreciate the comparison.

She pushed away from the door and crossed to the dressing table, where Jenny had laid out one of the new evening gowns from Madame Fontaine's. It was a deep plum silk with a modest neckline and sleeves that tapered to her wrists, simple in cut but rich in colour. Isabel changed out of her ash-dusted day dress and slipped into it, fastening the small buttons at her cuffs before sitting down to attend to her hair.

She studied herself in the mirror as she picked the last of the cobwebs from her hair and brushed the ash from her temples, then tucked a loose curl back into place. The plum suited her colouring, she had to admit. It brought warmth to her pale skin and made her eyes appear more violet than blue. She adjusted the pin at her temple, angled her head, frowned, and adjusted it again.

Since when did she fuss over her hair?

She lowered her hands and met her own gaze in the glass. The finely dressed woman staring back at her looked rested, the colour returning to her cheeks. A far cry from the hollow-eyed creature who had been led onto an auction stage a mere week ago.

Drawing her gaze from the mirror, Isabel rose. Yielding to old habit, she took the time to tidy her dressing table and put the room back into proper, polished order before finally making her way downstairs.

Lord Whitmore and Vera were already seated in the dining room when she entered. The earl stood at once, as he always did, and drew out the chair beside his own. Isabel thanked him and sat, smoothing her skirts beneath the table.

She still had not grown accustomed to this. The small courtesies, the pulled-out chairs, the way he rose every time she entered a room. No master she had served had ever treated her with such consideration. And that was what he was, she reminded herself. Her master. Her business partner at best, until their arrangement concluded and he granted her freedom.

Freedom. The word that had sustained her through twelve years of servitude. She had dreamed of it, plotted for it, clung to it on the darkest nights. And yet, sitting here at this table, in this house, with these people who had somehow become more than strangers to her, the thought of leaving settled heavy in her chest.

What would she do? Where would she go? To the Free Isles, perhaps. She had always imagined the Free Isles. But the image felt distant now, abstract, and stripped of the urgency that had once driven her.

"Miss De Clare?"

She blinked. The earl was watching her, his brows slightly drawn.

"Forgive me." She straightened in her chair. "I was lost in thought. Did you say something?"

"I was wondering if you could spare a moment after dinner. There is a matter I would like to discuss with you."

"Of course, my lord."

Dinner passed in pleasant conversation, Vera driving most of it as she recounted the details of her afternoon at Lady Deacon's. There was talk of the guest list, of which gowns the other ladies had worn, of the baroness's new wallpaper, which Vera declared an improvement over the last and Damien had apparently declared ghastly.

Isabel ate and listened, offering the occasional smile or comment when Vera drew her into the conversation. Across the table, Lord Whitmore sat cloaked in a silence that was dense even by his own stoic standards.

When the last course was cleared, Vera rose with a graceful yawn.

"I believe I shall retire early. It has been a full day." She kissed her brother's cheek and squeezed Isabel's hand. "Good night, both of you."

She swept from the room, and Isabel was alone with the earl.

He stood. "Shall we move to the drawing room and take a drink?"

Isabel followed him down the corridor and into the drawing room, where the fire had been banked and the lamps turned low. He poured two glasses of brandy, handed her one, and gestured toward the armchairs by the hearth.

They sat, and for a while, Lord Whitmore merely turned his glass between his fingers and said nothing.

Isabel took a sip and waited. When the silence stretched beyond what felt natural, she spoke.

"You said there was something you wished to discuss."

He looked up, and she thought she saw a flicker of hesitation in his expression. How she wished she could read his mind, and not for the first time.

"I have been thinking," he said slowly, "about... the connection between us. What happens when we touch." He paused, choosing his words. "When we first discussed it, I suggested it might be worth exploring, to see if it could give us an advantage against Delacroix."

Isabel said nothing, though her pulse had quickened.

"The autumn ball is approaching, and there will be further investigations ahead," he continued. "If there is a way for us to benefit from this connection, it could prove invaluable." He drew a breath and met her eyes. "What I am asking is whether you are still willing to explore it."

Isabel had not expected this. After the alley, after his rigid distance all day, she had assumed the subject was closed. That he had sealed it away along with whatever else he had felt in that moment when his face had hovered inches from hers.

And now here he sat, asking her to take his hand again.

She told herself the flutter in her stomach was professional interest. The connection could indeed prove useful. It was only logical to explore it. A strategic thing to do.

The fact that she longed to feel his silence wrap around her again was utterly irrelevant.

"Yes," she said. "I agree, it is worth exploring."

He nodded, and his shoulders eased, just slightly.

"Shall we begin right away?" she asked.

His brows rose. "Now?"

"Why not? Didn't you say yourself that we cannot afford to waste time?"

He set his glass aside. "You are right."

"So." Isabel set her own glass down and folded her hands in her lap. "How do we do this? Do we simply hold hands?"

"To start with, yes. I would suggest we hold the connection longer than before. See if anything changes, or if we can shape it through conscious effort."

Isabel held out her hand.

Alexander looked at it for a moment. Then he reached across the space between their chairs and took it in his own.

The silence settled over her like a velvet mantle, sudden and absolute. Every voice, every hum, every whisper of thought from the servants in distant rooms, from Vera upstairs, from the coachman in the stable yard, was gone. Wiped clean in an instant.

Isabel closed her eyes. A sigh escaped her lips, and she could not help the smile that followed. That blessed, perfect quiet. She had spent twenty-four years drowning in other people's thoughts, and here, in the warmth of his hand, she could finally breathe.

When she opened her eyes, he was watching her. His gaze was fixed on her face with an intensity that made her breath catch, and a small smile rested on his lips, as if her relief had given him something too.

"Tell me what you feel," he said. "Describe it."

"Silence," she said. "Complete silence. Every mind around me has gone quiet. It is as if the rest of the world has simply ceased to exist."

"You hear nothing? No one?"

"No one."

"Can you sense me?" he asked. "Within the silence. Is there anything there at all?"

Isabel concentrated, reaching out with her gift into the quiet. She searched for the familiar brush of another consciousness, the way she would search for a voice in an empty room. But there was nothing. Only stillness.

She shook her head. "I'm trying, but I can't find you."

"Perhaps you are trying too hard." His thumb shifted against her knuckles, a small, absent movement she was not sure he was aware of. "Do not reach with your mind. Just feel. Because I can feel you in this space. I cannot hear your thoughts, but your presence is there, somewhere beside my own."

Her heart stumbled at those words. She nodded and closed her eyes again.

She stopped searching and simply sat in the silence, let it hold her.

And there he was.

A faint but unmistakable presence, like warmth from a fire in an adjoining room. A consciousness resting alongside her own, steady and calm and undeniably him.

Her eyes flew open.

He was already watching her. And she saw in his gaze the moment he knew, the exact instant he felt her find him.

His grey eyes softened, and the small smile returned. "There you are."

Chapter Six

Alexander had to suppress a yawn.

They had been in the library since breakfast. The desk was buried beneath ledgers, naval registries, and shipping manifests he had pulled from his office the night before. The morning had stretched into afternoon, the tea had gone cold in its pot, and the fire had burned down to ash without anyone noticing.

Damien had arrived at a remarkably civilized hour, which had startled everyone. He had strolled in before ten o'clock and deposited himself in the armchair nearest the fire with the announcement that he had intelligence to share.

"The Jensons know Delacroix," he had said, accepting a cup of tea from the tray Hartley had brought up. "Sir Reginald Jenson does business with him from time to time. Nothing sinister, as far as I could tell. Import contracts, shipping agreements, the usual commerce."

"How convenient," Vera had said from the settee, not looking up from the fashion plates she was leafing through. "And I suppose you will need to call on Miss Jenson again to pursue this lead further."

"The thought had occurred to me."

"I'm sure it has. Along with several other thoughts that likely have nothing to do with the investigation."

"You wound me, Lady Vera. My motives are entirely honourable."

"Your motives are entirely transparent."

"Which, one might argue, is a form of honesty."

Alexander had let the exchange wash over him. His attention was elsewhere.

Isabel sat across from him at the desk, a heavy ledger open before her, tracing columns of figures with the tip of her finger. She had pulled a strand of hair behind her ear, and the morning light from the window caught the copper in her dark curls. Her brows were drawn in concentration, her lips pressed together as she worked through the entries.

He looked away. Looked back. Looked away again.

He had slept badly. The hours after Isabel had retired to her chamber had been spent staring at the ceiling of his own bedroom, his mind refusing to settle. He kept returning to the drawing room, to the firelight, to the warmth of her hand in his and the extraordinary experience that had followed.

He had felt her, in that private space within his shield. Had felt her presence settle beside his own, and then, that breathtaking moment when her awareness had locked onto his own. It had been the most intimate experience of his life, and they had done nothing more than hold hands.

He had told himself his reasons for suggesting the experiment were tactical. The connection could give them an advantage. It could be used as a tool for the investigation.

And if he also craved the nearness of her, the peace that her presence brought to a space that had been solitary for twenty-eight years — well. That was a matter he preferred not to examine too closely.

Even now, hours later, he could barely concentrate. His gaze kept drifting to her hands on the ledger, to the line of her jaw, to the way she tucked that strand of hair back each time it fell forward. Across the room, Damien and Vera had resumed their skirmish over whether the viscount's interest in Miss Jenson constituted espionage or courtship, but Alexander could not have recounted a word of it.

"Here."

Isabel's voice cut through his thoughts. She looked up from the ledger, her violet eyes sharp, and tapped the page with her finger. "Look at this."

Alexander blinked and sat forward, leaning across the desk to see where she pointed. Two columns ran down the page: incoming ordnance shipments logged at the Crown arsenal in Greyport, and outgoing distributions to naval vessels and coastal fortifications.

"These entries," Isabel said, tracing a line of figures. "The September intake lists forty-two barrels of gunpowder received from the foundry at Kingsbridge. But the outgoing ledger for the same month only accounts for twenty-six distributed to ships and garrisons." She looked up at him. "That leaves sixteen barrels unaccounted for."

Alexander took the ledger from her and studied the columns. She was right. The numbers did not reconcile. Sixteen barrels of military-grade gunpowder had entered the Greyport arsenal and simply vanished from the books.

"That is more than enough to fill a warehouse," he said.

"And more than enough to destroy a harbour," Isabel added quietly.

He met her eyes. "An astute observation, Miss de Clare."

She held his gaze for a moment, and he thought he saw a faint flush rise in her cheeks before she looked back down at the ledger.

Alexander scanned the page for a name. Each entry was initialed by the officer responsible for logging the transaction. The September intake bore the same set of initials throughout: *H.C.*

He cross-referenced the initials against the registry of arsenal staff filed in the back of the volume. His finger stopped on a line halfway down the list.

"Lieutenant Harold Crowe," he read aloud. "Quartermaster, Greyport Naval Arsenal."

He closed the ledger and looked up. Across the room, Damien and Vera had gone quiet, their attention drawn by the shift in his tone.

"That is our next lead," Alexander said. "Lieutenant Crowe is the man who signed for those barrels. He either knows where they went, or he was the one who made them disappear."

Damien straightened in his chair. "What do you need from me?"

"What I asked of you yesterday. Keep your ears open in the clubs and the drawing rooms. See if anyone has heard of Crowe, or if his name surfaces in connection with Delacroix. Any link, however small."

"Consider it done."

"And what shall I do?" Vera set down her fashion plates, her expression a mixture of eagerness and frustration. "Sit here and wait while the rest of you are out chasing leads?"

Alexander considered his sister. "The ball is a week away. There are preparations to make. Gowns, arrangements, guest lists to study. You have a talent for that sort of thing, and I need you ready when the evening comes. Delacroix's associates will be there, and we will need background information."

Vera's eyes lit up. "You want me to coordinate the ball strategy?"

"I want you to ensure that when we walk into that room, we know exactly who is there and where they will be positioned. Can you do that?"

"Can I do that." Vera rose from the settee, her face alight with joy. "I will need access to the seating chart. And I shall have to call on Lady Deacon again. And I will need a new gown, obviously."

"Obviously."

"And Isabel will need one too. Something striking. If she is going to read half the room, she best look the part."

Alexander did not argue. He turned to Isabel, who had been quietly watching the exchange.

"Miss de Clare." He rose from behind the desk. "Are you ready for another tour to the harbour?"

Isabel stood as well. "Lead the way, my lord."

The naval district occupied the northern end of the harbour, set apart from the commercial docks by a high stone wall and a gatehouse manned by two marines in crisp blue uniforms. Alexander presented his credentials, and the younger of the two guards straightened visibly when he read the name.

"Lord Whitmore. Of course, my lord. How may we be of assistance?"

"I am looking for a Lieutenant Harold Crowe. Quartermaster of the Greyport arsenal."

The guard nodded. "Lieutenant Crowe's office is in the stores building, my lord. Second door on the left past the main yard. I'll have someone escort you."

They were led through the yard, past rows of stacked crates and coils of heavy rope. At the far end stood a squat brick building. The escort knocked on a door marked with a brass plate — *H. Crowe, Quartermaster* — and left them to it.

"Come in," called a weary voice from within.

The office was small and cluttered. Ledgers lined the shelves from floor to ceiling, stacked two deep in places, and the desk was buried beneath a landslide of loose papers and what appeared to be the remains of a meat pie. Behind this fortress of paperwork sat a thin man of perhaps forty, with wire spectacles perched on a long nose and ink stains on both cuffs. He looked up from his work, his eyes narrowing.

"Lieutenant Crowe?" Alexander stepped forward. "Alexander Kensington, Under-Secretary of State for the Home Office. This is Miss de Clare, my associate. We are conducting a further investigation into the harbour fire and would appreciate a moment of your time."

Crowe's eyebrows rose above his spectacles. He muttered something under his breath that sounded like "more bloody paperwork" and set down his pen with a resigned sigh. "Of course, my lord. What do you need?"

"Your records show that forty-two barrels of gunpowder were received from the Kingsbridge foundry in September. Only twenty-six were distributed to ships and garrisons. I need to know what happened to the remaining sixteen."

Crowe pulled a heavy ledger from the shelf behind him and thumbed through the pages, licking his finger at each turn. He found the entry, squinted at it, then leaned back in his chair.

"Ah. Yes, I remember this. There was an additional requisition that month. An out-of-the-ordinary order." He tapped the page. "Normally, barrels come in from Kingsbridge, we log them, and they go straight onto the ships at the dock. Standard procedure. But this lot was different. The order specified collection by private transport."

"Private transport," Alexander repeated.

"Horse-drawn wagons. They didn't have naval markings, and there was no military escort. Two men with carts showed up, loaded the barrels, and left." Crowe shrugged. "I thought it odd at the time, but the requisition came through proper channels. Stamped and signed by my supervisor's office."

"Who authorized it?"

Crowe spread his hands. "That I cannot tell you, my lord. The order was passed down through the chain of command. There was no individual name attached, just an official directive with the right seals on it. I am a quartermaster, not a detective. When an order comes from above with the correct authorization, I fulfill it. That is how the navy works."

Alexander met Isabel's eyes across the cramped office. She gave a small, firm nod.

"Thank you, Lieutenant. You have been most helpful."

Crowe looked doubtful. "Will there be additional paperwork?"

"Not from me."

"Small mercies," the quartermaster mumbled, reaching for his pen as they closed the door behind them.

They stepped out into a bright afternoon. For the first time in days the wind had dropped to a gentle breeze, the low November sun casting a pale shimmer across the water.

"We haven't learned much," Isabel said as they passed back through the gatehouse.

"I disagree." Alexander fell into step beside her as they turned onto the quayside. "We now know the order came through official naval channels. The requisition carried proper authorization, and it was passed down from above. That is not the work of a lone criminal. Delacroix could not have arranged this without allies in positions of real authority."

"Someone high-ranking."

"Very high-ranking. Someone powerful enough that a quartermaster would not dare question the order." He frowned, turning the implications over in his mind. "This goes deeper than we thought."

They walked in silence for a stretch, past merchant vessels unloading cargo and fishermen mending their nets on the quayside. The harbour bustled around them, alive with the shouts of dockhands and the creak of rigging, and the salt air carried the smell of tar and fresh fish.

Alexander glanced at Isabel. The afternoon light brought out the copper in her hair and warmed her pale skin. She had turned her face toward the sun, her eyes half-closed.

"Shall we walk a while?" he heard himself say. "The weather is fine, and the carriage can wait."

She looked up at him, a rare smile softening her lips. "I would like that."

He offered his arm, and she took it. They strolled along the waterfront with no destination in mind, and for a few minutes Alexander allowed himself to simply enjoy himself in her company.

It was dangerous, this feeling. He knew it. And he did not care. Not right now. Right now, on this sunlit quay, with this woman at his side, he could pretend they were just two people taking an afternoon walk. Nothing more complicated than that.

Isabel stopped.

Her hand tightened on his arm, and the smile vanished from her face.

"What is it?" he asked.

"We are being followed."

Alexander's gaze swept the quayside, taking in the noisy blur of commerce and daily toil. Nothing seemed out of place.

"Are you certain?"

"I wasn't, at first. Someone noticed us earlier, and their attention lingered, but that happens. People stare."

"They do?"

"More often than you might think, my lord." She kept her voice low, her eyes forward. "But this is different. The mind I perceive now is the same one that noticed us before. Whoever it is must have been following us."

Alexander scanned the crowd again. A man hauled rope near a fishing boat, briefly glancing as they walked past. A group of sailors smoked near a warehouse entrance. Any one of them could be watching.

"We should go back to the carriage," he said.

Isabel nodded, and they turned, quickening their pace.

The quayside grew congested as they neared a merchantman taking on freight. Dockhands swarmed the area, hauling cargo up gangplanks and rolling barrels across the cobblestones. The crowd thickened, closing around them from both sides, and Alexander felt Isabel's grip loosen on his arm as they were forced to move single file between the workers and the stacked goods.

He stepped around a tower of crates, glancing back to check that she was still behind him.

A labourer stumbled into his path, a heavy load tipping in his arms. Alexander sidestepped, caught his balance, and turned.

Isabel was gone.

The space where she had been standing was occupied by two dock workers rolling a barrel between them, their broad backs blocking his view. He pushed past them, searching the crowd.

"Isabel!"

A muffled cry. Brief and sharp, cut off almost instantly, from somewhere to his left. His head snapped toward the sound. There was a narrow gap between two warehouses, dark where the afternoon sun did not reach.

He ran.

The gap opened into a loading bay at the rear of the warehouse, shadowed and reeking of fish oil. A figure was dragging Isabel toward a black carriage waiting at the far end, one arm locked around her waist, a gloved hand clamped over her mouth. She was fighting, clawing at the arm that held her, her boots scraping against the cobblestones, but the man was twice her size and moving fast.

Alexander closed the distance in seconds. He seized the man by the collar and wrenched him backward, driving his fist into the side of his jaw. The impact jarred up through his knuckles and the man staggered, his grip on Isabel breaking. She stumbled free, gasping.

Alexander hit him again. The man's head snapped to the side and he dropped to one knee, blood at the corner of his mouth.

With a crack of the driver's whip, the black carriage lunged into a sudden, jolting sprint, its wheels clattering over the cobblestones as it tore out of the loading bay and vanished around the corner. The vehicle bore neither crest nor insignia upon its dark lacquer, making it look indistinguishable from any other carriage in Greyport.

The man on the ground scrambled to his feet. Alexander lunged for him, but the attacker was already running, sprinting through the gap between the warehouses and disappearing into the crowd beyond.

Alexander took two steps after him and stopped. Isabel was behind him. Alone. Unprotected. If this was coordinated, if there were others waiting—

He turned back.

She stood where the man had released her, one hand braced against the warehouse wall, the other pressed to her throat where the attacker's arm had been. Her hair had come loose from its pins, dark strands falling across her face. Her eyes were wide, her breath coming in short, ragged gasps.

He was at her side in two strides. His hands found her shoulders and he held her at arm's length, searching for injury.

"Are you hurt? Isabel. Look at me. Are you hurt?"

She shook her head. "I'm all right." Her voice was thin, but steady. "I'm all right."

She was shaking. He could feel the tremors running through her beneath his hands, and the sight of it cracked something open in his chest.

He pulled her to him.

His arms closed around her and he held her tight against him, one hand cradling the back of her head, the other pressed flat between her shoulder blades. She was rigid for a heartbeat, her whole body taut with shock. Then she exhaled, a long shuddering breath, and her forehead dropped against his shoulder. Her fingers curled into the lapels of his coat and held on.

"You are safe," he said, his voice rough against her hair. "I have you. I am not going to let you go."

She did not answer. She did not need to. Her grip on his coat tightened, and he felt her breathing begin to slow, steadying against the rhythm of his own.

"That was too close," he said. "It was my fault. I should not have suggested we walk. I got careless."

She pulled back just enough to look up at him. Her violet eyes were bright, her cheeks flushed, but the shaking had begun to ease. "It wasn't your fault. I should have seen it coming. I don't know why I didn't." She dropped her gaze. "I was distracted."

The word landed between them, heavy with everything it did not say.

Alexander drew a breath. "Can you walk?"

"Yes."

He released her shoulders but kept his arm around her waist. She did not object. They made their way back through the gap between the warehouses, past the loading bay, and out onto the quayside where the afternoon sun still shone as if nothing had happened.

People stared. A woman with a basket on her arm turned to whisper to her companion. A dockhand paused mid-step, his gaze following them down the quay. Alexander did not care. Let them look. Let them talk.

He tightened his arm around Isabel's waist and walked her to the carriage.

This would not happen again. Whatever it cost him, whoever he had to fight, he would keep her safe.

After handing her up into the carriage, he climbed in behind her and pulled the door shut.

"Home," he called to the driver. And this time, he did not sit across from her. He sat beside her, close enough that her shoulder rested against his, and he did not move away for the entire ride back.

Vera was in the entrance hall when they came through the door, arranging flowers in a tall vase on the side table, chattering to Mrs. Hartley about ribbon colours for the ball. She looked up with a bright smile that died the instant her eyes found Isabel's face.

"What happened?" The chrysanthemums she had been holding fell forgotten onto the table. Vera was across the hall in three strides, her hands reaching for Isabel's arms. "You are white as a sheet. Alexander, what happened?"

"Mrs. Hartley," the earl said from behind Isabel, his voice clipped, "chamomile tea, if you would. In the drawing room."

"At once, my lord." The housekeeper disappeared down the corridor without another word.

Vera took Isabel by the arm and steered her firmly away from her brother, guiding her through the drawing room door and settling her into the chair nearest the fire. She pulled a shawl from the back of the settee and draped it around Isabel's shoulders, her hands gentle but her expression fierce with concern.

"Sit."

Lord Whitmore followed them in and closed the door. He remained standing, one hand braced against the doorframe, and began to explain.

Isabel listened to his account as if from a great distance. The words washed over her as he spoke about the arsenal, Lieutenant Crowe, the walk along the harbour, the man who had seized her from behind, and she found herself drifting, her mind circling back, not to the attack itself, but to the minutes before it.

Not only had she been careless, she had been willingly blind.

The earl's silence had always been a distraction. From the first moment they met, his presence had tugged at her awareness, muffling the noise around her, making it harder to read the minds in their vicinity.

Until now she had managed to compensate with concentration, but today she had let herself be absorbed by him. By his nearness, the rare and precious quiet that surrounded him. She had tilted her face toward the sun and, for the briefest moment, had stopped paying attention to everything else.

And someone had almost taken her because of it.

She had dealt with danger before. She had survived solely because she had always kept one ear turned toward the thoughts around her, staying three steps ahead of anyone who might wish her harm. Her gift had been her armor. Her advantage. The one thing that kept her safe when nothing else could.

But ever since she had come to Whitmore Hall, that armor had been slipping. Because she kept letting her guard down. Around him. For him. Because she let herself be drawn in by that silence of his which she had come to crave.

She had to be more careful. Had to rebuild her walls, stop letting the Earl of Whitmore cloud her judgement. She could not afford this. Her freedom depended on surviving long enough to earn it, and freedom would be of little use to her if she was snatched off a quayside and delivered to Delacroix.

Because it had to be Delacroix. Who else would want her badly enough to orchestrate an abduction in broad daylight? A black carriage had been waiting for them. The follower had tracked them from the arsenal. Every detail spoke of coordination, of planning.

The marquis had not forgotten about her...

"Isabel?"

Vera's voice pulled her back. The younger woman was leaning toward her, a cup of chamomile tea extended in her hands. Isabel had not even noticed Mrs. Hartley enter and leave again.

"Have some tea. You still look very pale."

Isabel took the cup. The porcelain was warm against her fingers, and she wrapped both hands around it, letting the heat seep into her skin. She took a sip. The chamomile was sweet and fragrant, and some of the tightness in her chest began to ease.

Lord Whitmore had taken the armchair beside her. He sat forward, his elbows on his knees, his expression grim.

A knock sounded at the door and Hartley entered, silver tray in hand. Upon it rested a folded note alongside two thick, gilt-edged cards.

"My lord. A message from Captain Raines. It arrived by courier just moments ago."

The earl frowned and collected the items. As Hartley withdrew, Lord Whitmore set the two unmarked cards on the side table, then broke the seal on the note. He scanned the contents, folded the paper, and set it down.

"The captain is back in port," he said, his brow creasing. "Sooner than expected. I hope nothing went wrong with Lena." He paused, gesturing to the table. "He is calling in his favour. There will be a naval reception at the Admiral's residence in two days' time. Raines requests that Isabel attend as his guest."

Vera's brow arched at the sound of her brother using Isabel's first name. The young woman's gaze flickered between them, but the earl did not seem to register the look at all.

"After what happened today," he continued, his voice hardening, "I am not inclined to put you in danger again, Isabel. I will speak with Raines and see if we can come to another arrangement."

Isabel set down her tea. "No."

He looked at her.

"I gave the captain my word," she said. "And besides, a reception filled with naval officers may be just what we need right now. If the order for those barrels came from someone high-ranking, there is a fair chance they will be in attendance. I could learn a great deal in a single evening."

Lord Whitmore held her gaze, and she could see the reluctance in his eyes, the tension in his shoulders. He did not want her there. In fact, she suspected, he did not want her anywhere that was not behind the walls of Whitmore Hall, preferably with an armed guard at every door.

"Very well," he said at last. "But the arrangement changes. You will not attend as the captain's guest. You will attend with me. Raines can have his favour, but I will be the one at your side." His grey eyes held hers. "I will be right beside you. The entire evening."

Vera and Isabel exchanged a glance. Vera's lips pressed together, fighting something that looked suspiciously like a smile. Alexander did not appear to notice.

"Well then," Vera said after a moment, gracefully rising from her seat. "I shall leave you to finalize the details. I have a great deal of work to do before the ball, and the fabric samples will not sort themselves." She paused at the door, glancing back at Isabel with a look that promised questions later, and then she was gone.

The drawing room was quiet safe for the crackling of the fire and the ticking of the clock on the mantelpiece. The earl's gaze was fixed on the flames, his expression grim.

"Lord Whitmore—" Isabel began.

"Please," he said as he turned to her, his voice softer now. "Call me Alexander."

She hesitated.

He had offered this before, and she had refused out of defiance, a small act of resistance against the man who held her papers.

But things were different now. She trusted him, however uncomfortable the admission felt. If she had harboured any remaining doubt, this afternoon had burned it away. He had come for her. Had fought for her. Had held her in his arms and told her she was safe, and she had believed him.

And it had not escaped her notice that he had been calling her Isabel ever since the attack. As if the formality between them had been stripped away in the moment he thought he might lose her.

She found that she did not mind. More than that — she found that she wanted to return the gesture.

"Alexander," she said.

His features eased at the sound of his name.

"I wanted to thank you," she continued. "For today. For coming after me. If you hadn't been there—" She stopped herself. The alternatives were not worth speaking aloud.

"Do not thank me." His voice was rough. "If I had been paying closer attention, it would never have happened. I failed you."

"I would say you very much succeeded, given that I am sitting here in one piece. So I will thank you whether you like it or not." She held his gaze. "Thank you, Alexander."

He gave a short nod, his throat working.

After a pause, he shifted forward in his chair. "I am sure you would like some rest after everything that has happened. I should give you some privacy."

He began to rise, but Isabel spoke before she could think better of it.

"Actually." She looked down at her hands, then back up at him. "If you don't mind, I would rather not be alone just now. Would you stay? Just for a while."

The tension drained from his shoulders. He settled back into the chair, and a smile crossed his face.

"Of course."

The brandy was good. Alexander barely tasted it.

He stood at the drawing room window, glass in hand, staring out into the darkness. The women had retired an hour ago, Vera pressing a kiss to his cheek and Isabel offering a quiet "good night, Alexander" that had settled warm in his chest.

The sound of his name from her lips, shaped by that slight northern inflection that softened the syllables, had lodged itself somewhere beneath his ribs and showed no sign of leaving.

He took a drink and let his mind drift back over the afternoon.

After the attack, after the tea and the conversation about Raines and the reception, they had simply sat together. He could not recall the last time he had done that with anyone, just existed in the same room without agenda or obligation. The fire had burned low and the daylight beyond the windows had slowly faded to dusk, and Isabel had eventually closed her eyes, her breathing evening out, her head tilting slightly toward the wing of the armchair. He had watched her sleep for longer than propriety permitted, noting how the tension left her face, how young she looked without the sharp wariness she wore during waking hours.

When she had stirred, he had pretended to be reading.

Dinner had passed pleasantly. Vera had dominated the conversation with her plans for the ball, cataloguing fabrics and seating arrangements with her usual enthusiasm for all things societal. Alexander had contributed the occasional nod or murmur of agreement, but his attention had been elsewhere. Beside him, Isabel had eaten quietly, her eyes lifting to meet his at intervals, and each time their gazes had caught and held for a beat longer than necessary. As if they shared a secret the rest of the room was not privy to. As if the events of the afternoon had woven a thread between them that only they could see.

He had not touched her again since they had arrived back home. Had not so much as brushed her hand when passing the salt. And yet the evening had felt more intimate than any he could remember.

He did not know what to do with that.

The front door opened across the hall, and he heard Hartley's measured voice in the entrance, followed by a familiar, less measured one.

"Frightfully sorry for the hour, Hartley. Is he still up?"

"In the drawing room, my lord."

Footsteps crossed the hall. The door opened, and Damien appeared, his golden hair windswept, his cravat loosened, his coat creased from a day spent in and out of carriages.

"Forgive me," he said, dropping into the armchair nearest the fire and stretching his legs toward the hearth. "I would have been here for dinner, but I was chasing a lead and could not let it go."

Alexander turned from the window. "You found something."

"I found something." He looked pointedly at the decanters on the sideboard. Alexander crossed the room, poured a second glass, and handed it to his friend. Damien took a long swallow and leaned forward. "I spent the afternoon at the Merchant Marine Club. Dreadful place, terrible wine, but excellent gossip if one knows whom to ask. I struck up a conversation with a shipping clerk named Fenwick, a thoroughly unpleasant man with a fondness for port and a tendency to talk when he's had enough of it."

"And?"

"He let slip that there is a large cargo shipment scheduled for the southern docks. A private consignment, arriving by sea, due to be unloaded the week after the ball." Damien's blue eyes were sharp. "The interesting part is who arranged it. The shipping contract was brokered through a merchant firm called Harlow and Sons."

Alexander went still. "The Harlow brothers. They are on the guest list for the ball."

"They are indeed. And according to my talkative friend Fenwick, the Harlows have been handling an unusual number of private shipments over the past year. Cargo that arrives at night, gets unloaded quickly, and disappears into warehouses before morning. No customs inspections are filed, and no manifests are submitted to the harbour authority."

"What kind of cargo are they moving?"

"That is the question Fenwick could not answer. Or would not." Damien took another drink. "But he did mention that the Harlows have been spending well beyond their means lately. They have acquired new carriages and a country house, and they entertain lavishly. That is not the kind of wealth one earns from honest shipping."

Alexander moved to the fireplace and leaned against the mantelpiece. The Harlow brothers were associates of Delacroix, they were on the guest list for the ball, and now they were linked to suspicious shipments arriving under cover of darkness.

"We need to be at those docks when that shipment arrives," he said.

"My thoughts precisely." Damien swirled his brandy. "But first, the ball. If the Harlow brothers are there, Isabel can read them. We may learn exactly what this cargo is before we ever set foot on the quayside."

Alexander nodded slowly. "I have something to tell you as well," he said. "We had an eventful afternoon."

Damien's brow rose. "More eventful than mine?"

"Someone tried to take Isabel."

Damien leaned forward, his glass forgotten, his face draining of colour. "What?"

Alexander recounted the events at the harbour. The walk along the quayside, Isabel sensing the follower, the separation, the man dragging her toward a black carriage.

Damien was silent throughout. When Alexander finished, his friend's expression was grave.

"Delacroix."

"Who else."

"Is she all right?"

"Shaken. But unharmed." Alexander paused. "I was careless, Damien. I let my guard down. I suggested a walk along the harbour as if we were out for a Sunday stroll, and she nearly paid for it."

"You could not have anticipated an abduction attempt in broad daylight."

"I should have. After everything we know about the marquis, I should have been prepared for exactly that." He pressed his thumb into the scar on his right hand. "It will not happen again."

Damien studied him. "You say that as though you were making a vow."

Alexander looked up. "What do you mean?"

"I mean that there is a difference between a man protecting his associate and a man swearing an oath over the woman he—" Damien stopped himself. He raised a hand. "Forgive me. It is not my place."

"You are right. It is not," Alexander said and turned back to the fire.

"Fair enough. I shall leave it alone." Damien raised his glass. "For now."

Alexander let the comment unanswered. He did not want to discuss Isabel. Did not want to examine, under the sharp light of Damien's observation, the thing that was growing between them. It was easier to keep it in the dark, unnamed, where he could pretend it was merely concern for a woman under his protection.

"There is one more thing," he said, steering the conversation back to safer ground. "Raines is back in port. He is calling in his favour. There is a naval reception at the Admiral's residence in two days."

"And you will let her go? After everything that's happened today?"

"I agreed to let Isabel fulfill her promise. But on my terms. She will attend with me, not Raines. After today, I will not let her out of my sight."

Damien opened his mouth, and Alexander could see the comment forming behind his eyes. But for once, the viscount exercised restraint.

"The reception could work in our favour," Damien said. "Isabel might overhear something useful. You still haven't told me what you learned at the arsenal today."

Alexander gave him a brief account of Lieutenant Crowe and the missing sixteen barrels, the official requisition that bore no individual name, and the unmarked wagons that had collected the gunpowder.

Damien let out a low whistle. "So someone of high authority within the Admiralty is involved in this. And they are connected to Delacroix."

"Yes. And the reception may put Isabel in a room with the very people who could tell us who gave that order."

"Clever woman, to see that."

"Yes." He cleared his throat. "She is."

Damien finished his brandy and set the empty glass on the side table. He rose, rolling his shoulders, and crossed to the sideboard to pour himself a second measure. He brought the decanter back with him and topped up Alexander's glass without being asked.

"So." He settled back into his chair. "We have a reception in two days. The ball will take place in a week, and the shipment the week after. We have a great deal to accomplish in a short time."

"We do."

"Then I suggest we both get some rest." Damien raised his glass. "You look terrible, by the way. When did you last sleep properly?"

Alexander did not answer. He could not remember.

"That's what I thought." Damien drained his glass in two swallows and stood. "Get some sleep, Alex. You are no good to anyone, least of all her, if you collapse from exhaustion."

He made for the door, then paused and looked back.

"For what it's worth," he said, "I am glad you were there today to protect her."

"So am I."

"And Alexander?"

"Yes?"

Damien held his gaze. "Whatever is happening between you and Isabel, do not fight it so hard that you strangle it. Some things are worth the risk. Even for men who have lost as much as you have."

He was gone before Alexander could respond, the door clicking softly shut behind him.

Alexander sank back down into his chair and thought of violet eyes meeting his across a dinner table. Of a voice saying his name for the first time. Of a woman who had asked him to stay, and the look on her face when he had said yes.

He finished his drink, extinguished the lamp, and climbed the stairs. This time, when he passed her door, he did not stop.

But he smiled.

Chapter Seven

Two days had passed in a blur of ledgers, maps, and late-night discussions around the library table, and suddenly it was the afternoon of the naval reception, and Isabel was sitting in the carriage beside Alexander, still adjusting to the fact that the hands folded in her silk-clad lap were the same ones that had worn iron shackles not long ago.

She smoothed the deep green silk across her knees and glanced at the man opposite her. He sat rigidly upright, his dark coat immaculate, his jaw set in that particular way that meant he was running through contingencies in his head.

"Are you certain the captain won't object to the change of arrangement?" she asked.

Alexander's gaze snapped to hers, the distant focus in his eyes clearing. "He will have no choice." He adjusted his gloves. "Once inside, we fulfill his request first. Then we use the remainder of the evening to engage the guests I have identified. You stay at my side. At all times."

Isabel gave a nod and pressed her lips together against a smile. Far be it from her to object, she thought, as she turned to the window, where the streets of Greyport's naval quarter were sliding past. Grand stone buildings lined the avenue, their facades hung with the blue and gold pennants of the Royal Navy. Carriages queued ahead of them, depositing officers in dress uniforms and their wives in evening gowns at the steps of an imposing Georgian mansion.

The Admiral's residence. Lamplight blazed from every window, and the sounds of music and conversation drifted out into the cold evening air.

Their carriage drew up, and a footman opened the door. Alexander descended first and handed Isabel down, his gloved fingers steady around hers. Together they climbed the steps to where Dominic Raines was waiting, leaning against one of the columns.

He straightened when he saw them, and his green eyes swept over Isabel, warm with appreciation.

"Lord Whitmore. Miss de Clare." He bowed, then offered Isabel a smile that was all charm and mischief. "I must confess, when I received your message informing me that the lady would be attending on your arm instead of mine, I was rather put out. I had been looking forward to the pleasure of her company."

"I am sure you will survive the disappointment, Captain," Alexander said.

Raines laughed. "Barely." He fell into step beside them as they entered the mansion. "I half expected this, you know," he murmured to Isabel as Alexander presented their invitations to the steward at the door. "The earl is not the most subtle man when it comes to guarding what he considers his."

Isabel felt heat rise in her cheeks. She caught Alexander glancing back at them, his eyes narrowing, but before he could speak Raines had already turned away, nodding to an acquaintance across the foyer.

Alexander caught the captain's arm before he could drift further. "A word, Raines. I was not expecting to see you back in port so soon. Should you not still be en route to the Free Isles with Lena? Has something gone wrong?"

Raines shook his head. "Yes and no. We were intercepted a day out by a naval frigate conducting routine inspections. We hid Lena below deck. My crew knows how to handle a search. But while the officers were aboard, I overheard two of them discussing this reception. The entire senior command of the Greyport fleet under one roof." His green eyes sharpened. "A chance like that does not come twice. I entrusted my first mate with seeing Lena safely to the Free Isles and I booked passage back to Greyport on the naval vessel."

"You left Lena with your first mate?" Alexander's brow creased.

"She is in the safest hands I know, outside of my own. And I could not let this opportunity pass." Raines's expression lost its easy charm. "The answers I need are in that room tonight, Lord Whitmore. I can feel it."

Alexander held his gaze for a moment, then nodded. "Very well. Let us make the most of it."

The reception hall was grand and crowded. Officers in blue dress coats mingled with merchants and shipbuilders, their wives and daughters circulating in jewel-coloured silks. Chandeliers blazed overhead, throwing warm light across polished marble, and a string quartet played from a gallery above the main floor.

Isabel tightened her walls. The hum of dozens of minds pushed against her awareness, and she let them wash past, filtering out the noise, searching for anything useful beneath the surface chatter. Most of it was mundane, nothing but gossip and complaints.

Raines confidently guided them through the crowd, introducing them to various officers and merchants, clearly knowing everyone and liked by most. Isabel smiled, inclined her head, and listened.

After an hour of pleasantries, Raines drew them into a quiet alcove near the far windows, his demeanour shifting.

"There." He nodded discreetly toward the centre of the room, where a grey-haired man in the decorated uniform of a senior officer stood surrounded by a small circle of subordinates. He was tall and lean, his face hard and watchful. "Admiral Fallon. Commander of the Greyport naval fleet."

Isabel studied him. His mind was controlled and guarded. Here was a man who had spent a lifetime practicing which thoughts to keep behind his teeth.

"This is about your brother," she said quietly and turned to the captain, whose underlying worry had caught her attention.

Raines's jaw tightened. "James has been missing for over three months. The official account is that his ship went down in the Serpent's Passage and all hands were lost." He paused. "I don't believe it. James was the finest navigator in the fleet. He knew those waters. And in the weeks before he disappeared, he told me he had uncovered irregularities in the Admiralty's accounts." His green eyes hardened. "He was investigating a cover-up. And then, conveniently, he was gone."

"What do you need from me?"

"I am going to engage the admiral in conversation. Ask him questions about the circumstances of James's disappearance. All I need is for you to tell me if he is lying. And anything else you might hear in his thoughts about James or the investigation he conducted."

Isabel nodded. "I understand."

Alexander leaned towards Isabel. "If anything feels wrong, signal me and we leave."

Raines led them across the room. The admiral saw them approaching and his expression shifted to a polite smile.

"Captain Raines." Fallon extended his hand. "What a pleasure. I did not expect to see you this evening."

"Admiral." Raines clasped his hand briefly. "I believe my invitation must have gone astray. Fortunately my parents were good enough to lend me theirs. They send their apologies, my father's health has kept them from attending in person." He gestured to his companions. "May I introduce Lord Whitmore, Under-Secretary of State for the Home Office, and Miss de Clare."

Fallon's gaze moved to Alexander, then to Isabel. His eyes lingered on hers a fraction too long, and she felt his mind harden, a door closing somewhere deep within his thoughts.

"Lord Whitmore. An honor." He inclined his head. "The Crown Prince has spoken of you often. It is a pleasure to finally make your acquaintance." His gaze returned to Isabel. "And Miss de Clare. What a striking colour your eyes are. Most unusual."

"You are too kind, Admiral," she said, keeping her voice steady.

The conversation began innocuously. Raines asked after mutual acquaintances, discussed the recent weather, complimented the reception. Fallon responded smoothly, his thoughts running a tight parallel to his words, revealing little.

Then Raines changed the topic.

"I trust the search for my brother's vessel is still under way," he said casually. "It has been three months, and I confess the family grows anxious for answers."

Fallon's smile did not falter. "These matters take time, Captain. The Serpent's Passage is notoriously difficult to survey. Rest assured, we are doing everything in our power."

Doing everything in my power to ensure no one finds a damned thing.

The thought slipped through a crack in his composure, gone almost as quickly as it came.

"I have heard rumours," Raines pressed, his poise wavering just slightly, "that James had submitted reports to the Admiralty in the weeks before his final voyage. Reports concerning certain irregularities in fleet operations. Have those been reviewed?"

Fallon's expression cooled. "I am not at liberty to discuss the details of internal matters, Captain. I'm sure you understand."

The reports were destroyed the day they arrived on my desk. Along with every copy that fool sent to the Naval Secretary.

Isabel's pulse quickened. She kept her eyes forward, her face composed, but with her fingers she pressed hard against Alexander's arm. He glanced down at her hand, then at her face, and she saw the shift in his expression as he understood that she had found something.

"Of course," Raines said, and Isabel could hear the strain in his voice now, his thoughts churning with grief and fury held barely in check. "Though I find it curious that the shipping logs for James's final voyage have not been made available to the family. Standard procedure, I believe, in cases of vessels lost at sea."

"The Passage is under restricted jurisdiction." Fallon's tone had gone clipped. "Certain records are classified."

If that pup pushes any further I will have him disposed of, too. The brother was trouble enough.

"Forgive me, Admiral, but my brother was—"

"Your brother," Fallon interrupted, his voice quiet but carrying an unmistakable edge, "was a fine officer who met an unfortunate end in dangerous waters. I grieve his loss, as we all do. But I will not discuss classified naval operations at a social function." He turned to

Alexander. "Lord Whitmore, if you will excuse me. I see the harbour Master requires my attention."

He inclined his head and withdrew into the crowd.

As the admiral turned away, a final cascade of thoughts reached Isabel, spilling through his composure in the wake of his irritation.

I should have taken the marquis up on his offer to handle the whole affair. But then again, the evidence is at the bottom of the sea, along with that nosy captain and his ship. No one will ever reach it...

Isabel glanced at Raines. His restraint was fraying. She could hear the turmoil in his thoughts, grief and fury tangling together, his control slipping with each breath.

Alexander noticed it too. He stepped closer to the captain and lowered his voice. "We have what we need. Let us step outside."

"I'm not finished with him," Raines said through his teeth, his gaze still fixed on the spot where Fallon had disappeared into the crowd.

"You are for tonight." Alexander's tone was firm. "You will gain nothing by confronting him here, in a room full of naval officers. Come. We can discuss what Isabel learned on the way."

Raines stood rigid for a moment, his jaw working. Then he exhaled, a slow, controlled breath. "Fair point."

They made their way toward the exit, Alexander guiding Isabel and Raines following close behind.

They collected their coats and descended the steps to the drive, where the carriage stood waiting among a row of others.

"Ride with us," Alexander said. "We should talk."

Raines was cursing before the carriage door had fully closed behind him.

"That smug, self-satisfied son of a—" He dropped onto the bench opposite Isabel and slammed his fist against his knee. "Did you see his face? Standing there, smiling, shaking my hand, while my brother—" He broke off, pressing his knuckles against his mouth.

Isabel could hear his thoughts clearly. They were a storm of grief and rage battering against the walls of his composure. Images of James flashed through his mind, and one question repeated over and over: *Where are you?*

Alexander had taken the seat beside Isabel, his expression grave. He let Raines spend himself for a moment before he spoke.

"Dominic. Look at me."

The captain raised his head. His green eyes were bright with fury, but the use of his first name seemed to anchor him.

"We went there for a reason," Alexander said. "And Isabel has answers for you. But I need you to hear them clearly. Can you do that?"

Raines drew a long breath. Then another. His fists unclenched, and he sat back against the bench, jaw still tight but listening.

"The admiral was lying," Isabel said. "About nearly everything. When you asked about the search for James's vessel, his thoughts were clear: he has no intention of finding your brother. The reports James submitted about irregularities in the fleet were destroyed the day they reached Fallon's desk."

Raines eyes went wide.

"There is more." Isabel chose her words carefully. She could see how close he was to the edge, and she did not want to be the one to push him over it. "In his thoughts, Fallon referred to James as trouble. And when you pressed about the shipping logs, his first instinct was to consider having you silenced as well."

"Silenced." The word left Raines's lips flat and hollow. "So he is behind James's disappearance. I knew it."

"I cannot confirm that directly. His thoughts did not spell it out so plainly. But he is clearly concealing the truth about what really happened to your brother. Also..."

Both men looked at her as Isabel paused.

"As the admiral walked away," she continued, "his thoughts turned to the marquis. He was thinking that he should have accepted his offer to handle the affair. But then he reassured himself that it no longer mattered, because the evidence of whatever James had been documenting is now at the bottom of the ocean, along with your brother and his ship, where no one will ever find it."

“Fallon is working with Delacroix?” Alexander asked.

“He didn’t name him specifically,” Isabel admitted, “but I highly suspect that he was referring to the Marquis of Darkwater.”

The carriage was silent save for the rattle of wheels on cobblestones.

Isabel watched Raines, his green eyes distant, his jaw working as his mind was turning from grief to sharp focus as he calculated his next move.

There may be one person who can help with finding that evidence. She caught the thought as it surfaced, fierce and defiant. *If I can find her, I can reach that wreck.*

Raines looked up, his expression determined. "James kept records of everything. If there is proof of what Fallon has done, it will be wherever my brother's ship went down. And I will find a way to reach it."

Alexander leaned forward. "Where can we set you down?"

"The harbour." Raines straightened, his composure reassembling itself. "I have preparations to make."

The carriage changed course at Alexander's instruction, and within twenty minutes they had pulled up at the quayside. Through the window, Isabel could see the forest of masts rising against the night sky, dark hulls rocking gently at anchor along the docks.

Raines reached for the door handle, then paused. He turned back to them.

"Until our paths cross again, Lord Whitmore."

"Be careful out there, Raines," Alexander said.

"Always am." A ghost of the old grin surfaced. Then he turned to Isabel, and his expression softened. "Miss de Clare. Thank you. I owe you a debt I am not sure I can repay." He tilted his head toward Alexander. "And if you ever tire of this one's company, you know where to find me."

"Good luck, Captain," Isabel said. "I hope you find what you're looking for."

Raines inclined his head, stepped down from the carriage, and disappeared into the dark of the quayside. The door closed, and the driver urged the horses onward.

Isabel sat back against the cushions. Beside her, Alexander remained where he was, close enough that she could feel the warmth of him.

"Fallon," he said after a moment. "The commander of the Greyport fleet is involved in this. And with the authority to issue orders through the naval chain of command, he is most likely the one who arranged for those gunpowder barrels to be diverted from the arsenal."

"And he is connected to Delacroix," Isabel added. "Whether he is working for the marquis or alongside him, I cannot say. But there is a link." She frowned. "What I still cannot see is how it all fits together. A corrupted admiral, a marquis who chases magic users, a warehouse of military gunpowder used to discredit them. What is the common thread?"

"I do not know." Alexander's brow creased. "But we are closer to the truth than we have ever been. And all thanks to you."

He met her eyes for a brief moment, then leaned back and turned his head to look out the window and onto the gaslit streets of Greyport.

Isabel hesitated. An idea had been forming in her mind since they left the reception, and she had been weighing it from every angle, looking for a reason not to suggest it. She could not find one. Or perhaps she simply did not want to.

"Alexander."

He turned to her.

"We still have a good while before we reach Whitmore Hall. I was wondering—" She paused, steadying herself. "Would you like to practise our bond? We haven't had a chance since the other evening, and if we are to use it at the ball, we should be better prepared."

His brows rose, and then his expression eased. "I think that is a very good idea."

"We could try to build on what we achieved last time," she continued. "Find each other within the bond, and then see if we can go further. If you were to concentrate on a specific thought, a word or an image, I could try to receive it. A way to communicate without speaking."

"That would be invaluable."

"Then shall we?"

She removed her gloves and held out her hand.

Alexander looked at it. Then he pulled off his own glove, finger by finger, and took her hand in his.

The silence descended upon her, and it was as if her mind recognised the sensation and opened to it willingly. The noise of the city, the distant thoughts of the driver and the passers-by on the street, all of it fell away until there was nothing left but the warmth of his hand and his vast, all-encompassing quiet.

Isabel closed her eyes and breathed.

She did not reach out this time. She simply settled into the stillness, let it hold her.

And there he was. Faint but steady. His presence beside her own in that silent space, warm and constant as a heartbeat.

"I've found you," she said, and opened her eyes.

He was watching her, his grey eyes intent, and a smile rested on his lips. "Well done," he said softly.

"Now try. Think of a word. Hold it clearly in your mind and direct it toward me."

He closed his eyes. Isabel watched his face, the slight furrow between his brows, the way his fingers tightened fractionally around hers. She let her awareness drift toward his presence in the bond.

At first there was nothing but the steady pulse of his consciousness beside hers. Then, faint as a whisper carried on the wind, she caught it.

Safe.

Her breath hitched. She opened her mouth, closed it, and swallowed.

"Safe," she said. "You thought 'safe.'"

Alexander's eyes opened. The smile that spread across his face was unguarded and warm, and it made her chest ache in a way she did not want to examine.

"You heard it."

"Faintly. But yes."

"Remarkable." He shook his head, and the wonder in his expression made him look younger, the hard lines of his face softened by something close to delight. "We should make this a daily practice. If we can strengthen this, the advantages at the ball would be considerable."

Isabel nodded. She was aware, suddenly, of how warm his hand was around hers, of how close they were sitting, of how the lamplight from outside the carriage caught the grey of his eyes and turned them silver. She was aware of how much she wanted to lean closer, to lose herself in the silence that surrounded him and stay there.

She was aware, with a sharp and sudden clarity, that she was in danger of wanting far more than his silence.

Heat rushed to her cheeks. She released his hand and looked away, reaching for composure.

"That was good progress," she managed.

If Alexander noticed the flush in her face, he had the grace not to remark on it. "It was," he agreed.

They rode in silence for a minute, Isabel's hand resting in her lap where his warmth still lingered against her palm.

Then his voice came, quiet and steady beside her.

"Shall we try again?"

She felt a flutter low in her stomach as she turned to find him watching her, his hand extended between them.

Isabel met his eyes. Then she placed her hand in his.

The days since the naval reception had settled into a rhythm Alexander had not expected to find comfortable.

Mornings were spent in the library, the four of them bent over guest lists and floor plans of Lady Deacon's ballroom. Vera had taken command of their preparations, drilling them on the names of every guest, their political leanings, their connections to Delacroix, and their likely positions in the room. She had procured a seating chart from the baroness herself and pinned it to the wall beside the fireplace, annotating it with notes that would have impressed a spymaster.

Damien came and went, bringing scraps of intelligence gathered from his social rounds. Alexander reviewed naval registries and cross-referenced shipping records. Isabel studied the guest profiles, committing names and descriptions to memory so she would recognise the people whose minds she needed to read.

But it was the evenings Alexander had come to look forward to most.

After dinner, when Vera retired and Damien took his leave, he and Isabel would retreat to the drawing room. The fire would be lit, two glasses of brandy poured, and they would sit in the armchairs by the hearth and practise their bond.

The progress had been steady. What had begun as a faint sense of each other's presence had sharpened into a clearer, more defined awareness. They could now exchange short messages, a word or a brief phrase sent from his mind and received by hers. He would think *left* and she would turn her head. He would think *careful* and she would straighten in her chair. Simple commands, clear as speech, transmitted through nothing more than the contact of their hands.

But it worked only in one direction. She could hear him. He could not hear her.

He had tried. Had opened himself as fully as he knew how, had quieted his thoughts and reached for hers the way she described reaching for his. Nothing. His shield blocked every attempt to reach him, making no distinction between friend and foe, welcome and unwelcome. The wall that protected his mind was absolute, and he could not lower it even when he wished to.

What he could feel, however, was her. Not her thoughts, not words or images, but her emotions. He could sense when she was amused, a lightness that danced at the edge of his awareness. When she was concentrating, a focused stillness. When she was anxious, a tightening that echoed in his own chest.

And he could feel her growing affection.

It was there every evening, woven through the bond like a thread of gold through dark cloth. A tenderness that deepened each time their hands met, each time their eyes held across the quiet room. He had not told her he could sense it. Could not bring himself to acknowledge it aloud, because acknowledging it would mean confronting his own feelings, and those were a territory he was not prepared to enter.

But even without the bond, he could see how she felt. In the way her gaze lingered on his when she thought he was not looking. In the way she said his name now, naturally, as if she had been saying it her whole life.

She trusted him. He was certain of it. He could feel it through their bond, clear and unwavering, and the weight of that trust pressed against his conscience like a hand against his chest.

Because it was precisely that trust that forbade him from acting on what he felt. She depended on him. Her papers sat in his desk. Her freedom was his to grant or withhold. Whatever she felt for him, however genuine it might be, was shaped by a power imbalance he could not pretend did not exist. To reach for her now, to pull her close the way he ached to do every evening when their fingers intertwined by the fire, would be to take advantage of a woman who had already been taken advantage of by every man who had held power over her before him.

He would not be another name on that list.

And so he held himself in check. Let go of her hand when propriety demanded. Said good night at the drawing room door and climbed the stairs alone. Lay in the dark and thought of violet eyes and did not sleep.

"Alexander? Are you listening?"

He blinked. Vera was watching him from the chair beside his, her fork poised mid-air, her expression expectant. Across the dinner table, Damien was grinning into his wine glass, and Isabel sat at Alexander's right, her gaze lowered to her plate.

"Forgive me," he said. "My mind was elsewhere."

"Clearly." Vera set down her fork. "As I was saying, the dancing arrangements for tomorrow night. Damien will partner me, naturally, and Isabel will dance with you."

"If my feet survive the ordeal," Damien murmured, setting down his glass. "Your sister has a habit of leading, Alexander. And stepping on toes when contradicted."

Under the table, Alexander heard Vera's foot connect sharply with Damien's shin. The viscount flinched and reached for his wine again.

"We are supposed to dance?" Isabel's voice drew Alexander's attention. She looked at Vera, alarm plain on her face.

"But of course," Vera said, as if the question were absurd. "It is a ball, Isabel. Dancing is rather the point."

"I had lessons as a child. When I was still living with my parents." Isabel set down her knife. "But that was over a decade ago. I haven't danced since. I'm not certain I remember the steps well enough to be convincing."

"Nonsense." Vera waved the concern away. "Dancing is like riding. Once learned, never forgotten. It will come back to you the moment you hear the music." Her eyes lit up. "Which gives me a wonderful idea. Alexander, you must give Isabel a practice lesson."

Alexander opened his mouth.

"Tonight," Vera continued. "After dinner. The ball is tomorrow, so there is no time to waste. Hartley can prepare the gramophone."

"Vera—"

"While my brother likes to pretend he loathes dancing," Vera informed Isabel, ignoring him, "he is in truth an excellent partner. Our mother taught us both when we were children, and he has a natural grace that he goes to great lengths to conceal beneath all that brooding."

"I do not brood."

"You brood magnificently. It is one of your finest qualities." Vera beamed at Isabel. "So. Shall we?"

Alexander looked at Isabel. She looked back at him, a faint crease of worry between her brows.

"It would be my honour," Alexander said.

He did not allow himself to dwell on the prospect of holding her, of guiding her through the steps, of standing close enough to feel her breath and smell the lavender in her hair. No, he did not think about any of that.

"Wonderful!"

Vera clapped her hands together and launched back into her briefing on the guest list, rattling off names and seating positions. Damien rubbed his shin under the table and offered the occasional sardonic comment. Isabel returned to her plate.

Alexander met her gaze one more time across the candlelight and gave a helpless shrug.

Her worried expression softened, and her lips curved into a small smile. Those lips, he thought. How lovely they were when she smiled. How close he had been to kissing them in that alley, how close he came to thinking about them every single—

He reached for his wine and drank deeply.

The ballroom at Whitmore Hall was a grand, echoing space that looked as though it had been waiting years for someone to remember it existed.

The nearest dust covers had been pulled from the furniture and some of the chandeliers lit, their crystals throwing fractured light across the polished parquet floor. Tall mirrors lined the walls, reflecting the glow of a mere dozen candles and the four figures standing somewhat uncertainly in the centre of the room.

"Why should Damien and I not have some fun as well?" Vera was saying, adjusting the cuff of her sleeve. "Besides, this poor ballroom gets used far too little. It is practically begging for company."

"The ballroom is not begging," Damien said. "I, on the other hand, am. My feet are begging you, Vera, to reconsider."

"Your feet will survive. Hartley, if you would?"

The butler, who had stationed himself beside a small table near the doorway, lowered the needle onto the gramophone. A waltz filled the room, tinny and distant from the brass horn but unmistakably elegant, the strings rising and falling in three-quarter time.

Vera seized Damien by the hand and pulled him toward the far end of the floor. He went with theatrical reluctance, muttering about the sacrifices required of loyal friends, but his hand found her waist easily enough and within moments they were moving together, Vera leading half the time and Damien pretending not to notice.

Their bickering faded to a pleasant hum as they danced further away, and Isabel found herself standing alone with Alexander in a pool of candlelight.

He turned to her and held out his hand.

"Shall we?"

She placed her hand in his. His fingers closed around hers, skin against skin, and the silence swept over her at once, blotting out the vibrant swirl of Vera's mind, the warm undercurrent of Damien's, and the butler's measured, contented thoughts by the door. The world contracted to the warmth of Alexander's hand and the quiet space they shared.

"We may as well use this as further practice," he murmured as he pulled her closer. "Try to reach each other under harder conditions, with other people in the room, music, distractions. Try to keep the bond open while we dance."

She nodded, a smile tugging at her lips as he placed his other hand at her waist and she rested hers on his shoulder.

Then they began to move.

She was clumsy at first. Her feet remembered the shape of the steps but not the timing, and twice she trod on his boot before finding the rhythm. Alexander guided her patiently, his hand steady at her waist, adjusting his stride to match hers, and gradually the old lessons surfaced from wherever they had been sleeping for the past twelve years. The turns came back. The count settled into her bones. And her body began to follow his without her mind having to instruct it.

Vera was right. She did remember.

But the steps were secondary to everything else.

Alexander had held her before. In the dark alley outside the prison, pressing her against the wall to shield her from the watchman. After the abduction attempt at the harbour, when he'd pulled her against his chest and she'd gripped his coat and let herself be sheltered. And they had touched many times since, their hands meeting each evening in practice, their bond deepening with each session. But those moments had been brief, or still, or both. They had never been this close for this long, moving together, his hand warm and firm at her waist, her fingers resting on the solid breadth of his shoulder, their bodies separated by inches that felt like nothing at all.

She didn't need to examine the ache in her chest or the heat spreading through her where his palm pressed against the small of her back. She'd long since admitted to herself that she was drawn to him. Attracted. Perhaps even falling for him, God help her. But tonight she didn't want to weigh the implications or count the reasons it could never work. Tonight she wanted to close her eyes and feel the music carry them and pretend, just for a little while, that this was all there was.

So she did.

"See? I told you she would remember!" Vera's voice sailed past them as she and Damien swept by in a wide arc, and Isabel's eyes flew open. Vera flashed her a triumphant smile before Damien spun her away toward the far mirrors.

Isabel met Alexander's gaze. He was watching her with an expression she'd come to recognise: intent, guarded, and an underlying tenderness that he was trying very hard to contain.

Through the bond, she felt it. The warmth of his enjoyment, his pleasure at holding her, a quiet contentment.

It felt so good to be held by him. So safe.

Safe.

The word echoed back to her through the bond, his voice in her mind, clear and immediate. Isabel's eyes went wide.

"Did you just hear me?" she whispered, low enough that the others wouldn't catch it over the music.

Yes.

She stared at him. He stared back, his grey eyes bright with the same astonishment she felt.

"How?" she breathed.

"I do not know." His lips barely moved, the words meant only for her. "Try again."

She thought of a colour. Blue. Concentrated on it, held it in her mind and pushed it toward him through the bond.

Nothing. His expression didn't change. He shook his head slightly.

Disappointment tugged at her. She frowned and tried again. A number. The image of a candle. Her own name. Nothing reached him.

"Try something genuine," he whispered, his mouth close to her ear, his breath warm against her skin. "Not a word. A feeling. Something you feel right now, in this moment. I have a theory."

Isabel's pulse quickened. She searched for something true, something she could send without revealing the full depth of what was churning beneath her composure. Though she suspected he already knew. She suspected he'd known for some time.

She thought of gratitude.

Not the word, but the feeling itself. She let it rise from the place where she kept it, the bone-deep thankfulness for everything he had done. For bidding on her at the auction when he could have looked the other way. For pulling her from the grip of a kidnapper on the docks. For opening his home and treating her as a guest when others only saw her as property.

She let the feeling fill her and directed it toward him.

Alexander's face changed. The guarded expression fell away, and a smile broke across his features, wide and warm.

"You are most welcome," he said aloud.

Isabel looked at him in wonder. "You heard that?"

"I felt it." His eyes held hers. "Your feelings seem to carry your thoughts when they are aligned. Emotion amplifies the message. That is why the other words did not come through, but the gratitude did."

"We should explore this further," she whispered. "If I can learn to send feelings along with words, perhaps I can reach you the way you reach me."

Agreed.

His thought rang through the bond, and at the same moment the music swelled and he turned her beneath his arm, spinning her out and drawing her back. She came to rest against his chest, closer than before, and his arm curved around her waist as he dipped her backward in the final bow of the dance.

She looked up at him. He looked down at her. Their faces were close, his grey eyes silver in the candlelight, and she could feel his heartbeat through his waistcoat, steady and strong and just slightly faster than it should have been.

The music faded. They held the position, suspended, his arm supporting her weight, her hand gripping his shoulder, and the silence between them was full of everything they had not yet said.

"Well." Damien's voice broke through from somewhere behind them. "I believe my feet have suffered quite enough for one evening. Vera, you are a menace to footwear, and I must regretfully excuse myself before I am permanently lamed."

Isabel straightened. Alexander released her, his hand lingering at her waist for just an instant before falling to his side. She stepped back, her cheeks burning, and busied herself with smoothing a crease in her skirt that didn't exist.

Vera appeared at Damien's elbow, pink-cheeked and bright-eyed. "You are a dreadful complainer, Damien. But I suppose you have earned your reprieve." She turned to Isabel. "I knew you had it in you. You were wonderful."

"She was," Alexander said quietly.

Isabel glanced up. He was looking at her, and the expression on his face was one she would carry with her long after the candles burned out.

Chapter Eight

Alexander checked his pocket watch for the third time.

"They have been up there for two hours," he said, snapping the case shut. "How long does it take to put on a dress?"

"You have clearly never observed the process." Damien stood at the sideboard, pouring himself a second measure of brandy with deliberate ease. A lifetime of waiting for women to come downstairs had evidently granted him complete immunity to impatience. "There are layers involved, Alexander. Corsets. Petticoats. Pins. The hair alone can take an hour. I once waited three hours for a lady, and she emerged looking exactly as she had when she went up."

"That is not reassuring."

"It wasn't meant to be." Damien raised his glass. "Patience, my friend. The results will be worth the wait."

Alexander moved to the fireplace and leaned against the mantelpiece, adjusting the cuff of his coat. He had dressed with more care than usual tonight, though he would not have admitted it. His dress coat was black, cut close to the shoulders, his waistcoat a deep charcoal silk, his cravat tied in a precise knot. He looked, he supposed, like a man attending a ball. Which was precisely the point.

He heard a door open and close on the second floor, followed by the soft rustle of skirts. Damien set down his glass and moved toward the drawing room door. Alexander followed him out into the entrance hall.

Vera descended first, her hand trailing the banister, her confidence suggesting she had been rehearsing the entrance all afternoon. Her gown was a rich emerald green, cut low across the shoulders, with a fitted bodice that flared into a full skirt. Her dark hair was swept up and pinned with small jewelled combs, and she wore their mother's pearl earrings, the ones she saved for occasions she deemed worthy of them.

Alexander glanced at Damien to make some remark about his sister's theatrical arrival and stopped.

Damien had gone still. His blue eyes followed Vera down the staircase, and for the first time in the many years Alexander had known the man, the viscount appeared to have lost the capacity for speech.

It lasted only a moment. Then Damien blinked and arranged his features into their usual pleasant lines.

Vera reached the bottom of the stairs and gave a small curtsy, her eyes bright. "Well? Will I do?"

"You look..." Damien paused, cleared his throat, and tried again. "You look very well, Lady Vera."

"Very well?" Vera's brow arched. "That is the best you can manage? I spent two hours getting ready and all I receive is 'very well'?"

"Radiant. Magnificent. A vision that would make the angels weep with envy." Damien recovered himself with admirable speed. "Is that more to your satisfaction?"

"It will suffice." But she was smiling.

Alexander opened his mouth to comment, but the words died on his lips.

Isabel had appeared at the top of the stairs.

She wore a gown of midnight blue silk, shimmering in the candlelight with each step as she descended. The bodice was fitted close, the neckline modest but elegant, edged with delicate silver embroidery that traced the line of her collarbone. Her dark hair had been swept up in an arrangement of soft curls, a few loose strands framing her face. The deep blue of the silk made her eyes burn violet, luminous and striking, and the colour in her cheeks owed nothing to rouge.

She looked like a lady. She was no longer the hollow-eyed woman who had been led onto an auction stage just two weeks ago, but the woman she had been born to be. The daughter of a noble house, dressed in silk and finery, descending a grand staircase as if she had been doing it her whole life.

Alexander forgot to breathe.

She reached the bottom step and stopped, her gaze finding his. "My lord?" A small, uncertain smile. "How do I look?"

He realised he was staring. "You look..." His voice came out too rough, and he had to clear his throat. "You look beautiful."

The word did not do her justice, but it was the best he could manage in his current mental state. Isabel's cheeks flushed, and she dropped her gaze to the gloves she was pulling on. Alexander reached for his own gloves and occupied himself with them, aware that Damien was watching the exchange with obvious delight.

"Before we leave," Alexander said, reaching into his coat pocket. He withdrew a small velvet case and held it out to her. "I had these made for you. For this evening."

Isabel opened the case. Inside, resting on a bed of dark silk, lay a sapphire pendant on a fine silver chain, with matching earrings. The stones were a deep, velvet blue. The exact colour of her eyes.

"Alexander, I..." She looked up at him. "I cannot accept these."

"Please, I insist," he said, his voice quiet but firm.

She held his gaze, then lifted the pendant from the case, and Vera stepped forward to fasten the clasp at the nape of her neck. Isabel fitted the earrings, and when she turned back to him the sapphires sparkled in the candlelight and gleamed as bright as her eyes.

"Thank you," she said, and the smile she gave him sent a sudden pulse of heat through his veins.

"Shall we?" Alexander offered her his arm. Damien did the same for Vera, and the four of them swept out into the cold November night, where the carriage waited in the drive.

The ride to Lady Deacon's estate took the better part of an hour. Vera filled most of it with last-minute instructions, reminding them which guests to seek out. Damien contributed sardonic observations. Isabel sat beside Alexander, her gloved hands folded in her lap, her expression composed, though he noticed the way her fingers tightened against each other when Vera mentioned Delacroix.

He leaned close, his voice low enough for only her to hear. "I will be right beside you. The entire evening."

She glanced at him, and the tension in her hands eased.

Lady Deacon's country estate blazed against the dark as they arrived. Every window was lit, and carriages lined the drive, depositing guests in furs and jewels at the foot of a grand stone staircase. Music spilled from open doors, and the air carried the scent of perfume and the sharp resinous tang of the yew hedges that lined the approach.

Whispers rippled through the crowd as the steward announced their names at the door. Alexander was accustomed to being watched, but tonight the attention was different. It was Isabel they were looking at. The telepath. The magic user on the Earl of Whitmore's arm. He could see the curiosity and the judgement and the poorly concealed fascination of the other guests as they entered the ballroom, and he felt his jaw tighten.

Isabel walked beside him with her chin raised and her spine straight, giving no sign that she heard every thought in the room. He admired her for that more than he could say.

The ballroom was magnificent. Lady Deacon had outdone herself. Crystal chandeliers threw cascading light across a marble floor, banks of white roses lined the walls, and a full orchestra played from a raised dais at the far end.

They made their first circuit of the room together, greeting acquaintances, exchanging pleasantries with Lady Deacon herself, who looked Isabel up and down and declared her "absolutely charming," before separating and moving on to other guests. Vera and Damien approached the refreshment tables, where several of the people on their list had gathered. Alexander guided Isabel toward the dance floor.

"We should dance," he said. "It will look less conspicuous than standing in a corner scanning the room."

Though deep down he knew that was not the only reason for his suggestion.

He took her hand and led her into the waltz. The orchestra was excellent, the melody sweeping and full, and after their practice session last night Isabel moved with confidence, her steps sure, her body following his lead with ease. Her hand rested on his shoulder, his palm pressed against the small of her back. Isabel had decided to keep her gloves on throughout the evening so that she could read the guests' minds without Alexander's shield interfering. If they needed to communicate through the bond, she would simply slip them off and take his bare hand. A discreet manoeuvre that would draw no attention.

He found himself almost hoping for an excuse to use it. The evenings of practice in the drawing room had made him crave her touch with an intensity that unsettled him.

He was in trouble. The way her lips curved whenever he turned her beneath his arm sent a jolt of warmth through his chest, and he knew that he was losing the battle he had been fighting ever since the night he had pulled her from the smuggler's tunnel and pressed her against a wall in the Warrens.

The music carried them across the floor, and for a while Alexander forgot about Delacroix and all the reasons that had brought them to this ballroom. There was only Isabel in midnight blue, her violet eyes holding his, her body warm beneath his palm where his hand rested at her waist, and the ache in his chest that was becoming impossible to ignore.

A hand clapped his shoulder as they passed the edge of the dance floor.

"A word, if you please." Damien appeared beside them, his smile fixed, his eyes sharp. He drew Alexander aside while Isabel stepped toward Vera, who had joined them with two glasses of champagne.

"You are meant to be investigating, not courting," Damien said, his voice pitched low. "And I say this as a man who is thoroughly delighted to see you behave like a creature of flesh and blood for the first time in eight years. But this is not the night for it, my friend. We have work to do."

Alexander straightened his coat. "You are right."

"Now then." Damien nodded toward a cluster of men near the card room entrance. "The Harlow brothers are here. Both of them. They have been at the wine steadily for the past half hour and seem in excellent spirits. I suggest we make our approach before they lose the capacity for coherent thought."

Alexander took a breath and locked his feelings away where they could not interfere.

The Harlow brothers were twins, though one would not have guessed it from looking at them. Edgar was tall and gaunt, restless as a greyhound, while Hector was stocky and florid, his cheeks flushed from wine. They stood near the card room entrance, deep in conversation with a merchant Alexander recognised from the shipping registries.

He approached with Isabel at his side, Damien following a step behind.

"Mr. Harlow. Mr. Harlow." Alexander inclined his head. "I believe we have not been formally introduced. Alexander Kensington, Earl of Whitmore."

Edgar Harlow straightened, his eyes darting between Alexander and Isabel before settling on the former. "Lord Whitmore. An honour. We have heard a great deal about you."

"All good things, I trust."

"Naturally." Edgar's smile was thin and unconvincing. Hector, the stouter twin, simply drank.

Alexander engaged them in conversation about their shipping concerns, steering the discussion toward trade routes and harbour schedules. Damien flanked them, contributing observations about the state of the merchant marine that kept the brothers nodding and talking while Alexander guided the current.

Beside him, Isabel stood quietly, her gloved hand resting on his arm, her expression pleasant and blank. To anyone watching, she was merely the earl's companion, decorative and disengaged. Alexander knew better. Behind those violet eyes, she was working.

After fifteen minutes of polite manoeuvring, during which Hector Harlow consumed two additional glasses of wine and Edgar grew visibly more relaxed, Isabel's fingers pressed against Alexander's arm. She had found what they needed.

Alexander brought the conversation to a graceful close, made his excuses, and guided Isabel away toward the far side of the ballroom, Damien veering off toward the refreshment table.

"Well?" Alexander asked, keeping his voice low as they walked.

"The shipment arrives next Thursday. After midnight. The southern docks, warehouse fourteen." Isabel kept her gaze forward, her lips barely moving. "Edgar was thinking about it the entire time you were talking. He is terrified that Delacroix will discover how much they have been embezzling from the operation. Hector is too drunk to guard his thoughts and was running through the logistics in his head. Six crates, arriving by a vessel named *Nightshade*."

"Six crates of what?"

"He did not think specifically about the contents. But his anxiety was considerable." She paused. "I suspect that is what has him drinking so heavily. Whatever is in those crates, it frightens him."

Alexander filed the information away. Thursday. Midnight. Warehouse fourteen. This was what they had come for.

He was about to respond when Isabel's hand tightened on his arm, her fingers digging into his sleeve. Her face had gone pale.

"He is here," she said.

Alexander followed her gaze across the ballroom. The crowd parted as naturally as water around a stone, and through the gap walked a man dressed almost entirely in black.

The Marquis of Darkwater cut a striking figure. His coat was impeccably tailored, dark as a moonless night, relieved only by the silver-grey silk of his waistcoat and the white of his cravat. His pale blue eyes, cold as a winter sea, swept the room as he made his way through the crowd, cane in hand.

Alexander watched Isabel. She had gone rigid beside him, her jaw clenched, her breathing shallow.

"His mind," she whispered. "I cannot read him. I can feel the edges of his thoughts, but nothing clear."

Delacroix navigated the room seemingly unhurried, exchanging greetings, accepting a glass of champagne from a passing footman. But his progress across the ballroom was deliberate, and Alexander could see that it was carrying him directly toward them.

"Lord Whitmore." The marquis arrived before them, his voice smooth and cultured. "What a pleasure. I had hoped you would attend."

"Lord Darkwater." Alexander kept his voice even. "I did not realise you had confirmed your attendance."

"A last-minute decision. I find myself drawn to occasions where interesting company is expected." His pale gaze moved to Isabel, lingered, then returned to Alexander. "I must confess, Lord Whitmore, I am surprised. When last I saw Miss de Clare, she was in Lord Daventry's possession. Or was that arrangement always rather more... flexible than it appeared?"

Alexander held the marquis's gaze. "Miss de Clare is under my protection. She always has been."

"How fascinating." Delacroix's smile widened a fraction. "I do admire a man who knows what he wants and takes the trouble to conceal it. We are not so different in that regard, you and I."

Delacroix turned his attention back to Isabel, a smile curling at the edges of his mouth. "Miss de Clare. How lovely to see you again. That gown is exquisite. Blue suits you."

"You are too kind, my lord," Isabel said. Her voice was steady, but Alexander could feel the tremor in her hand on his arm.

"I wonder," Delacroix continued, his eyes never leaving Isabel's, "whether I might have the honour of a dance. It has been some time since I have had the pleasure of such distinguished company on the floor."

Alexander stepped forward before Isabel could respond. "I am afraid Miss de Clare's dances are spoken for this evening."

Delacroix's smile did not waver. "What a pity." He inclined his head to Isabel. "Another time, perhaps."

As he turned to leave, he gave her one last look, and from the corner of his eye Alexander could have sworn he saw the cane's dark crystal head in the marquis's hand pulse with a faint light.

Isabel flinched, her grip tightening on his arm, and for an instant her violet eyes blazed bright before she controlled herself.

Delacroix walked away, melting back into the crowd as smoothly as he had emerged from it.

"Isabel." Alexander turned to her, lowering his head close to hers. "What is it? What happened?"

"He spoke to me." Her voice was barely audible. "Through whatever is shielding his thoughts."

"What did he say?"

Isabel met his eyes, and in them he saw her fear. "He said not to think myself safe because his men failed once. That next time, he would see to it personally."

Cold fury flooded Alexander's chest. His hand covered hers on his arm, and he felt his jaw lock so tightly his teeth ached.

"We are leaving," he said.

"Alexander—"

"We have the time and the place for the shipment. That is all we need." He guided her toward the edge of the ballroom, his arm firm around hers. "I will not stay another minute in the same room as that man. Not after he stood three feet from you and threatened to take you from me."

He did not notice Isabel's sharp intake of breath, or the way her eyes widened at what he had just said. His focus was on the door, on getting her out, on the cold calculation already forming in his mind about what he would do to the Marquis of Darkwater when the time came.

They found Damien and Vera near the entrance to the card room. Vera's face fell when Alexander told her they were leaving.

"Already? But we've barely been here two hours. I haven't danced nearly enough, and Lady Deacon has promised to introduce me to—"

"Vera." Alexander's tone stopped her mid-sentence.

Damien read his expression and straightened. "What happened?"

"Delacroix made a direct threat against Isabel. I want her away from here."

Vera's protest died on her lips. She looked at Isabel, saw the pallor in her face, and her expression hardened into the same fierce protectiveness Alexander had seen the day they returned from the harbour.

"Go," Vera said. "Take her home. Damien and I will stay. We still have people to speak with." She squeezed Isabel's hand. "Rest. We will finish what we started and be right behind you."

Damien met Alexander's eyes. "I will not let her out of my sight. You have my word."

Alexander hesitated a moment, then nodded. "I will send the carriage back for you. Lewis will remain at the door in case you need him." He glanced at the footman who had accompanied them from Whitmore Hall, a broad-shouldered young man in dark livery standing near the entrance. Lewis inclined his head.

Alexander took Isabel's arm and led her through the foyer. He collected their coats from the attendant, helped Isabel into hers himself, and guided her past the late arrivals still streaming through the entrance. The night air hit them on the steps, and Isabel drew a sharp breath.

The carriage was waiting. Alexander handed her up, climbed in after her, and pulled the door shut.

"Home," he told the driver.

The carriage lurched forward, and the lights of Lady Deacon's estate began to shrink behind them. Isabel sat across from him, her hands folded in her lap. She was not shaking. But she was very quiet, and her eyes, when they met his in the dim interior, were wide with fear.

Alexander leaned forward, his elbows on his knees.

"He will never touch you," he said. "I swear it."

The house was quiet when they returned.

Hartley met them at the door with his usual composure, took their coats, and enquired whether they required anything. Alexander asked for a fire to be lit in the drawing room. Hartley inclined his head and withdrew, and within minutes the hearth was blazing and they were alone.

Isabel stood near the window, her arms crossed, watching the dark garden beyond the glass. The marquis's words still echoed in her mind. That sharp, pointed message, forced though whatever force field kept his mind shielded. *Next time, I will see to it personally.* She had faced threatening men before. Had heard worse from masters who wished her harm. But the marquis was different. His threats were not born of temper or rage. They were calculated. The promises of a man who had all the time in the world and no intention of failing twice.

"Brandy?"

Alexander's voice pulled her back. He stood at the sideboard, a decanter in his hand, already pouring two glasses. His waistcoat was unbuttoned at the top, his cravat loosened, and his hair slightly dishevelled. He looked tired, she thought. Tired and angry and trying very hard to keep his emotions contained.

"Yes, please."

He brought her the glass. Their fingers brushed as she took it. The contact was too brief for the connection to fully open, but she felt the edge of it, a flutter of warmth at the threshold of the silence before it faded.

She took a sip. The brandy burned, welcome and steadying.

"Are you alright?" he asked.

"I will be."

"Isabel—"

"I don't want to talk about the marquis." She met his eyes. "Not tonight. Right now I would very much like to drink this brandy and not think about him for five minutes."

Alexander held her gaze. Then he nodded and raised his glass. "Five minutes."

They drank in silence. The fire crackled. The clock on the mantel ticked. Isabel felt the tension in her shoulders begin, slowly, to ease. The brandy was good and rich, and the room was warming from the fire in the hearth.

Alexander had finished his glass and set it on the mantelpiece, and now he was standing close enough that she could feel the faint pull of his silence at the edges of her awareness.

She drained the last of her own brandy and reached past him to set her glass beside his on the mantelpiece. As she withdrew her hand, she caught the edge of the small silver clock that sat there. It tipped, and she reached for it instinctively, the same moment Alexander did.

Their hands collided over the clock. His bare fingers closed around hers, and the connection opened like a door thrown wide.

The silence flooded in. Every foreign thought vanished in an instant, and she was standing in the vast quiet of his shield with his presence blazing beside her own, warm and vivid.

But tonight, through the connection, she felt more than his presence.

She felt his longing.

It poured through the bond, raw and unguarded, and the force of it stole the breath from her lungs. He wanted her. The wanting was enormous, far deeper and fiercer than she had dared to imagine. It saturated the connection, a hunger that had been building with every touch, held down by sheer force of will and the rigid architecture of his self-control.

And beneath the wanting, she felt his restraint. The iron discipline that kept him from acting.

Isabel looked up.

The clock had toppled from the mantelpiece and lay forgotten on the carpet beneath them. Their clasped hands had lowered between them, but neither let go. His grey eyes were fixed on hers, and in them she could see everything the connection was showing her. The want, the restraint, the ache of holding both at once.

His gaze dropped to her mouth.

She felt the impulse flare through the bond, hot and immediate, followed instantly by the clamp of control as he crushed it down. He was going to step back. She could feel it building in him, the withdrawal, the retreat to safety. In another heartbeat he would release her hand and clear his throat and say something appropriate, and the moment would pass, and they would climb the stairs to their separate chambers, and nothing would change.

Isabel decided it was time something did.

She closed the distance between them and pressed her lips to his.

The world came undone.

The connection, already open, blazed into a brilliance she had no name for. Every sensation doubled, trebled, until she could not tell where her feelings ended and his began. She felt his shock, a bright flare of disbelief at what she had just done. And she felt the last of his restraint shudder, crack, and fall away.

And then he was kissing her back.

A sigh escaped her as his free hand came up to cradle the side of her face, his fingers sliding into the curls at her temple. His mouth moved against hers, tentative at first, then desperate. He kissed her as though he had been drowning and she was the surface of the water. She felt his hunger and his overwhelming tenderness, all of it pouring through the bond in a torrent she could not have dammed if she tried.

She kissed him back with everything she had. Twelve years of loneliness and walls built so high she'd forgotten there was anything on the other side. She kissed him and let him feel what she felt, let her own wanting flood the connection, and she felt the moment it reached him because he made a sound against her mouth, low and broken, and his hand tightened in her hair.

His other arm came around her waist, pulling her against him, and she went willingly, her fingers curling into the silk of his waistcoat, feeling his heartbeat hammering beneath her palm. The kiss deepened, his lips parting hers, and she tasted brandy and warmth.

Through the bond, she could feel his shield wavering. A deep layer, the very foundation of it, shaking loose under the force of what was passing between them. For one staggering instant, she caught a glimpse of him, the whole of him, raw and unguarded.

It lasted only a breath. Then his shield snapped back into place, and she felt the shift before his body followed.

The withdrawal began somewhere deep inside him, a cold current cutting through the warmth. She felt it through the connection: his guilt, his shame. The crushing weight of obligation reassembling itself around him.

He pulled back.

Not far. An inch. His eyes were closed, and the expression on his face was one of a man in physical pain.

"Isabel." His voice was wrecked. "I am so sorry. I should never have allowed myself to... this should not have happened."

She stared at him. The warmth of the bond was still there, and through it she could feel the war inside him with agonising clarity. The part of him that wanted to pull her back. The part of him that was already building the wall again, brick by brick, mortaring it with all the noble reasons he used to keep himself caged.

"Please accept my apology," he said, releasing her. His hand fell from her hair. He stepped back, and the connection severed, and the noise of the world crashed back in.

"Alexander—"

But he was already moving. He turned and crossed the room without looking back, his stride uneven, his hand gripping the doorframe as he passed through it.

The door closed behind him, and she heard his footsteps climb the stairs, then fade into silence.

Isabel stood alone in the drawing room, the only sounds the crackling of the fire and the quiet tick of the fallen clock on the carpet beside her feet.

She bent down, picked it up, and set it back on the mantelpiece. Her fingers lingered on the cool metal casing for a moment.

Then she pressed those same fingers to her lips, where she could still taste his mouth.

She had kissed him. And for one magnificent moment, he had kissed her back.

Isabel stood outside the breakfast room door for a full minute before she could bring herself to open it.

She had barely slept. The hours after the kiss had been spent in her chamber, curled up in her bed, replaying every second of it until sleep had finally claimed her sometime before dawn.

She smoothed her dress, lifted her chin, and pushed open the door.

The breakfast room was bright with morning light. Vera sat at the table with a cup of tea and a plate of toast, speaking animatedly to Lord Daventry, who occupied the chair beside her and appeared to be only half listening. And at the head of the table, holding his newspaper up before him like a barricade, sat Alexander.

He didn't look up when she entered.

"Good morning," Isabel said.

"Good morning, Isabel!" Vera stood and pulled out a chair for her. "Come sit."

Alexander lowered a corner of the newspaper. "Good morning, Miss de Clare." His voice was polite, yet utterly devoid of warmth. He raised the paper again.

Miss de Clare.

She settled into the chair and poured herself a cup of tea with unsteady hands. The distance Alexander had placed between them was as tangible as a wall. She could feel it in the rigid set of his shoulders, in the deliberate way he avoided eye contact. He was fortified. Every stone back in place, every gate barred shut.

"We were just telling Alexander what else we learned last night," Vera said, oblivious to the temperature in the room. "After you left, Damien and I continued to circulate. And I had the most interesting conversation with a friend of mine. Charlotte Campbell. Do you remember her, Alexander? Lord Campbell's youngest daughter?"

The earl turned a page of his newspaper. "Vaguely."

"Well, Charlotte told me about her maid. A healer named Sarah. Charlotte adored her. They were close, far closer than Charlotte's parents would have approved of, had they known. For Charlotte, Sarah was a friend. She treated her as family."

Isabel reached for a roll and broke it apart, grateful to have an occupation for her hands.

"A few weeks ago," Vera continued, "Sarah vanished. One morning she simply did not report for her duties. Charlotte's parents dismissed it as a wayward servant, hired a replacement, and refused to discuss it further. But Charlotte doesn't believe Sarah would have left willingly."

"Did she say why?" Isabel asked, forcing herself to engage.

"Sarah had been happier than ever in the weeks before she disappeared. She had met someone. A man. She was quite secretive about it, wouldn't give Charlotte a name, but she was clearly smitten." Vera set down her tea. "Charlotte warned her to be careful, but Sarah laughed it off. She said he was a gentleman and would never do her any harm. An older man, she said. Distinguished."

Isabel's attention sharpened. "Did Charlotte give any indication of who this man might have been?"

"Not directly. But Sarah had mentioned once that he had the most extraordinary blue eyes she had ever seen. And that he had a way of making her feel as though she were the only person in the room."

The table went quiet. Isabel met Vera's gaze and saw the same recognition she felt in her own chest.

"Delacroix," she said.

"That is what I suspect," Vera said. "Though we cannot prove it."

Alexander folded his newspaper and set it beside his plate. "Another magic user gone. Another trail leading to the same door." He rose from the table and pushed in his chair. "If you will excuse me. I have work to do in my study. I suggest we regroup in the library this afternoon. We need to discuss our approach to the warehouse delivery."

He left without another word, shutting the door behind him with finality.

Vera frowned after her brother. "He is in a peculiar mood this morning." She shook her head and stood, gathering her tea. "Well, I have correspondence to attend to." She paused at the door. "Isabel, are you alright? You look tired."

"It was a late night."

"It was indeed." Vera gave her a warm smile before she made her own departure.

Isabel stared at the roll she had barely touched. Next to her, Lord Daventry had not moved. He sat with his elbows on the table, his chin resting on his laced fingers, watching her with an unusually serious expression.

"A word?" he asked.

She nodded.

They moved to the drawing room. The viscount closed the door behind them and gestured toward the armchair nearest the fire. Isabel sat while he remained standing by the mantelpiece, studying her.

"He kissed you, didn't he?"

Isabel's head came up. "How did you—" She stopped and drew a breath. "No. Actually. I kissed him."

Lord Daventry's eyebrows rose. "You did? Why am I not the least bit surprised by that." He folded his arms. "But he kissed you back."

"Yes."

"And then he panicked and left you standing there."

Isabel said nothing, which was in itself answer enough.

The viscount sighed and moved to the chair beside hers, lowering himself into it. He leaned forward, his elbows on his knees, his expression serious.

"Miss de Clare. Isabel. There are things you need to understand about Alexander. Things he would never tell you himself, because telling you would require admitting that they are true." He paused. "When Marianne died, Alexander did not simply grieve. He dismantled himself. The man I had known since boyhood, the one who laughed easily and wore his heart where people could see it, ceased to exist. What remained was the guarded man you met at the auction, driven by a single purpose and unwilling to let anyone close enough to compromise it."

Isabel listened, her hands folded tightly in her lap.

"He has spent eight years convincing himself that caring for someone is a liability. That if he allows himself to feel anything beyond duty and vengeance, he will suffer, just like he did after losing his parents and Marianne."

Damien's gaze drifted to the fire.

"I know what grief does to a man, Isabel. When my own parents died, I was seventeen." He said it without flinching. "My uncle became my guardian and informed me that I was now responsible for the estate. I was a boy who had just buried his mother and father, and the world expected me to become a man overnight."

"Lord Daventry, I am so sorry. I had no idea—"

"Damien," he said, and gave her a brief smile. "I think we are well past formalities." The smile faded. "And do not feel sorry for me. I did not rise to the occasion. I buried my grief in card halls and brandy bottles, and my only solace was the company of whichever woman would have me for the night." The corner of his mouth lifted, but there was no warmth in it. "The drinking and the women were always part of my nature, I will not pretend otherwise. But after my parents died it stopped being an indulgence and became a ruin. I was drowning, and I was perfectly content to let the current take me."

"What changed?" Isabel asked.

He looked at her. "One particular bad night, Alexander dragged me out of a gambling house at three in the morning, threw me into a carriage, and brought me to Whitmore Hall. His parents took me in, sobered me up. They gave me a room beside Alexander's, and treated me as if I had always belonged there. Vera was only young back then. She stole biscuits for me from the kitchen and sat on the floor outside my door until I came out."

He paused, his gaze becoming distant. "Not long after that, Alexander suffered his own tragedy. I tried to do for him what he had done for me. Pull him back. But he did not drown the way I did. After the accident, he closed himself off and has kept everyone at arm's length ever since. Even me. Even Vera." He met her eyes. "Until you."

Not knowing what to say to this, Isabel looked down at her hands.

"He will try to shut you out, too," Damien continued. "He is doing it right now, as we speak, sitting in that study of his, building walls and telling himself it was a mistake." He leaned closer. "But you must not let that discourage you."

Isabel pressed her lips together. She could feel the old familiar burn behind her eyes. But she hadn't cried in twelve years, and she wasn't about to start now.

"You are kind to say so, Lord Dav—Damien." She met his gaze. "But perhaps Lord Whitmore is right."

The viscount frowned. "What do you mean?"

"What do I have to offer him? Even if I am freed, I will never be a suitable match for an earl. Society would never accept me, and the people would make his life a misery for choosing me." Her voice was steady, though each word cost her. "After everything he has done for me, after how many times he has put himself at risk on my behalf, the last thing I want is to cause him grief."

She drew a breath. "I thought about it all night. And the truth is, the kindest thing I can do for him is to help him finish what he started. Find the evidence he needs to bring down Delacroix and free the magic users the marquis has taken." She paused. "And then I will leave. As was always intended. And the Earl of Whitmore will be free to follow his duties without the burden of a woman who was never meant to be part of his world."

Damien leaned back and folded his arms across his chest.

"I think you are wrong," he said. "Both of you. But I will not presume to tell you what to do." He held her gaze. "I want you to know, Isabel, that whatever happens, you have a friend in me. If you ever need anything, for any reason, you have only to ask."

The burn behind her eyes intensified, and she had to blink hard. "Thank you, Damien. If I could ever call anyone a true friend, it would be you." She paused. "And Vera. I would not want her to feel left out."

The viscount's familiar smile resurfaced. "She would be furious."

Isabel smiled back, and it was genuine, even if it hurt. She rose from the chair.

"If you will excuse me. I would like to rest before this afternoon. It was a very late night."

Damien stood as she did, inclining his head. "Of course."

She walked to the door and pulled it open. As she turned to close it, the viscount was already crossing to the sideboard, reaching for the decanter.

The Kensingtons may have pulled him back from the edge, but grief, Isabel knew, never truly left a person. One simply learned to wear a better disguise.

Chapter Nine

Alexander had not slept.

He had lain in the dark for hours, staring at the ceiling of his chamber, his mind circling the same moment over and over. The warmth of her mouth against his. The sound she had made when he kissed her back, a soft, breathless sigh that had undone something fundamental inside him.

And then the cold flood of clarity settling in his mind. The words he had forced through his throat.

I am so sorry... This should not have happened.

He had walked away from her. Had climbed the stairs to his chamber and stood with his back against the closed door, breathing hard, his hands shaking, the taste of her still burning on his lips. And he had told himself, over and over, that he had done the right thing.

It did not feel like the right thing. It felt like tearing out a part of himself and leaving it on the drawing room floor.

But the alternative was worse. The alternative was taking advantage of a woman who depended on him. Whose life was legally his to control. Who had spent twelve years in the power of men who used their position to take what they wanted from her, and who deserved, at the very least, a protector who did not do the same.

He had kissed her back. That was the unforgivable part. She had kissed him, and he could have stopped it, could have gently set her aside and explained why it could never happen. Instead he had pulled her against him and kissed her as though the world was ending, and through the bond he had felt everything. Her longing, her courage, her fierce determination, and her deep affection for him. And he had let her feel his own, and now she knew. She knew what he felt for her, because the connection did not lie.

Which made his retreat all the more cruel.

He had spent the morning in his study, surrounded by shipping reports and naval registries he could not concentrate on, rehearsing what he would say when he saw her again later on this day. He would be courteous. Professional. He would re-establish the boundaries he should never have allowed to blur. And he would not, under any circumstances, look at her lips.

Now it was afternoon, and they were gathered in the library, and Alexander was discovering that his plan was considerably easier in theory than in practice.

Isabel sat in the armchair across from his desk, her posture straight, her hands folded in her lap. She wore a simple grey day dress, her hair pinned back, no jewellery. She looked as she had in the first days after the auction: composed and unreachable.

She had not called him Alexander once since entering the room. It was "my lord" and "Lord Whitmore" and the occasional clipped nod, and every syllable landed like a door closing.

He told himself this was what he wanted. What was necessary.

It did not explain why it felt as though someone had reached into his chest and removed a vital organ.

"The Harlow brothers confirmed the shipment," Isabel was saying, her voice steady and matter of fact. "Thursday after midnight. An expected delivery of six crates, contents unknown, though Hector Harlow's anxiety suggests they contain something significant."

"That aligns with what Fenwick told me at the Merchant Marine Club," Damien added from the settee where he sat with one ankle crossed over his knee. "The Harlows have been handling private consignments for months. Cargo that arrives at night and disappears before dawn."

Vera sat beside Damien, perched on the arm of the settee, a notebook open on her knee. "And then we have Charlotte Campbell's maid, Sarah. A healer, vanished without warning, lured by a man matching Delacroix's description. That makes forty-four confirmed disappearances."

"Forty-four that we know of," Alexander said. He looked down at the ledger before him, turning a page he had already read three times. "The true number is almost certainly higher."

Isabel shifted in her chair. "The question is, what do we do with it. We have the details for the shipment. But we still lack physical evidence."

"Which is why we need to be at that warehouse when the cargo arrives," Damien said.

Alexander nodded. "Damien and I will go, along with a few of my men. We observe the delivery, document what we find, and if possible, we seize evidence before it can be moved."

"I am coming with you," Isabel said.

Alexander looked up. Her violet eyes met his, firm and unyielding.

"That is out of the question."

"My abilities would be invaluable. I can detect approaching minds before you see or hear anyone. I can tell you whether the men inside are armed, how many there are, and what they intend. Without me, you are walking in blind."

"It is too dangerous."

"More dangerous than the auction? The prison? The harbour?" Her voice did not rise, but the edge in it was sharp enough to cut. "I have been at your side for every step of this investigation, Lord Whitmore. I do not intend to sit at home while you finish it."

Damien glanced between them but wisely said nothing.

Alexander held her gaze. The coldness in her expression was new, and it stung in ways he could not afford to examine. This was the Isabel he had met at the auction: guarded, defiant, trusting no one. She had retreated behind her walls, and he had no one to blame for that but himself.

"Very well," he said at last. "But you stay in the background. If we are discovered, you leave immediately. No arguments."

"I am perfectly capable of defending myself, my lord."

"That was not a request."

They stared at each other across the desk. Vera's gaze moved between them, her brow creased, and Alexander could see the moment comprehension dawned in his sister's eyes. She pressed her lips together and looked down at her notebook.

Damien cleared his throat. "Well then. Thursday. I suggest we finalize the details once I have had a chance to survey the warehouse district." He stood, offering Vera his hand. "Lady Vera, shall we? I believe Mrs. Hartley mentioned something about fresh scones."

Vera rose, casting one more troubled glance at Isabel before allowing Damien to escort her out. The door closed behind them.

Alexander and Isabel sat alone in the library, and the silence between them was brittle and cold.

"There is one more matter," Alexander said. He kept his voice level. "The operation would benefit from our ability to communicate through the bond. If we continued to practise over the next few days, we might—"

"That will not be necessary."

Isabel met his eyes. Her expression was composed, her voice steady, but beneath the composure he thought he caught a flicker of resolve that went beyond mere stubbornness.

"I have resources of my own, Lord Whitmore. If the situation at the warehouse requires intervention beyond what your men can provide, I will deal with it." She rose from the chair and smoothed her skirts. "You need not concern yourself with my safety. I have been looking after myself for a very long time."

Her message was clear: *I managed before you. I will manage after.*

"If that is all," she said, "I would like to excuse myself. I have reading to do before dinner."

Alexander looked at her. She stood before him in her plain grey dress, her chin raised, her violet eyes cool and distant, and he wanted to tell her that he was sorry. That walking away from her last night had been the hardest thing he had done since the day he pulled his hand from a burning carriage. That the taste of her was still on his lips and he could not stop thinking about it and he was terrified that he had destroyed the only good thing that had happened to him in eight years.

"Of course, Miss de Clare," he said instead.

She inclined her head and walked out without another word.

The days blurred together.

Isabel had settled into a routine that kept her occupied and, more importantly, kept her away from the earl. Mornings she spent in the library, working through the ledgers and accounts that had accumulated over eight years of investigation. Afternoons she walked in the gardens when the weather allowed, or read in her chamber when it did not. She attended meals with the others, contributed to debriefs when her input was needed, and retreated the moment propriety permitted.

She told herself it was for the best. The investigation was all that mattered now, and sentiment had no place in it.

She told herself this frequently. It did not become more convincing with repetition.

The only relief came from Vera.

Two days after the ball, on one of those rare November afternoons when the clouds parted and the sun lay golden across the frosted gardens, Vera had found her on the stone bench beneath the bare oak tree, her coat pulled tight against the cold, staring at nothing in particular.

"May I join you?"

Isabel had nodded, and Vera had settled beside her, tucking her skirts beneath her.

"Isabel." Vera's voice had been gentle but direct. "Has my brother done anything to offend you?"

Isabel had kept her gaze on the garden. "Lord Whitmore has always treated me with the utmost respect."

"That is not what I asked."

Isabel had turned to look at her then. Vera's grey eyes had held no judgement, only concern.

"Nothing happened," Isabel had said. "I simply want to focus on concluding the investigation. For your brother's sake, and for yours. And for mine."

"And after, when everything is over? What will you do then?"

Isabel had been quiet for a moment. "I thought I might ask Captain Raines for passage to the Free Isles. Start over somewhere new. Somewhere no one knows who I am."

"That sounds terribly lonely, Isabel. And I would miss you dreadfully."

Isabel had managed a smile. She could not manage an answer.

Vera had not pressed further. But from that afternoon onward, she had made it her quiet mission to keep Isabel company. She appeared in the library with tea and biscuits. She sat beside her during meals and steered the conversation to safe ground when the tension between Isabel and the earl grew too pointed. And she talked, openly and warmly, about things Isabel had never asked about but found herself grateful to hear.

She learned about their parents. How they had been passionate advocates for magic user rights, pushing for reforms that went far beyond the Protection of the Realm Act. They had petitioned the crown for full equality, had argued that the current laws were a half-measure that preserved the appearance of progress while changing nothing of substance.

"They even conducted research," Vera had told her one afternoon. "Into magical abilities, bloodlines, the history of magic in Elthera. They believed that understanding magic was the first step toward acceptance." Her expression had clouded. "Most of their work was lost. After they died, someone broke into Whitmore Manor and ravaged Father's study. Alexander believes it was Delacroix, though he has never been able to prove it."

"What did the marquis want with their research?"

"I don't know. But apparently he showed an unusual interest in it. Which was curious, given that he is known as a staunch conservative, very much opposed to the reforms. Why would a man who despises magic users care so deeply about understanding their abilities?" Vera had shaken her head.

Isabel had turned this over alongside everything else she had learned. The pieces of the puzzle were accumulating, but the picture they formed remained incomplete. Delacroix's interest in magical research. Admiral Fallon's complicity. Forty-four people gone without a trace. How did it all connect?

Vera had also spoken of the Crown. The Kensingtons had maintained strong ties to the royal family for generations, she explained, both politically and in private. Vera herself had met Crown Prince Finian on several occasions. "A handsome man," she had said, her eyes going briefly dreamy. "Very charming. Very attentive. Alexander speaks with him from time to time about political matters. The prince has always been sympathetic to our cause."

Isabel had nodded and filed the information away.

On the day of the cargo shipment, they were gathered in the library for a final briefing. Lord Whitmore stood behind the desk, a map of the southern docks spread before him. Damien occupied the armchair to his left, dressed in dark, sombre clothing that stood in jarring contrast to his usual bright attire. Vera sat on the nearby settee, her notebook open, though she would not be joining them tonight. Isabel had taken the chair furthest from the desk, her hands folded in her lap.

The earl went through the plan. They would depart after nightfall, taking two carriages to avoid attention. His men would position themselves around warehouse fourteen before midnight. The earl, Damien, and Isabel would approach from the quayside. Once the *Nightshade* arrived and the cargo was unloaded, they would observe and gather what evidence they could before withdrawing.

Isabel listened, her eyes on the map, tracing the layout of the docks, the positions Lord Whitmore had marked for his men, and the escape routes he had planned.

She couldn't help watching his hands as he pointed to positions on the map. Those hands that had cradled her face. That had tangled in her hair as he kissed her.

She looked away.

Even now, seated across the room, she could feel the pull of his silence. That magnetic stillness that had drawn her in from the very first night. She had tried to build her walls against it, the way she built walls against every other mind. It did not work. His silence was not noise to be blocked out. It was an absence, a void, and her gift leaned toward it the way a compass needle leaned toward north.

She hated it. She also craved it with a ferocity that frightened her.

"Miss de Clare."

She blinked. He was looking at her. The others were looking at her. She had missed a question.

"Forgive me. Would you repeat that?"

"I asked whether you will be able to detect approaching minds from the position I have indicated." His tone was formal, his gaze steady on hers, but she caught the faintest crease between his brows.

"Yes," she said. "I will be able to cover the full perimeter from there."

He nodded and returned to the map.

"We leave in two hours," he said. "Everyone should eat, rest if they can, and dress warmly. It will be a long night."

The others rose. Vera crossed to Isabel and squeezed her hand without a word. Damien caught the earl's eye and gave a short nod. They filed out, and Isabel stood to follow.

"Miss de Clare."

She stopped at the door.

"A moment, if you please."

She turned. He stood behind the desk, and for the first time in days his expression was not guarded. Suddenly, who stood before her, was the man who had held her after the harbour. Who had danced with her in the ballroom. Who had whispered *safe* into her mind.

"You do not have to come tonight," he said. "I mean that sincerely. We have enough men, and Damien and I are capable of handling the operation without—"

"I am coming."

"Isabel." Her name slipped from him the way it used to, natural and unthinking, and she saw him register it the moment it left his lips. He did not correct himself. "This could be dangerous. If Delacroix is there, if anything goes wrong—"

"Then you will need me all the more." She held his gaze, and for one treacherous moment she felt her resolve waver. The warmth in his voice, the concern in his eyes — this was the Alexander she had come to know. The one she had come to trust. The one she had kissed in the firelight and who had kissed her back.

God help her. She could not shut off what she felt for him. She had tried for days, had buried herself in evidence and routine and the cold logic of self-preservation, and still the wanting was there, stubborn and relentless, rising every time she heard his voice or caught his scent across a room.

But it did not change anything. The circumstances remained the same. She would help him. He would free her. And then she would leave.

She composed herself. "The sooner we bring this to a close, the better. For all of us."

The warmth in his expression dimmed. He heard what she meant, the finality beneath the words, and she watched him absorb it.

"Very well," he said. "Two hours."

She inclined her head and left the library.

In the corridor, out of sight, she stopped. She pressed her back against the wall and closed her eyes, and the ache in her chest was so sharp she had to press her fist against it.

It didn't matter what she felt. It didn't matter that his silence still called to her, that the memory of his mouth on hers would haunt her for the rest of her life.

Some things were not meant to be. And wanting them did not make them possible.

She drew a breath, straightened her shoulders, and climbed the stairs to change.

The southern docks were black and silent under a moonless sky.

Alexander crouched behind a stack of shipping crates, his breath forming pale clouds in the freezing air. Beside him, Damien pressed his back against the wood, pistol in hand. Around the warehouse, six of Alexander's men waited in the shadows, armed and alert.

Isabel knelt at his other side, her dark coat pulled tight around her shoulders, her face pale in the faint light that reached them from a distant harbour lamps. She had been shivering for the past hour, though she had said nothing about it. He had noticed, of course. Had noticed the way she tucked her hands into her sleeves, the way her jaw clenched to keep her teeth from chattering.

He shrugged off his overcoat and held it out to her without a word.

She looked at the coat, then at him. For a moment he thought she would refuse. Then she took it and pulled it around her shoulders.

"Thank you," she murmured.

He nodded and turned his attention back to the harbour.

They had been in position since ten o'clock. It was now past midnight, and the *Nightshade* had not yet appeared. Warehouse fourteen, a long, low-roofed structure of blackened brick, sat dark and apparently empty at the end of the quay. Two of Alexander's men had scouted the perimeter an hour ago and reported no signs of activity.

Alexander did not like it. The stillness felt wrong.

"Anything?" he asked Isabel, keeping his voice low.

She closed her eyes, her brow creasing with concentration. Then her face brightened.

"Minds inside the warehouse," she said. "Six. They are waiting. Anxious." She paused. "One of them is Edgar Harlow. He is thinking about the cargo. He hopes—" Her expression tightened. "He hopes they are not in as poor a condition as the last ones. He is remembering having to carry them because most of them were unconscious when they arrived."

Alexander's stomach turned. "Carry whom?"

Isabel opened her eyes. The glow in them was vivid, bright violet in the dark. "The crates don't contain goods. They contain people. Magic users."

Beside him, Damien swore under his breath.

"We cannot leave them in there," he said.

Alexander looked at Damien. His friend's face was grim.

"No." Alexander's mind was already working through the options. Six men inside, plus however many crew would come off the ship. His own force numbered eight, including himself and Damien. The odds were not favourable, but they were not impossible either, provided they had the element of surprise.

"There." Isabel pointed toward the harbour mouth. A dark shape was moving through the water, running without lights, its sails furled. The *Nightshade*, sliding into port silent as a ghost.

They watched as the ship manoeuvred alongside the quay. Lines were thrown, the hull bumped against the stone, and within minutes a gangplank was lowered. Men began emerging from below decks, carrying freight between them. Six wooden crates, each large enough to hold a person, hauled down the gangplank and into the warehouse through a loading door that had been opened from within.

The whole operation took less than ten minutes.

Alexander felt sick.

"Can you sense Delacroix?" he asked Isabel.

She closed her eyes in concentration. "No. He is not here. I cannot feel his mind anywhere in the vicinity."

"The men inside — are they armed?"

"Pistols and cudgels. But they are not expecting trouble. Their thoughts are focused on the cargo and the schedule. They want this done quickly."

Alexander made his decision. "We go in. Free the captives, subdue anyone who resists. Damien, you take the left flank with Lewis and Brayden. I will take the right with Landon and Morris. The rest hold the perimeter."

"Wait." Isabel gripped his arm. "Let me create a distraction first. If they scatter before you enter, you will face fewer men inside and reduce the risk of the captives being harmed in a fight."

"How?"

"Leave that to me." Her violet eyes held his, steady and certain. "I will stay outside the warehouse. I will be safe there. They cannot see me. Just give me a moment, and you will know when to move."

Alexander hesitated. Every instinct told him not to let her out of his sight, not after Delacroix's threat at the ball.

"Trust me," she said.

The phrase hit him in the chest as he remembered the dark alley where he had first said those exact same words.

"Very well." He held her gaze. "But if anything goes wrong—"

"It won't. Go."

He signalled to his men, and they began moving toward the front of the warehouse, keeping low, while Isabel made her way towards the side of the building, where wide, dirt-streaked panes afforded a glimpse inside. Damien split off to the left with his pair. Alexander took the right, angling toward the loading door.

He glanced back once. Isabel had found cover behind a stack of crates, her dark figure barely visible, the bright violet glow of her eyes being the only thing that gave her away.

When he turned back to the warehouse, the screaming started.

From inside the building came shouts of alarm, panicked and overlapping. "The Watch! The harbour patrol! We've been sold out!" Men burst through the loading door, stumbling over each other, weapons abandoned, their faces white with terror. They scattered across the quayside, running for the alleys, the side streets, anywhere that was away.

Alexander stood frozen for an instant, his hand on his pistol. There was no Watch. No harbour patrol. The quay was empty except for his own men, who looked at each other in bewilderment as the warehouse emptied itself in a frenzy of shouting and fleeing.

What had she done?

He did not have time to wonder. The loading door stood open, the interior now visible in the light of the lanterns the fleeing men had left behind.

"Move!" Alexander ordered, and his men surged forward.

They entered the warehouse at a run. The interior was cavernous, stacked with ordinary cargo. Barrels and sacks of grain were piled against the walls, alongside coils of rope and heaps of tarred netting. And in the centre, arranged in a row, stood six wooden crates.

Alexander crossed to the nearest one and wrenched the lid free.

Empty.

He moved to the next. Empty. The next. Empty. All six, opened one after another, their interiors bare.

"Alex." Damien's voice was sharp as he came running toward him from the far end of the warehouse. "Something is wrong."

A slow, measured clapping echoed through the space.

From the shadows beyond the cargo stacks, a figure emerged, pale blue eyes catching the lantern light, the cane tucked away under his arm.

The Marquis of Darkwater walked toward them, smiling.

And in front of him, a pistol pressed to the side of her head by one of his men, stood Isabel.

Alexander's blood turned to ice.

"Lord Whitmore." Delacroix's voice was conversational, as though they were at a dinner party. "How gratifying that you came. I must confess, I wasn't sure you would. But then, men of principle are so dreadfully predictable."

Isabel's face was chalk-white. Her eyes were open but unfocused, her body swaying slightly, and Alexander could see that she was barely standing. Whatever she had done to create that diversion had cost her dearly.

"Let her go, Delacroix." Alexander's voice came out flat and cold, though his heart was slamming against his ribs so hard he heard it pounding in his ears.

"I think not." The marquis drew his cane from beneath his arm and brought it down against the stone floor with a sharp crack, the dark crystal head glowing faintly in the sparse light as he squared his shoulders.

"Did you truly believe I was unaware of your little investigation?" Delacroix continued, still smiling. "The very reason I wanted this woman was her telepathic gift. It did not take a great leap of imagination to deduce that you would use her to read my associates. So I arranged matters accordingly. The Harlow brothers believed this shipment was genuine. Their thoughts were authentic. Everything your telepath read from them was the truth. They did not know that I staged this little performance."

Alexander said nothing. His mind was racing through options and finding none. His men stood behind him, weapons drawn, but Delacroix had a man hold a pistol against Isabel's head, and at this range he would not miss.

"And what a performance she gave in return," Delacroix murmured, his gaze turning to Isabel with an expression that made Alexander's skin crawl. "That projection. Magnificent. An entire warehouse full of armed men, fleeing from an illusion. I had suspected she possessed the ability, but I had not dared hope it would be so potent." He looked back at Alexander. "You have no idea what you have been harbouring, Lord Whitmore. She is extraordinary."

Projection. The word snagged in Alexander's mind. Isabel had projected an illusion into the minds of those men, had made them see and hear a harbour patrol that did not exist. That was what she had meant when she said she had resources of her own.

But it had exhausted her. She could barely stand. And he was the one who had driven her to such desperate lengths.

"If you will excuse me, gentlemen." Delacroix took Isabel's arm and pulled her against his side, his cane planted against the ground as he began to back toward the rear of the warehouse. The man who had held the pistol to Isabel's temple swung it toward Alexander and his men. "I will take my leave. My men will see to the rest. I have never had the stomach for violence. Such an ugly business."

From the shadows on both sides of the warehouse, armed men stepped into the light. A dozen at least. Pistols drawn, faces hard. Alexander's men shifted into defensive positions, weapons raised, but they were outnumbered badly.

"We are going to have to fight our way out," Damien said beside him, his voice low and urgent.

Alexander did not answer. His eyes were fixed on Delacroix and Isabel who was stumbling alongside him.

The marquis turned his back and walked toward the rear exit, dragging Isabel with him.

Alexander moved.

"Take them!" he shouted to his men, and then he was running, pistol in hand, straight for the back of the warehouse. Behind him, the crack of gunfire erupted as his men engaged the Marquis's fighters.

Damien was at his side for the first few strides, then Alexander heard a grunt and the sound of a body hitting the ground. He glanced back. Damien was on one knee, a hand pressed to his side, blood seeping between his fingers. A man with a knife stood over him.

Lewis was already moving, bringing the attacker down before he could strike again.

"Go!" Damien shouted, his face contorted with pain. "I'll be fine. Go after her!"

Alexander ran.

He burst through the rear door of the warehouse and into the night.

The loading yard behind the building was narrow and dark, hemmed in by the high brick walls of adjoining warehouses. A small lantern hung from a hook above the door, throwing a weak circle of light across the cobblestones. Beyond it everything was in shadow.

Alexander stopped, his breath ragged, pistol drawn, and listened.

Footsteps. Ahead and to the right, moving fast but uneven. One set heavy and measured, the other stumbling, dragging. He followed the sound, rounding the corner of the warehouse at a sprint.

There.

Delacroix was thirty paces ahead, hauling Isabel toward a black carriage that waited at the end of the alley, its horses stamping in the cold. Two men flanked the carriage, armed, watching the approach.

Isabel's feet caught on the cobblestones with every step, her head lolling, and the marquis's grip on her arm seemed to be the only thing that held her upright.

Terror seized Alexander as he watched the woman he loved being dragged away from him. It rose in his chest like a tide, tearing down every wall he had built between himself and the world.

He had been here before. Arriving too late. Watching through smoke and flame as the people he loved were taken from him. He had failed once, the scar on his right hand being proof of it.

He would not fail again.

Something shifted inside him.

It began in his chest, a pressure building behind his ribs, expanding outward. A gathering of energy he had never consciously summoned but had carried his entire life, coiled and dormant, waiting for the moment it was needed.

His shield.

He had always known it as a passive thing. A wall around his mind that kept others out. A barrier he had never learned to lower, never learned to shape, never understood beyond the simple fact of its existence.

But in this moment, with Isabel thirty paces away and slipping further with every second, the shield responded to his desperation the way a muscle responds to a scream.

It expanded.

Alexander felt it surge outward from his body in a wave. It rolled across the cobblestones, and when it hit Delacroix, the marquis staggered.

Isabel sank to the ground as his grip on her loosened.

Delacroix stumbled backward. "What — how—"

Alexander was already closing the distance. He covered the thirty paces in seconds, seized the marquis by the collar, and drove his fist into the man's jaw. Delacroix's head snapped sideways and he went down.

The two men by the carriage drew their weapons and advanced. Alexander stepped over Delacroix's crumpled form and planted himself between them and Isabel, his own pistol raised, his chest heaving.

"Come, then," he said.

They hesitated. Behind Alexander, Delacroix scrambled to his feet. Blood ran from the corner of his mouth, and his pale eyes were wild, the polished composure shattered.

"Take her!" he snarled at his men. "Take her now!"

Alexander met the first with a sharp blow to the wrist that sent his pistol clattering to the ground, then drove his elbow into his throat. The second came from the right, swinging a cudgel, and Alexander pivoted, caught the man's arm, and twisted. He kicked the man's knee and heard something crack as he went down.

The first attacker recovered and lunged again. Alexander sidestepped, caught his wrist, twisted, and drove a punch into the man's temple. He went sprawling.

When Alexander turned back, Delacroix was gone. The black carriage was already moving, wheels clattering over the cobblestones, the driver whipping the horses into a gallop. Alexander took two steps after it, then stopped.

Isabel.

She lay where Delacroix had released her, crumpled on the cold stones, her dark coat spread around her, Alexander's overcoat still draped over her shoulders. She was not moving.

He was beside her in an instant, dropping to his knees on the cobblestones, gathering her into his arms. She was limp, her head falling against his shoulder, her skin cold beneath his fingers. Blood traced a thin line from her nose to her upper lip, dark in the lamplight.

"Isabel." He pressed his fingers to her throat and found a pulse. Faint, but there. "Isabel, open your eyes. Look at me."

Her lashes fluttered. Her eyes opened, glassy and unfocused, the violet glow reduced to a faint flicker.

"Alexander...?" Her voice was a thread.

"I am here. I have you." He pulled her closer, one arm beneath her shoulders, the other cradling her head against his chest. "Stay with me. Do you hear me? Stay with me."

Running footsteps behind him. Lewis and Brayden rounded the corner, pistols drawn, their faces taut with urgency.

"My lord! Are you—"

"The carriage," Alexander ordered, his voice raw. "Bring it here. Now."

Brayden sprinted off. Lewis crouched beside them, his gaze moving over Isabel with concern. "Is she—"

"She is alive. Where is Damien?"

"Lord Daventry has been taken to the first carriage, my lord. Landon and Morris are with him. The wound is to his side. Serious, but Landon says he will live if we get him to a surgeon quickly."

"Send them ahead. Do not wait for us. Get Damien to Dr. Barrett immediately and tell him to send his nurse to Whitmore Hall at once."

"Yes, my lord."

Lewis disappeared. Alexander sat on the cold cobblestones, holding Isabel, listening to her shallow breathing, feeling her heartbeat against his chest. Delacroix had escaped, and they still had no evidence.

But Alexander had Isabel. She was alive. She was in his arms. And he was never going to let go again.

The carriage arrived. Lewis helped him lift Isabel inside, and Alexander climbed in after her, settling onto the bench and drawing her against him. Her head rested on his shoulder, her body curled into his, and he wrapped both arms around her and held her as the carriage set off.

The streets of Greyport slid past the windows, dark and empty at this hour. Alexander stared at nothing, his cheek against her hair, his hand pressed flat against her back where he could feel the faint rise and fall of her breathing.

He had almost lost her. Another few seconds, and Delacroix would have had her in that carriage and she would have been gone. Another person he loved, taken from him.

He had promised her she would be safe. Had said the words to her face, more than once. And tonight he had almost proved himself a liar.

He had been a fool.

He had pushed her away because of duty. Because of power imbalances and legal papers and the fear that wanting her made him no better than the men who had used her before. He had kissed her and apologised for it, as though the most honest moment of his life had been a mistake. He had retreated behind his walls and watched her retreat behind hers, and they had spent days circling each other in formal silence while the distance between them grew broader.

And for what? To protect her? She had nearly died tonight because he was too consumed with protecting her feelings to notice that she had been hiding a dangerous secret from him. To protect himself? He had spent eight years protecting himself, and it had earned him nothing but empty rooms and sleepless nights and a scar he touched when he had no one else to hold.

Damned be propriety. Damned be society and its rules. Damned be every voice in his head that told him he had no right to love this woman.

The lights of Whitmore Hall appeared through the carriage windows, glowing golden through the dark. Alexander held Isabel closer and watched them grow brighter with every turn of the wheels.

Home. He was bringing her home.

And he was never going to walk away from her again.

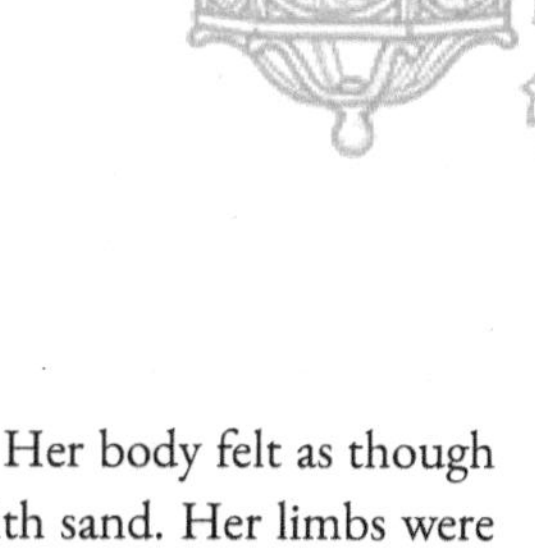

Chapter Ten

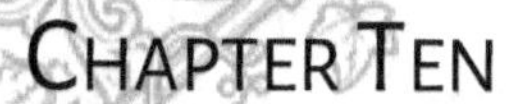

Isabel blinked, her vision slow to focus. Her body felt as though it had been emptied out and refilled with sand. Her limbs were heavy, her head throbbed with a dull, persistent ache, and when she tried to lift her hand, the effort made her arm tremble.

She turned her head on the pillow, struggling to make sense of her surroundings.

Pale afternoon light filtered through gaps in the curtains, a fire crackled steadily in the hearth, and she was buried beneath layers of blankets that someone had tucked carefully around her.

Her room. She was in her room at Whitmore Hall.

And on the chair right beside her bed sat Alexander.

His coat was gone, and he appeared to have changed into a fresh set of clothes since she'd last seen him. So had she, apparently, or someone had done it for her, she realised, heat flushing her cheeks as she felt down her sides and recognised the soft cotton of her nightgown beneath the blankets.

The earl had rolled up his shirtsleeves to the elbows. He was half-leaning on the edge of the mattress, one arm folded beneath his head, asleep. His dark hair fell across his brow, and the hard lines of his face had softened in rest, the tension that lived permanently in his jaw and his shoulders loosened for once.

He looked younger. He looked exhausted.

How long had he been sitting there?

Isabel shifted beneath the blankets, and the small movement was enough. Alexander's eyes flew open. He sat up, disoriented for an instant, then his gaze found hers and the relief that flooded his face was so unguarded that it stole the breath she had only just recovered.

"Isabel." He leaned forward, his hands gripping the edge of the chair. "Thank God. You are awake."

"How long have I been asleep?"

"Nearly a full day. It is Friday evening." He reached for a glass of water on the side table and held it to her lips. She drank, the cool liquid easing the rawness in her throat. "How do you feel?"

"As though someone filled my bones with lead." She managed a weak smile. "But alive. What happened? After I..."

She trailed off. The memories were fragmented. They'd been at the warehouse. She had projected, reaching into many minds at once. Too many. Then the exhaustion had hit her, sudden and total, her legs giving way. And suddenly Delacroix had been beside her, his man grabbing her arm and pressing a pistol against her temple.

"Delacroix took you," Alexander said. His voice was steady, but his hands were not. She could see his knuckles turn white where he gripped the chair. "The marquis had the entire operation staged. The Harlows believed it was real, which is why you read genuine thoughts from them. But the crates were empty. It was a trap, designed to draw us in and capture you."

"What happened, after he..."

"I came after you. The marquis was dragging you toward a carriage in the alley behind the warehouse. I could not reach you in time, not by running." He paused, and she saw him frown. "My shield... did something I did not know it could do. It expanded outward. I felt it surge from me, and when it reached Delacroix, he staggered. His grip on you loosened, and you fell free."

Isabel stared at him. "You projected your shield? In an attack?"

"It would seem so."

"Alexander, that is... I didn't know that was possible."

"Me neither." He rubbed the back of his neck. "I was not thinking about magic or shields or abilities. I was thinking about you. About losing you." His grey eyes met hers. "And then it just... happened."

She held his gaze.

"There is something I need to tell you as well," she said.

He waited.

"The diversion at the warehouse. The men who fled, screaming about the Watch." She drew a breath and tried to push herself upright against the pillows. Alexander rose at once, easing an arm behind her shoulders and adjusting the cushions until she was propped up comfortably. She murmured her thanks, and he settled back into his chair.

"That was me," she continued. "I projected an illusion into their minds. I made them see and hear a harbour patrol that was not there."

Alexander said nothing, but she noticed that he didn't look surprised.

He knew.

"It is called projection," she continued. "I can plant thoughts, images, even sensations into other people's minds. It is far more powerful than simply reading thoughts, and far more dangerous." She looked down at her hands, weak and pale against the dark wool of the blanket. "I have only used it a few times. Once, when I was..." She stopped. "It doesn't matter. The point is, it nearly killed me then. On one of these occasions I was unconscious for three days."

"Why did you never say anything?"

"Because it is my last defence. The one advantage no one knows about." Her voice was quiet. "I have survived twelve years by keeping it hidden. If the wrong person learned what I could do, I would never be safe again. Delacroix must have suspected. Now he knows for certain."

"You should have told me, Isabel."

"I know." She met his eyes. "I nearly did. But I was angry with you..." She paused. "I thought I could manage it on my own. I was wrong."

Alexander leaned forward. "You did manage it. Those men fled. Your projection worked. You gave us the opening we needed."

"And then I collapsed and was captured."

"Because it was a trap. It was not your fault. I just wished you had not put yourself in danger like that."

"I couldn't let you walk in there without an advantage. I couldn't risk you or Damien or any of the others getting hurt." Her throat tightened. "Not when I had the power to prevent it."

"Damien..." Alexander frowned.

Her heart lurched. "Is he—"

"He will be fine. He suffered a wound to his side. It was quite serious, but the surgeon has seen to it. Vera is with him now."

"Vera is nursing him?"

"She insisted. Refused to leave his bedside."

Isabel felt her lips curve despite the ache in her body. "She cares about him."

"Yes." Alexander's expression grew thoughtful. "And I think he cares about her, too. More than either of them has been willing to admit."

The words hung between them.

Alexander moved from the chair to the edge of the bed. He sat carefully, as though she were made of glass, and looked down at his hands for a long moment before speaking.

"Isabel. I owe you an apology."

"You have already apologised. After the kiss. Rather extensively."

"Not for that." He raised his eyes to hers. "For walking away. For spending these past days pretending I did not feel what I feel. For calling you Miss de Clare when your name was the only word I wanted to say."

Her breath caught.

"I was terrified," he continued. "When Delacroix had you, when I saw the pistol at your head, I understood with absolute clarity that every reason I had given myself for keeping my distance was a lie. I was not protecting you. I was protecting myself. From caring too much. From losing someone I—" He stopped and drew a breath. "From losing you."

He reached for her hand where it rested on the blanket. His fingers closed around hers, and the connection opened, immediate and full. The silence washed over her, and with it came the torrent of everything he had been holding back. His fear of losing her at the warehouse, his murderous fury at Delacroix, and the thing he could not say aloud but could no longer hide.

Tears burned behind her eyes. She blinked them back, as he lifted her hand to his mouth and pressed his lips against her knuckles.

"I am not going to walk away again," he said against her skin. "That I can promise you."

She reached up and touched his face. Her fingers were trembling, weak from the projection's aftermath, but she traced the line of his jaw and felt the muscles there ease under her hand.

He leaned into her touch, his eyes closing for a moment. When he opened them, they were dark and intent, and his gaze dropped to her mouth.

He didn't move until she let her thumb trace the corner of his mouth. Until she aimed one wordless feeling through the connection.

Yes.

He drew a slow breath. Then he lowered his head and kissed her.

Gently, at first, his lips soft against hers, his hand cradling her face as though she were precious beyond reckoning. She kissed him back, and through the connection she felt his relief. His hunger.

The kiss deepened. His hand slid into her hair, and she pulled him closer, and for a few breathless moments there was only the warmth of his mouth and the silence they shared.

Then he pulled back.

Isabel tensed.

"I should let you rest," he said.

She waited for the retreat. The apology. The step backward. But instead he leaned down once more and kissed her forehead.

"I am not leaving," he said. "But you need to eat. And then you need to sleep. Your body needs time to recover."

She wanted to argue. Her body, however, sided firmly with Alexander. The kiss had left her breathless for reasons that went well beyond exhaustion, but the exhaustion was there all the same, heavy in her bones, pulling her toward the pillows.

"Will you come back?" she asked.

His expression softened into a smile. "I will be here."

A knock sounded at the door, and Mrs. Hartley appeared with a tray bearing a bowl of steaming broth, fresh bread, and a pot of chamomile tea.

"There she is," the housekeeper said, her face creasing with relief. "Back with us at last. Now then, let us get some food into you."

Alexander had not intended to fall asleep.

He had withdrawn while Mrs. Hartley tended to Isabel, crossing the corridor to his own chamber to wash and change. He had spent most of the day at her bedside, leaving only twice — once in the early hours when Jenny and the nurse had arrived to tend to her, and once to change out of his soiled clothes. He had not eaten, had not rested, had done nothing but sit in that chair and watch her breathe and wait for her eyes to open.

Now, having finally forced himself to eat from the tray Hartley had brought to his room, he had washed, changed into a more comfortable clean shirt and trousers, and returned to her chamber as promised.

He had found her asleep, her face peaceful against the white pillow, the colour already returning to her cheeks. The broth bowl on the tray was empty, and the chamomile tea had been drunk. Mrs. Hartley had left a candle burning on the bedside table, and the fire had been built up against the cold.

He had sunk into the chair beside her bed and sat watching her. The rise and fall of her breathing. The steady, fragile beat of her pulse at the base of her throat.

He had promised himself he would not sleep. Would stay awake through the night, standing guard over her the way he should have stood guard over her at the warehouse. But even as he made the resolution, he could feel his body betraying him, the exhaustion of the past thirty-six hours weighing down on him.

His eyelids grew heavy. His head dipped forward. And at some point, without knowing when, he had leaned against the edge of the mattress and let the dark take him.

He woke with a start.

The room had changed. The fire had burned down to glowing coals, their faint light the only illumination save for the candle stub guttering on the bedside table. Beyond the curtains, the windows were black. The small hours, he judged — well past midnight.

He sat up in the chair, his neck stiff, his senses sharpening. He was not sure what had woken him. The house was silent, no sounds came from the corridor beyond the door.

Then he heard it.

A low moan from the bed beside him. Isabel stirred beneath the blankets, her body tensing, her head turning sharply on the pillow. Her fingers clawed at the sheets.

"No." The word was ragged, torn from sleep. "No — let me go—"

Alexander rose from his chair and sat on the bed beside her, his hands finding her shoulders. "Isabel. Isabel, wake up. You are safe. You are home."

Her eyes flew open, wild and unseeing. She thrashed upright, her hands shoving against his chest, and for a terrible instant she fought him. Then recognition flooded her face and she collapsed forward against him, her arms wrapping around his neck, her cheek pressing hard against his shoulder.

"Alexander."

"I am here." He held her close, one hand cradling the back of her head, the other flat against her spine. He could feel her heart racing against his chest, fast and frantic. "It was a dream. Only a dream. You are safe."

She did not speak. She simply held on, her breath hot against his throat, her fingers gripping the collar of his shirt as though letting go would send her back to whatever dark place she had just escaped.

Alexander was acutely aware of her. He could feel the warmth of her body radiating through the thin cotton of her nightgown, registering every curve pressed against him as she clung to him. He breathed in the scent of lavender from her hair, felt the sheer softness of her beneath the palm he rested against her back. His body responded on its own accord, and he clenched his jaw and held himself still, willing the heat in his blood to subside. She was frightened, vulnerable, barely recovered. This was not the moment.

He held her until the trembling eased. Until her breathing slowed and the rigid tension in her body began to loosen. Drawing back from her cost him more than he cared to examine. He eased away just enough to see her face, and the loss of her warmth against his chest left a cold ache in its place.

Her eyes were open, luminous in the near-dark. Strands of hair had fallen across her cheek, and he reached up and brushed them aside, tucking them behind her ear. His fingers lingered at her temple, tracing the line of her jaw.

She turned her face into his palm.

The connection opened at his touch, and what he felt from her made his chest tighten. Her fear had vanished after the nightmare had released its grip, and what remained was a longing so raw and intense that it stole the air from his lungs. A need for closeness, for warmth, for him. She was looking at him and wanting him and making no effort to hide it, and through the bond he felt it pour into him, undiluted and fierce.

She knew that he could feel it. He saw the awareness in her eyes, the deliberate choice not to pull back.

He cradled her face in both hands, his thumbs tracing the line of her cheekbones, and lowered his mouth toward hers. He stopped an inch away. His breath was unsteady, his pulse hammering, and every fibre of his discipline was screaming at him to pull back, to be the man who exercised restraint, who did not take advantage of a vulnerable woman under his protection.

Then he felt the warmth of her hand settle at the back of his neck, the fraction of a pull, and with it came a wave of feeling so clear it needed no words.

She wanted this. Wanted him.

He closed the distance and kissed her.

The kiss was deep and slow, a surrender of two people who had come too close to losing each other. Her mouth opened beneath his, and the tenderness of her kiss broke something loose inside him that he had been holding in check for far too long.

Her hands moved to his chest, fingers spreading against the linen of his shirt, and he felt her touch like a brand. She was tentative, her palms tracing the shape of him through the fabric, and the hesitancy of it made his blood sing. When her fingers found the open collar of his shirt and brushed the bare skin of his throat, he drew a sharp breath against her mouth.

Through their connection, every sensation was doubled, reflected and returned. He could feel what his touch did to her as clearly as he felt her hands on his skin. It was a current that built on itself, amplifying each point of contact until the boundary between giving and receiving pleasure dissolved altogether.

His body was ahead of his mind, his desire rising so fast it frightened him. He pulled back, breathing hard, and searched her eyes. The restraint was fraying, and he could feel himself losing the fight.

"Isabel." His voice was rough. "If we do not stop now, I will not be able to turn back."

She held his gaze. "I don't want you to turn back."

He kissed her again, and this time there was nothing measured about it. His mouth found hers with a hunger that had been caged for weeks and was finally, irrevocably free. His hands moved as though released from chains, tracing the line of her throat, the curve of her shoulder beneath the thin cotton of her nightgown. She arched into his touch, a soft moan escaping her lips, and through the bond he felt exactly where she wanted him, the map of her desire drawn as clearly as any chart he had ever read.

He followed it.

His mouth found the hollow beneath her ear, and she gasped. His lips traced her collarbone, and she sighed. When his hand skimmed her waist and settled against the curve of her hip, she pressed closer, her body flush against his, and the sound she made was small and wanting and undid him entirely.

He eased the nightgown from her shoulders, slowly, giving her time to stop him. She did not stop him. She helped, pulling the fabric over her head and tossing it aside. He lowered her gently back against the pillows, and then she was bare before him, her skin pale in the fading candlelight, her dark hair spilling across the white linen, her violet eyes burning bright.

The word beautiful was insufficient to describe her. He had thought her striking the night of the auction, had called her beautiful at the ball, but those had been observations made from behind walls. Now, with every wall down and the connection wide open between them, he saw her truly, and the sight of her left him speechless.

He bent and kissed the pulse point at her throat. His mouth trailed lower, along the slope of her collarbone, down to the swell of her breast. He cupped her gently, his thumb brushing across the sensitive peak, and she arched into him with a gasp. He took her into his mouth, tasting her skin, feeling through the bond the sharp spike of pleasure that raced through her, and the echo of it sent heat flooding through his own veins. He lavished attention on one breast, then the other, until she was trembling beneath him.

His mouth continued its descent. He kissed the valley between her ribs, explored the soft curve of her stomach, lingered on the jut of her hip. When he settled between her thighs, she tensed for an instant, and he paused, lifting his eyes to hers. Their gazes held, and he felt her body ease beneath him, her trust flowing through the bond, warm and absolute.

He kissed her inner thigh. Then higher. And when his mouth finally found her centre, she cried out, her back lifting from the mattress, her fingers twisting in his hair. He explored her with his tongue, slow and deliberate, guided by the bond, following every tremor and shift of her body, every surge of sensation that flowed between them. When he found the rhythm that made her gasp his name, he held it, steady and relentless, until her body coiled tight and broke.

She came apart beneath him with a cry, her body arching, her hands fisting the sheets on either side of her. He felt her release echo through the connection, a wave of blinding sensation that crashed through him and left him shaking.

He kissed her through it, murmuring her name against her skin, until the tremors subsided and she lay breathless beneath him, her eyes heavy-lidded, her lips curved in a dazed smile that made his heart turn over.

He moved back up beside her, settling on his side, and she turned toward him at once, her hand finding his chest. Her fingers traced slow circles against the linen, then drifted to the top button of his shirt. She unfastened it, then the next, her eyes following her hands as though memorising the terrain. When the shirt fell open she pressed her palm flat against his bare chest, and the contact sent a jolt through the bond that made them both draw breath.

She pushed the fabric from his shoulders, and he shrugged it off. Her hands explored him, tentative and wondering. She traced along the line of his collarbone, down to the muscles of his arms, found the ridged scar on his right hand and forearm. When her fingers reached the waistband of his trousers, she hesitated, then met his eyes.

He covered her hand with his and helped her.

When the last of the fabric was tossed aside and they lay skin to skin, the connection deepened to a place he had not known existed. He could feel her heartbeat as though it were his own, could feel the warmth of her body not just where they touched but everywhere, as if the boundary between them had been erased.

He positioned himself above her, his weight braced on his arms, and kissed her slowly, deeply. Through the bond he sent her a question, giving her the final choice.

Her answer came back clear and warm.

He entered her slowly. She drew a sharp breath and her hands tightened on his shoulders, and through the connection he felt the briefest flash of discomfort followed by her determination to push past it. He stilled, giving her time to adjust, pressing kisses to her neck.

Then, deeper within the bond, he felt it. A truth she had not spoken aloud.

She had never done this before.

Alexander went rigid. The realisation struck him so hard he stopped breathing. He raised his head and looked down at her, and she met his gaze without flinching, though colour had risen high in her cheeks.

He stared at her, and alongside his shock came a surge of possessiveness that took him by surprise. She had kept this. Through twelve years of servitude, through every cruelty and degradation, she had guarded her innocence with everything she had.

And now she had given it to him.

"Isabel..." His voice was hoarse. "You... I did not know. I thought—"

"You thought wrong." Her voice was steady, though he could feel her heart hammering. "I told you I defended myself, Alexander. No man ever touched me. I made certain of that."

"Isabel, do you understand what this means? I have... in the eyes of society—"

"I don't care about society." Her hands cupped his face, holding him still, her violet eyes fierce. "I care about you. About this."

He searched her face for doubt, any sign that she was doing this out of obligation or gratitude. He found none. Through the connection, he felt only her desire and her trust and her absolute certainty that she had chosen exactly what she wanted.

He kissed her, long and deep, and began to move.

Slow at first, careful not to hurt her. He let the bond guide him, reading every silent signal until he could feel her pleasure building alongside his own. He paused when she gasped, deepened when she pressed closer, and when she whispered his name against his throat, he answered with his body.

The connection amplified everything. Each touch, each breath, each pulse of emotion reflected between them, building until the sensation was almost too much to bear. He felt her approaching the edge and held himself there with her, their bodies moving in synchrony.

She broke first, her back arching, his name torn from her lips, and the force of it swept through the bond and pulled him over with her. He buried his face against her neck and let go, and for one searing moment they were not two separate beings but one. Two hearts fused in a pleasure so intense it left no room for grief or fear.

Moments later, they lay tangled together, breathing hard, the sweat cooling on their skin. Alexander gathered her against his chest and pressed his lips to her hair.

He pulled the blankets over them both. She settled against him, her head on his chest, her arm across his waist, and within minutes her breathing had evened out into the deep, steady rhythm of sleep.

Alexander held her and watched the first pale light of morning creep through the cracks in the curtains.

He was not the same man who had walked into that auction house three weeks ago. That man had been a ghost, driven by vengeance, haunting his own life.

The woman sleeping in his arms had changed everything. She had walked right through every wall he had built and shown him that the bravest thing a broken man could do was let himself be held.

His eyes grew heavy. He tightened his arm around Isabel, felt her breathing against his chest, and followed her into sleep.

"I am a grown man, Vera. I don't need another cup of tea."

"You need rest, and you need to stop reaching for that decanter. Doctor's orders."

"The doctor said nothing about brandy."

"The doctor said no spirits for a month. I was there."

"You may have misheard."

"I have exceptional hearing, Damien. Drink your tea."

Alexander sat in the library's armchair by the fire, watching the exchange with a quiet contentment he would not have believed himself capable of a fortnight ago.

Damien was ensconced on the settee, a cushion propped behind his back and a blanket draped across his lap that he had tried to remove on three occasions and that Vera had replaced each time. He looked better than he had any right to, given the wound to his side that had kept him bedridden for the better part of a fortnight. The colour had returned to his face, and the sharp wit had never left, but he moved carefully, and Alexander noticed the way he braced himself against the armrest whenever he shifted position.

Vera perched on the corner of the settee, close enough to refill Damien's teacup whether he wanted her to or not. She had spent the first week of his recovery at his townhouse, refusing to leave despite Damien's protests and Alexander's concerns about propriety. When

Damien had finally been well enough to be brought to Whitmore Hall for the afternoon, Vera had supervised the transfer with eagle eyes.

"You are enjoying this," Damien said, glaring at his tea.

"Maybe a little," Vera admitted.

Alexander had noticed Damien watching Vera when she was not looking, his blue eyes tracking her every movement.

In the armchair beside him sat Isabel. She had her feet tucked beneath her, a cup of tea balanced on her knee, and she was watching Vera and Damien's performance with a faint, knowing smile. Her dark hair was loose tonight, falling past her shoulders in soft waves, the copper in it reflecting in the firelight.

He reached over and handed her a biscuit from the plate on the side table. Their fingers brushed, and she looked up at him, her smile widening by a fraction. He held her gaze for a moment, and the warmth that passed between them required no bond and no words.

It had been two weeks since the warehouse and the night that followed. A night that had changed everything, and Alexander could still scarcely believe the life he was living.

He had not left Isabel's side since that morning he had woken with her in his arms. She had recovered quickly from the projection's toll.

Their days had been spent side by side in the library, working through evidence, cross-referencing files, building a case that would hold up before the Crown. He had not let her out of his sight, and she had not seemed to mind.

And the nights. God, the nights.

He had spent eight years sleeping alone, dreaming about the faces of people he could not save. Now he fell asleep with Isabel's body warm against his and woke to the scent of lavender and the sound of her breathing, and the dreams did not come. For the first time in eight years, he slept through until morning.

During the days he found it almost impossible to keep his composure. The urge to reach for her was constant. All he wanted was to take her hand, find any excuse to be near her. The restraint required to conduct himself appropriately in front of the servants and visitors was considerable, and on more than one occasion he had caught himself contemplating carrying her off to his chamber in the middle of the afternoon.

He had not told Vera or Damien what had happened between them. But he suspected they knew.

"Alexander." Damien's voice pulled him back to the present. The viscount had abandoned his campaign for brandy and was looking at him with an expression that had shifted from playful to serious. "You were going to tell us about your plans."

Alexander straightened in his chair. "Yes. I have written to Crown Prince Finian."

The room grew quiet. Vera set down the teapot.

"The warehouse made one thing clear," Alexander continued. "I underestimated Delacroix. We all did. He anticipated our moves, staged an elaborate trap, and very nearly succeeded in taking Isabel. If we continue as we have been, the four of us against a marquis with influence and resources we cannot match, someone is going to get killed." He paused and looked at Damien. "Someone very nearly did."

Damien's jaw tightened, but he did not argue.

"I cannot carry this alone any longer," Alexander said. "We need the authority to search Darkwater Manor and seize whatever Delacroix is hiding there. That can only come from the Crown."

"And the prince has agreed to see you?" Vera asked, her eyes bright.

"He will be in Greyport shortly before Christmas for diplomatic engagements. He has granted me an audience. I intend to present everything we have gathered and petition for a warrant to search the marquis's estate."

Vera clasped her hands together. "The Crown Prince. Here in Greyport." A flush crept into her cheeks. "Will there be a formal reception? I should think so, for a royal visit. We shall need to prepare—"

"Vera." Alexander gave his sister a look.

Across the settee, Damien took a slow sip of his tea. His expression was blank, but Alexander caught the way his fingers tightened around the cup at Vera's enthusiasm for the prince's arrival.

"Until further notice," Alexander continued, "we cannot afford to act rashly. We still do not know what Delacroix is doing with the magic users he takes. The Harlows believed the warehouse delivery was genuine, which means shipments like it have happened before and will likely happen again. People are being held and used for purposes we have not yet uncovered."

"All the more reason to get that warrant," Isabel said quietly.

"Agreed. Which is why I am placing all my hope in the audience with the prince."

Damien set down his teacup. "For the time being, I think we have all earned some rest. Christmas is two weeks away. I propose we use the time to recover and prepare ourselves for whatever comes next."

"Damien is right," Alexander said and turned to his friend. "And I want you to know that I will not ask anything of you until you are fully recovered. You have done more than enough."

"Nonsense. I have barely begun." Damien waved the concern away. "But I will concede that a few more days of Vera's tyrannical nursing might not go amiss."

Vera beamed. "I am glad you are finally seeing reason."

"I am seeing no such thing. I am merely too weak to resist." He reached for the teapot himself this time and poured a fresh cup, wincing slightly at the stretch. "Though I must say, the eligible young ladies of Greyport will be bereft without me on the social circuit. I do hope they survive the deprivation."

"I'm sure they'll manage," Vera said sweetly. "Most of them had already given up hope."

"You wound me, Lady Vera."

"That is the surgeon's handiwork, not mine."

Isabel set down her teacup and rose from her chair. "If you will excuse me," she said. "It has been a lovely evening, but I think I shall retire."

Her eyes found Alexander's as she turned toward the door.

"Good night, Isabel," Vera said.

"Good night, Miss de Clare," Damien added. "I must say, your company has done more for my recovery than any tonic the surgeon prescribed."

"Then you shall have to visit more often," Isabel said, and smiled at him before slipping through the door.

Alexander let a reasonable interval pass. He finished his brandy, contributed a few more observations about the prince's visit, and then stood.

"I should retire as well. It has been a long day."

"Of course." Vera's expression was perfectly composed, though her eyes danced. "Good night, Alexander."

"Good night." He crossed to the door.

"Alexander."

He turned.

Damien was watching him from the settee, his teacup cradled in his hands.

"I am happy for you, my friend. I knew you would come to your senses eventually."

Alexander held his friend's gaze. A dozen responses came to mind, deflections and denials that had served him for years. He discarded them all.

"Thank you, Damien," he said instead.

He left the drawing room and climbed the stairs, his stride quickening with each step. The corridor was dim, the sconces burning low, and at the far end Isabel's door stood slightly ajar, a sliver of warm light spilling across the floorboards.

He pushed it open and stepped inside, pulling it shut behind him, and the woman waiting for him in the firelight smiled.

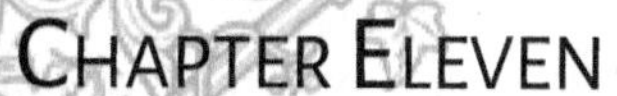

Chapter Eleven

Isabel woke to the warmth of Alexander's breath against the back of her neck, his arm draped across her waist, his chest pressed against her spine. She lay still for a moment, savouring the feeling of being held.

How quickly she had grown accustomed to this. Four weeks ago she had slept alone, as she had slept every night for twelve years, her walls up, her mind braced against the constant hum of other people's thoughts. Now she slept in his arms, wrapped in his silence, and the peace of it was so complete that waking felt like surfacing from the deepest, warmest water.

She turned in his embrace to look at him.

Alexander slept on his side, one arm folded beneath his head, the other still holding her. His dark hair fell across his brow, and his face in repose bore no resemblance to the one he wore during waking hours. The furrow between his brows had smoothed. The hard set of his jaw had softened. He looked young, she thought. He looked like the man he might have been if grief had not carved its marks so early and so deep.

But even during the days now, that heaviness was lifting. She could feel it through the connection whenever they touched, a slow unburdening, as though something that had been clenched inside him for eight years was gradually learning to let go. He smiled more. Laughed, even, at Damien's barbs and Vera's teasing. His grey eyes, once so guarded, now found hers across room and held them with an openness that flooded her chest with warmth.

He was coming back to life with her. Just as she was coming back to life with him.

The thought terrified her as much as it thrilled her.

Four weeks had passed since the warehouse. Since the night that had changed everything between them. Now, Christmas was less than a week away, and outside the window the December frost had painted the garden white.

Today was the day the Crown Prince would arrive in Greyport and pay his visit to Whitmore Hall. In a few hours, Alexander would present their case and petition for the authority to move against Delacroix. Everything they had worked toward came down to this.

And after that? After Delacroix was dealt with, after the papers were signed and her freedom granted? What then?

She knew what she wanted. She wanted this. Wanted him, and the family she had found within these walls.

But wanting and having were different things. She was a magic user. He was an earl. The law might grant her freedom, but it would never grant her equality. If Alexander married her, it would mean scandal, ostracism, the destruction of his political career. The council would turn on him. Everything he had built, every alliance he needed to continue the fight for magic user rights, would crumble.

She could not do that to him. Would not.

But she could not think about that today. Today she would live in this moment, in this bed, with this man whose heartbeat she could feel beneath her palm, and she would be selfish for a little while longer.

She let her fingers slide lightly across his chest. The steady rise and fall of his breathing shifted as she touched him.

She leaned up and brushed his lips gently with hers.

Through the bond, she felt his consciousness surface, rising from a deep sleep. A slow warmth spread through the connection, followed by awareness. Followed by pleasure.

Good morning.

She smiled as the thought arrived in her mind.

His eyes remained closed, but his mouth curved, and his arm tightened around her waist, drawing her closer. He lowered his head and found her lips.

She deepened the kiss, pressing herself against him, and felt his response through the bond before his body caught up. A surge of heat, a sharpening of focus, desire kindling in the space between sleep and waking.

His hand slid from her waist to her hip, then down to her thigh. She hooked her leg over his, pulling him closer, and felt his breath quicken against her mouth.

He pulled back just enough to look at her. His grey eyes were heavy-lidded, dark with want, and the smile on his lips was one she had come to know well in these four weeks. It was the smile that preceded the moments when restraint fell away and Alexander became someone only she had ever seen.

He rolled her onto her back and settled over her, his weight braced on his forearms, his mouth finding the hollow of her throat. She arched beneath him, her fingers sliding into his hair. He shifted his weight and with his free hand he skimmed her stomach, her ribs, the curve of her breast. He cupped her, his thumb circling, and the sensation echoed through the bond, doubling back on itself until she could not tell whose pleasure she was feeling.

She ran her hands down his back, feeling the muscles shift beneath his skin. He kissed her collarbone, the swell of her breast, drew the sensitive peak into his mouth, and she gasped, her hips rising to meet his.

"Alexander—"

He answered by shifting lower, his mouth tracing a path down her body that he had learned by heart over the past month but that never failed to undo her. He knew exactly where to linger, where to tease, where to press. The bond made him fluent in her body, and he used that fluency without mercy.

When his mouth reached the juncture of her thighs, she was already trembling. He parted her with his tongue and she cried out, one hand fisting in the sheets, the other gripping his shoulder. He worked her steadily, reading every flutter and shift through the connection, adjusting his rhythm to the crescendo building inside her.

She shattered with his name on her lips, her body convulsing, the pleasure so intense it whited out her vision. Through the bond she felt his own arousal spike at her release, fierce and urgent, and before the last tremors had subsided she was pulling him up, pulling him to her, wrapping her legs around his waist.

"Now," she whispered. "I want you now."

He entered her in one smooth stroke and they both groaned, the sensation amplified tenfold by the connection. He moved, and she moved with him, their rhythm instinctive, their bodies in a conversation that needed no words. She gripped his shoulders, her nails pressing into his skin, and he buried his face against her neck, his breath ragged, his hips driving into hers with a hunger that matched her own.

The bond blazed between them. She could feel his pleasure as her own, could feel the exact moment when his control began to fracture, and she leaned into it, sending her own desire flooding back through the connection.

He groaned her name, low and broken, and his rhythm faltered. She tightened around him, pulling him deeper, and they broke at the same moment, the climax crashing through them in a shared wave that left them both gasping, clinging to each other, trembling in the golden morning light.

For a long time afterward they lay tangled together, breathing hard, the sheets twisted around their legs. The sun had risen, pouring through the gap in the curtains and throwing a stripe of bright light across wall behind the bed. Isabel pressed her face against Alexander's chest and listened to his heartbeat slow.

"We should get up," she murmured.

"We should," he agreed, making no move to do so.

She smiled against his skin. "The Crown Prince—"

"Can wait."

"Alexander."

"Five more minutes."

A knock at the door.

Both of them froze.

"Isabel?" Vera's voice, bright and pointed, came through the wood. A deliberate clearing of her throat. "Isabel, I do hate to disturb you, but we have a great deal to prepare for the prince's reception, and my brother seems to have vanished. I have searched the drawing room, the library, and his study, and he is nowhere to be found." A pause, calibrated to perfection. "You wouldn't happen to have any idea where he might be?"

Isabel's cheeks blazed crimson. Beside her, Alexander was already out of bed, pulling on his trousers with one hand and reaching for his shirt with the other, his movements frantic and silent. He caught her eye and pressed a finger to his lips, and the absurdity of the Earl of Whitmore, Under-Secretary of State, creeping around her bedroom like an anxious stripling very nearly made her burst out laughing.

"I'm afraid I haven't seen him, Vera," Isabel called, biting the inside of her cheek. "But I will certainly help you look."

"How kind. I shall continue searching downstairs with the staff. Perhaps he has gone for an early walk."

Vera's footsteps retreated down the corridor, giving Alexander the chance to make his escape.

Isabel collapsed back against the pillows, a hand over her mouth, shaking with suppressed laughter. Alexander, half-dressed and thoroughly dishevelled, stood at the foot of the bed looking as flustered as she had ever seen him.

"That was not funny," he said.

"It was extremely funny."

"She knows."

"Of course she knows. She has known for weeks." Isabel sat up, grinning. "You will have to be quicker with your waistcoat if we are to keep up appearances."

He crossed back to the bed, leaned down, and kissed her, hard, deep, and thorough enough to make her head swim. When he pulled back, her grin had been replaced by something considerably more dazed.

"I will see you downstairs," he said, as he slipped through the door.

Isabel pressed her fingertips to her mouth and smiled. Then she rose and crossed to the wardrobe in search of a gown worthy of a prince.

They received him in the grand salon, a room Isabel had not seen used before.

It occupied the eastern wing of Whitmore Hall, its tall windows overlooking the frost-covered gardens, the walls hung with portraits of Kensington ancestors in gilded frames. Vera had spent the morning arranging fresh flowers and directing the staff to ensure that every surface gleamed.

Isabel stood beside Alexander near the fireplace, wearing the deep burgundy silk she had selected for the occasion. Vera occupied the settee, her posture perfect, her cheeks flushed with an excitement she was doing a poor job of concealing. Damien stood by the window, his hand resting lightly against his side where the wound was still tender, his expression pleasant but composed.

When the carriage arrived, they heard the commotion in the entrance hall before the doors opened: Hartley's formal welcome, the stamp of boots, followed by the murmur of an escort being dismissed.

Then Crown Prince Finian walked in, and Isabel understood immediately why Vera had spent two hours on her hair.

He was tall, broad-shouldered, and his presence filled the room in a way that left no question as to who held the authority within it. His hair was dark blond, cut short in the military fashion, and his features were striking: a strong jaw, high cheekbones, and warm brown eyes that crinkled at the corners as he smiled. He wore a simple but immaculately tailored coat of navy blue, a gold pin bearing the royal crest at his lapel, and no other adornment. He was, Isabel estimated, in his early thirties, and he looked every inch a future king.

"Lord Whitmore." The prince crossed the space and clasped Alexander's hand, his grip firm, his smile genuine. "It has been too long. I was glad to receive your letter, though I confess its contents troubled me."

"Your Royal Highness." Alexander inclined his head. "Thank you for coming. I know how demanding your schedule must be."

"Nonsense. When a man I respect asks for my time, he gets it." Finian turned to Vera and his smile broadened. "Lady Vera. What a pleasure to see you again. You look very well."

Vera dipped into a curtsy so graceful it might have been choreographed. "Your Royal Highness. Welcome to Whitmore Hall. May I say how honoured we are to receive you."

"The honour is mine, Lady Vera." He took her hand and bowed over it, and Vera's cheeks turned a shade of pink that Isabel had not seen on her before.

From the window, Damien watched the exchange. His expression remained pleasant. His thoughts did not. Isabel caught them clearly, surfacing unbidden, sharp with an emotion the viscount himself seemed determined not to acknowledge.

Very well... It seems those words are perfectly adequate after all, provided they come from a prince...

Isabel looked away, granting him the privacy he deserved.

"And Lord Daventry." Finian turned to Damien and offered his hand. "I was sorry to hear about your injury. I trust you are recovering well?"

"Tolerably, Your Royal Highness." Damien shook the prince's hand with his usual grace. "Though my nurse is rather more formidable than the surgeons." He cast a sideways glance at Vera that the prince did not appear to notice.

"Allow me to introduce Miss Isabel de Clare," Alexander said, stepping to Isabel's side. "She is assisting me with the investigation I mentioned in my letter. Her telepathic abilities and her contributions to our work have been invaluable."

Finian turned to Isabel. His brown eyes met hers, and she felt his gaze take her in with an attentiveness that missed neither the violet glow in her eyes, nor the burgundy silk she was wearing and the way she stood at Alexander's side.

"Miss de Clare." He bowed, a politeness he was under no obligation to extend to a magic user, and the gesture was so natural that Isabel found herself immediately warming to him. "Lord Whitmore speaks highly of you. I am delighted to make your acquaintance."

"The pleasure is mine, Your Royal Highness," she said and curtseyed in turn.

As she straightened, Isabel let herself brush the surface of his thoughts. What she found was remarkable focus. His mind was structured the way she imagined a well-run ship might be: every thought in its place, every impulse measured and controlled. It was a mind that had been trained from childhood to lead, disciplined by duty and a military education that had left its mark on every layer of his consciousness.

She found it oddly reassuring. In her experience, the most dangerous minds were the messy ones, full of dark corners where cruelty could easily hide. Finian's mind was the opposite, and he seemed to be genuinely concerned with the matters Alexander had brought to his attention.

She retreated from his thoughts and gave the prince a warm smile.

They settled into the salon. Hartley served tea and withdrew, and Alexander began to lay out their case.

He did so carefully. A marquis was not a man one accused lightly, and even with the prince's ear, Alexander weighed every word. He presented the evidence methodically: the pattern of disappearances, the auction, Delacroix's interest in Isabel, the warehouse operation, the link to Admiral Fallon and the naval gunpowder, the harbour fire.

The prince listened without interruption. He sat in the armchair across from Alexander, one ankle resting on his knee, his expression attentive and grave. Occasionally he asked a question. How many confirmed disappearances? What evidence connected the gunpowder to Fallon?

By the time Alexander had finished, Finian's expression had grown thoughtful.

"These are serious accusations, Lord Whitmore," he said at last. His voice was measured, his expression sombre. "Against a man of considerable rank and influence. I want you to know that I believe you. And I believe Miss de Clare." He inclined his head toward Isabel. "The account she has provided, the thoughts she has read, the threat the marquis made at the ball, I take all of it seriously."

"Thank you, Your Royal Highness," Alexander said.

"However." Finian paused, and Isabel saw the regret in his face before he spoke. "Without physical evidence, witnesses who can testify in open court, proof that can withstand legal scrutiny, my hands are tied. What you have is compelling, but it is circumstantial. The word of a magic user, however truthful, will not hold up before a magistrate. I do not say that to diminish Miss de Clare's testimony. I say it because I know the courts, and I know the men who sit in them."

Isabel could see Alexander's disappointment settle over him. While his posture remained straight and his expression composed, she noticed the way his hand tightened on the arm of his chair.

Vera, on the settee, pressed her lips together and looked down at her lap.

Damien alone seemed unsurprised. He leaned against the window frame, his arms folded, his expression attentive but resigned.

"I understand," Alexander said. "I had hoped that your authority might—"

"There is something I can do," Finian interrupted gently. He leaned forward, his elbows on his knees, his brown eyes earnest. "I am holding a reception here in Greyport on Christmas Eve. The usual, diplomatic affairs, council business." He paused. "I will have my own investigators look into the marquis. Discreetly. We cannot afford a scandal or a public accusation without proof, but a private enquiry, conducted by men loyal to the Crown, may uncover what you have been unable to reach."

Alexander straightened. "You would do that?"

"I would. And I will." Finian's expression was firm. "The reception is in three days. Come and join me on Christmas Eve. By then I should have my men's findings, and we can discuss how to proceed. If my investigators confirm what you have told me today, I will personally ensure that you have the authority you need to act."

Isabel saw the hope in Alexander's expression, his face bright after the initial disappointment, and she had to resist the urge to reach for his hand.

"Your Royal Highness, I am grateful," Alexander said. "More than I can express."

"You are fighting for justice, Lord Whitmore. For your family and for the people that have fallen victim to crimes no one else is willing to look into." Finian rose from his chair, and the others rose with him. "That is a fight I will always support."

He crossed to Alexander and gripped his shoulder. "Your parents would be proud of you, Alexander. I want you to know that. They were fine people, and their vision for a more just kingdom lives on in their son."

Alexander's throat worked. He nodded once.

The prince turned to Vera. "Lady Vera, thank you for your gracious hospitality. I look forward to seeing you at the reception."

"It would be our honour, Your Royal Highness."

Finian shook Damien's hand, wished him a swift recovery, and then turned to Isabel.

"Miss de Clare." He took her hand and bowed over it, the same courtesy he had shown on arrival. "It was a genuine pleasure. I have not forgotten my commitment to working with Lord Whitmore toward greater equality for magic users, and meeting you has only strengthened that resolve. I very much hope to see you at the reception."

"Thank you, Your Royal Highness. I will be there."

He held her gaze for a moment, then released her hand, nodded to Alexander, and made his way to the door, where Hartley waited to escort him to his carriage.

The front door closed. The sound of hooves on gravel faded into the December afternoon.

Vera exhaled. "Well. He is everything I remembered and more."

Damien said nothing. He crossed to the sideboard and poured himself a brandy, looking as though he had been counting the minutes until the prince departed.

Alexander turned to Isabel. "Christmas Eve," he said.

She took his hand and the connection opened. "Christmas Eve."

Christmas Eve arrived with frost on the windows and candles in every sill.

The Crown Prince's reception was held at Greyport's Royal Residence, a grand estate maintained by the Crown for occasions when royalty visited the city. The ballroom was magnificent. Vaulted ceilings bore celestial paintings that caught the light from enormous chandeliers dripping with crystal, and garlands of holly and ivy wound around every column. An orchestra played waltzes from a raised gallery, and the room was warmed by two great hearths blazing at either end, the air fragrant with mulled wine and pine.

Alexander stood near the entrance with Isabel on his arm, surveying the crowd. The room was filled with diplomats and naval officers, merchant lords and their wives. Half the peerage of Greyport seemed to be in attendance. He scanned the faces methodically, searching for the one he dreaded seeing.

Delacroix was not here. Nor, as far as Alexander could tell, were any of his known associates. The Marquis of Darkwater had, it seemed, chosen not to attend the Crown Prince's Christmas reception.

Alexander allowed himself a measure of relief.

He looked to Isabel at his side and felt the tension in his shoulders ease. She wore a gown of deep red velvet, the colour rich against her pale skin, her dark hair swept up and pinned with small gold combs. The sapphire pendant he had given her at the autumn ball rested at her throat. Her violet eyes were bright, and the smile she gave him was for him alone.

He offered her his hand. "Dance with me?"

Her smile widened. "I thought you'd never ask."

The music carried them across the floor, Isabel's hand warm in his, her body close, and for a few blissful minutes Alexander simply enjoyed dancing with the woman he loved on Christmas Eve.

Damien and Vera circulated nearby, moving through the crowd with their complementary skills. Vera charmed the wives and daughters, drawing out gossip and information with her natural warmth. Damien worked the men, trading quips over brandy and gathering intelligence disguised as small talk. They were good at this, both of them, and Alexander felt a surge of gratitude for the two people who had stood beside him through everything.

Halfway through the evening, the Crown Prince made his entrance to roaring applause. He wore the dark blue of the royal household, a gold sash across his chest, and drew every gaze in the room as he moved through the crowd. He greeted guests, shook hands, and eventually made his way toward their corner of the ballroom.

"Lady Vera." Finian bowed, his brown eyes warm. "Would you do me the honour of a dance?"

Vera's face lit up. "Your Royal Highness, I would be delighted."

He led her onto the floor, and Alexander watched his sister take the arm of a future king with a composure that utterly failed to conceal her elation.

Beside Alexander, Damien had gone still. He held a glass of champagne without drinking, his gaze fixed on Vera and the prince as they moved across the dance floor.

"She is enjoying herself," Alexander observed.

"Evidently." Damien's voice was clipped.

"You seem displeased."

"I am not displeased. I am merely observing that the prince is holding her rather closer than strictly required by a waltz."

Alexander raised an eyebrow. Damien took a sharp drink of his champagne, then set down the glass and crossed the floor to where a cluster of young debutantes stood chatting near the refreshment table. Within seconds he had charmed his way into their circle, his laughter bright and pointed, his attention conspicuously lavished on a pretty blonde in pale blue who blushed at every word he said.

The evening wore on pleasantly. Alexander danced with Isabel, exchanged words with several council members, and accepted a glass of mulled wine from a passing footman. Isabel stayed close, her hand on his arm, her presence a steady warmth at his side.

When the prince had completed his rounds of diplomatic conversations, toasts, and a brief address about the season and the kingdom's prosperity, he appeared at Alexander's elbow.

"Lord Whitmore. Might I have a word? In private?"

Alexander glanced at Isabel. She must have sensed his reluctance, because she gently squeezed his arm.

"Go," she said. "I will be perfectly fine here with Damien and Vera."

He hesitated a moment longer. Then he nodded, pressed her hand, and followed the prince through a side door into a private study. The room was wood-panelled and warm, a fire burning low in the grate, two armchairs drawn up before it. Finian gestured for Alexander to sit.

"My investigators have been busy," the prince began, settling into the opposite chair. "Much of what you told me has been corroborated. The pattern of disappearances is real. The link between Delacroix and several of the missing magic users is strongly suggested by the evidence, though not yet proven beyond doubt."

"And the shipments?"

"That is where it grows complicated." Finian leaned forward. "My men have confirmed that crates have been moving through the southern docks under false manifests, brokered through the Harlow brothers' shipping firm. The contents were never declared, and the destination records were falsified. But the trail leads through shipping routes that extend to the Free Isles and beyond. My investigators are currently tracking the vessels involved, but tracing where the shipments originated requires time."

Alexander leaned forward. "Then you have enough to—"

"Not yet." Finian raised a hand, his expression regretful. "I know this is not what you want to hear. We have a pattern. But we do not yet have proof that would hold up before a magistrate. If we move too soon, Delacroix will use his rank and his connections to bury us."

"How much time?"

"Weeks. Perhaps longer. These are international waters, and the merchants involved are not inclined to cooperate with royal enquiries." Finian met his gaze steadily. "I give you my word, Lord Whitmore, that I will not let this drop. My men will continue their work, and the moment they find what we need, I will act. But we must be patient."

Alexander sank back in his chair, unable to conceal his disappointment.

"I understand," he said. "And I am grateful. Thank you."

"You don't have to thank me. This is justice, and justice is my duty." Finian rose and clasped his shoulder. "Enjoy the evening, Lord Whitmore. It is Christmas. Allow yourself one night of peace."

They made their way back toward the ballroom. Alexander stepped through the doorway and scanned the crowd, searching for the dark hair and violet eyes that had become his true north.

He could not find her.

His gaze swept the room. She would stand out in any crowd. She was not in this one.

A cold weight settled in his chest.

He spotted Vera and Damien near the refreshment table, standing close together, their voices raised in what appeared to be an animated disagreement. He crossed the room, his stride quickening.

"Where is Isabel?"

They both turned. Vera's brow creased. "She was standing right beside me a moment ago. She said she suddenly felt hot."

"How long ago?"

"I don't — a few minutes, perhaps? Damien and I were discussing—"

"How long, Vera?"

"I don't know!" Vera's voice pitched higher, alarm bleeding through. "We were talking, and I turned around and she was gone. I assumed she had stepped out for fresh air."

Alexander turned to Damien. The viscount's face had gone pale.

"I didn't see her leave," Damien said. "I was—" He stopped, his jaw tightening. "I should have been watching."

Alexander was already moving. He pushed through the crowd toward the tall glass doors at the far end of the ballroom, Damien close behind him, Vera gathering her skirts and following. The doors were ajar, letting in a gust of cold December air.

Alexander stepped out onto the stone terrace. The night was clear and bitterly cold, the flagstones glazed with frost, the gardens beyond lay dark and still. Lanterns lined the balustrade, their flames guttering in the breeze.

The space was empty.

Alexander walked to the edge, gripped the stone railing and scanned the street below. The drive was quiet, carriages waiting in orderly rows, drivers huddled against the cold.

Then, at the far edge of his vision, a flicker of motion. A black carriage was rounding the corner at the end of the street. The horses were at a gallop, the driver whipping them hard, and the carriage swayed as it took the turn and disappeared from sight.

The blood drained from Alexander's face. His hands tightened on the railing until his knuckles went white, and the cold in his chest turned to dread.

"Alexander." Damien was beside him, hand on his shoulder. "What did you see?"

Alexander stared at the empty corner where the carriage had vanished. The street was quiet, illuminated only by the golden glow of the gaslamps.

"He has her."

Isabel woke to darkness, her head throbbing, a bitter taste coating her tongue.

Her mouth was dry, her tongue thick, and when she tried to move her arms, metal bit into her wrists. She blinked, willing her eyes to adjust, and gradually the blackness resolved into shapes. A half-spent torch, its flame ragged and low, flickered in a bracket outside the bars of her confined space, its weak glow barely reaching the far wall. But in the dim light she could make out rough stone walls and a low ceiling.

A cell. She was in a cell.

Isabel forced her breathing to slow and pieced together what she remembered. The last thing she could recall clearly was standing beside

Vera at the Crown Prince's reception, accepting a glass of mulled wine from a passing footman. She had never had mulled wine before. It had been stronger than she expected, but at the time she had attributed the sharp tang to the spices. Then she had suddenly grown hot, her skin flushing, the room swaying gently around her. She had stepped toward the terrace doors for air, and after that — nothing.

She looked down at her wrists. Heavy iron shackles were clamped tight around each forearm, their crude chains running to a ring bolted into the wall behind her. The iron pressed against her skin, and she could feel its undeniable effect, a dampening heaviness that settled over her gift like a wet blanket smothering a flame. Her telepathy was muted, reduced to a faint awareness of minds somewhere nearby but too distant and indistinct to read.

She tried to reach outward. Pushed against the iron's suppression, straining to feel beyond the walls of her cell. The effort sent pain lancing through her temples, and she gasped, sagging back against the cold stone.

Footsteps echoed from somewhere down the corridor, growing louder with each step, accompanied by the sharp tap of what sounded like metal against stone.

The Marquis of Darkwater appeared beyond the bars.

He looked immaculate, as always, wearing his customary black coat over a silver-grey waistcoat, and his pale blue eyes reflected the torchlight as he studied her. The silver-tipped cane in his hand looked oddly out of place against the rough stone floor of the dungeon, and Isabel found herself staring at it. He never seemed to go anywhere without it.

He regarded her through the bars, and his lips curved.

"Miss de Clare," he said smoothly. "Welcome to Darkwater Manor. I do apologise for the accommodations. They are temporary, I assure you."

"Alexander—"

His smile widened. "The earl will be most distressed to learn of your disappearance, I am sure. He is a compassionate man."

Isabel tested her shackles again, but the iron held firm.

"You should not exhaust yourself," Delacroix said, watching her struggle with clinical interest. "The iron will prevent you from projecting, and you will find that your considerable talents are, for the moment, perfectly contained."

"What do you want from me?" Isabel asked.

Delacroix tilted his head, as if surprised she had to ask. "What I have always wanted, Miss de Clare. Your gift. Your extraordinary, singular gift. I have spent twenty years assembling the finest magical specimens I can find, and you, a telepath who can not only read minds but project into them, are the crowning piece."

"I'm not a specimen."

"No. You are far more than that." His pale eyes softened, and for an instant Isabel caught a glimpse of genuine emotion beneath his coolness. Then he composed himself. "I have preparations to make. It should not take long. Tomorrow we should be ready for the procedure."

He turned to leave.

"Procedure," Isabel repeated. "What procedure?"

Delacroix paused at the edge of the torchlight. "All in good time, Miss de Clare. For now, I suggest you rest. You will need your strength."

He walked away, his footsteps and the steady tap of his cane receding down the corridor.

Isabel sat motionless, her back against the cold stone, her wrists aching beneath the iron. The torch beyond her bars swayed in the air the marquis had stirred, its flame shrinking, then recovering.

"He says that to all of them."

The voice, hoarse and scraped thin from disuse, came from the cell to her left. Isabel turned her head.

"He always tells them to rest." A pause. "None of us have rested since we arrived."

"Who are you?" Isabel asked.

"Sarah. I was a healer. Before."

Sarah. The maid Charlotte Campbell had lost. The young woman who had been lured by a charming older man with blue eyes.

"Sarah," Isabel said, rising from the cot she had woken up upon. The chains attached to her shackles rattled and pulled taut behind her as she crossed the small space to the barred iron door. "Your friend, Charlotte, she has been looking for you."

A sharp intake of breath echoed from the neighbouring cell, followed by a sound that might have been a sob.

"How long have you been here?" Isabel asked gently.

"Weeks. Months. I've lost count." Sarah's voice steadied. "There are nine of us. Ten, now, with you." She drew a breath. "Margaret is in the cell across from mine, she's a tide weaver. Silas is beside her, stone shaper. Dave is two cells down from you—"

"Dave is here?" Isabel's pulse quickened.

"Dave, can you hear me?" Sarah called softly down the corridor. "There's someone new. She knows your name."

After a moment of silence, a rough voice came from the dark, weary, as if drawn from sleep. "What?"

"Dave." Isabel pressed against the bars, straining toward the sound. "My name is Isabel de Clare. I am with Alexander Kensington. The Earl of Whitmore."

Another silence. Then: "Alexander sent you?"

"Not exactly. But he has been looking for you. And for Lena."

Dave made a sound that could have been a laugh or a cough. Sarah spoke again, her voice dropping. "He has a fever. It's been three days now. I've sent what healing I can through the iron, but it's nearly impossible. With the shackles blocking me and the distance between our cells..." She trailed off. "Some of the others are worse. I've tried to help them all, but I can barely reach anyone. And it doesn't matter much now anyway. He's taken most of it."

Isabel frowned. "Taken most of what?"

"My gift." Sarah's voice went flat. "That's what he does. That's what the procedure is. He has some kind of device, some technology. He straps you down and he... extracts it. Your magic. Pulls it out of you. I don't know how it works, only what it feels like." She paused. "It feels like having part of yourself torn out of you."

"Not all of them survive it," Dave said from down the corridor, his voice threadbare. "Some never come back from the laboratory. The ones who do are... less. Sarah used to be able to heal a broken bone from a distance. Now she can barely manage a bruise."

The horror of it settled over Isabel slowly, seeping into her bones. Delacroix was not merely collecting magic users. He was harvesting their abilities. Stripping them of the very thing that made them who they were.

But to what end?

"I will find a way to free us," Isabel said. "All of us. Alexander is looking for me right now. He will come."

"Don't." The voice from further down the corridor belonged to an older woman. Her tone was bitter and void of all hope. "Don't promise them things you cannot deliver. We have heard promises before. The marquis makes them too."

"I'm not the marquis."

"No. You are a woman in chains, in the same dungeon as the rest of us. Whatever rescue you think is coming, it's not."

Isabel pressed her lips together. She could feel the despair seeping in from the cells around her, the accumulated hopelessness of people who had been kept in darkness for months. Maybe longer.

"Listen to me," she said, and her voice carried more conviction than she felt. "The Earl of Whitmore knows what the marquis is doing. He has been investigating Delacroix for eight years. He has evidence. He has allies, including the Crown Prince himself. And he will not stop until he finds this place and everyone in it."

"Fine words," the old woman said. "Wake me when the door opens."

Silence fell across the depths of the dungeon.

"Isabel." Dave's voice sounded from the dark, barely audible. "Is Lena...?"

"She is alive," Isabel said. "She was brought to safety."

Dave let out a sigh of relief. He said nothing more, and after a moment Isabel heard him shift on his cot, and then only silence.

Footsteps echoed from the far end of the corridor. A guard rounded the corner, a stocky man with a truncheon at his belt and a face that bore no trace of conscience or kindness. He walked the length of the cells, peering in, and stopped at Isabel's.

She took several steps back, but kept her chin high, as his gaze moved over her slowly, lingering in places that made her skin crawl.

"So you're the one he's been so desperate to get his hands on," the guard said. "The mind reader." He leaned against the bars and grinned. "Enjoy your beauty sleep while you can, sweetheart. Once the marquis is done with you, the rest of us get a turn. If you survive, that is." He rapped his truncheon against the bars, making them ring. "Lights out. Any more chattering and I'll give you all something to cry about."

He unhooked the torch from its bracket and carried it with him as he left. The light faded as the man retreated down the corridor, leaving the dungeon in absolute darkness.

Isabel sat back on the narrow cot. The mattress beneath her was worn thin, the stone wall at her back cold and slick with moisture.

She was afraid. The fear sat in her stomach, cold and leaden, and she could not banish it with logic. She was chained in a dungeon, deprived of her abilities, surrounded by people who had given up hope, and the man who held her intended to do horrific things to her.

But she was also alive. And Alexander was out there. He would be looking for her already. She knew it as surely as she knew the sound of his heartbeat. He would tear all of Greyport apart if he had to.

He would find her.

Chapter Twelve

Alexander was halfway across the ballroom before Damien caught his arm.

"Alexander, stop. You cannot ride to Darkwater Manor in the dark, alone, with no plan—"

"Let go of me."

"Alex—"

He shook Damien off and kept moving, weaving through startled guests, making for the entrance hall. Vera was at his heels, her skirts gathered in both fists, her face white. The orchestra played on, oblivious. Couples waltzed beneath the painted ceiling as though the ground had not just fallen away beneath his feet.

Alexander reached the grand staircase and hurried down the steps. The front doors were thirty paces ahead...

"Lord Whitmore."

The voice carried an authority that bypassed thought and went straight to instinct. Alexander's stride broke. He turned.

Crown Prince Finian stood at the top of the staircase, flanked by two of his personal guard.

"Your Royal Highness, I do not have time—"

"I can see that." Finian descended and crossed to him. "Tell me what happened."

"Delacroix has taken Isabel. She stepped onto the terrace for fresh air, and now she is gone. I saw a black carriage leaving at speed. It was his. I am sure of it." Alexander's voice was ragged, his fingers raking through his hair in agitation. "I have to go after her. Now."

Finian studied his face. "Come with me. All three of you. Now."

"I do not have time for—"

"Lord Whitmore." The prince's voice dropped. "You will come with me, and you will hear what I have to say, and then if you still wish to ride into the night and get yourself killed, I will not stop you. But you will hear me first."

Alexander stared at him. Every second that passed was a second Isabel spent in Delacroix's hands. Every breath he drew was a breath she might be drawing in agony.

Vera grabbed his arm. "Alexander. Please."

He looked back toward the front doors. Thirty paces. He could be through them in seconds, on a horse in minutes. His whole body strained toward that exit.

But Finian's eyes held his, steady and unyielding, and somewhere beneath the roar of panic a quieter voice reminded him that the prince was right. A dead man could save no one.

Alexander turned from the doors and followed.

Finian led them through a private corridor to a study that appeared to be the prince's personal office. The room was lined with bookshelves, a massive oak desk dominating the centre, and the scent of burning pine drifted from the hearth. The Crown Prince closed the door behind them and turned to face Alexander.

"Darkwater Manor is an hour's hard ride on horseback. More than that by carriage. The road passes through open countryside with no cover and no settlements." Finian spoke crisply, laying out the facts. "If Delacroix anticipated this, and given the sophistication of his trap, we must assume he did, there will be men posted along that road. Riding out in the dark, in evening dress, with no escort and no weapons, is not courage, Lord Whitmore. It is suicide."

"I do not care."

"I know you don't. That is precisely why I am telling you." Finian moved closer, and his voice softened. "I can see what Miss de Clare means to you. I am not blind, and I am not a fool. But if you die on that road tonight, you cannot save her. And she will be lost."

Alexander pressed his knuckles against the desk and bowed his head, fighting for control. Deep from within him rose a fury so absolute it blurred his vision. The same fury he had felt in the alley behind the warehouse when Delacroix had dragged her toward that black carriage. The same desperation he had felt as a young man watching his parents' carriage burn, helpless and screaming, held back by Damien's arms. "What do you propose?" he asked through his teeth.

"At first light, I ride with you. Myself, and a company of my personal guard. Thirty men, armed and mounted." Finian braced his hands on the desk across from Alexander. "With the Crown at his door, the marquis will have no choice but to admit us. He cannot refuse a royal party. And once we are inside, we will find Miss de Clare and every other person he is holding, and we will bring them out."

"And if he has hurt her by then?"

"Then he will answer for it. To me. Personally." The prince's brown eyes held a hardness Alexander had not seen in them before.

Yet, every instinct screamed at him to run, to mount the nearest horse and ride until his horse dropped, to tear Darkwater Manor apart stone by stone until he found her.

"The prince is right, Alexander." Damien's voice came from behind him. "You will do Isabel no good dead in a ditch on the Darkwater road."

Alexander closed his eyes.

"First light," he said.

"First light," Finian confirmed. "I will have my men assembled and ready. We ride at dawn." He straightened from the desk. "In the meantime, I insist that all three of you remain here tonight. Guest chambers will be prepared for you. Lady Vera"—he turned to her with a gentle smile—"you will stay here, under the protection of my household guard, until we return."

Vera nodded, her composure barely held together. "Thank you, Your Royal Highness."

Finian turned to Damien. "Lord Daventry. Given your injury, I would advise you stay here as well. But if you insist on joining the company, I suggest you follow behind in a carriage rather than on horseback. The ride will be hard and fast, and I would not want to see your wound renewed."

Damien's jaw tightened. "I am perfectly capable of—"

"He is right, Damien," Alexander said. He turned to his friend, and the look on his face stopped the viscount's protest before it could form. "I need you whole, not bleeding from a reopened wound. Take the carriage. Follow behind with whatever additional men can be spared. I will have the Crown Prince himself and thirty armed riders at my side."

Damien held his gaze. The argument simmered behind his eyes, but eventually he exhaled and inclined his head. "As you wish."

Finian moved to the door. "I will send someone to show you to your chambers. Try to rest, if you can. You will need your strength tomorrow." He paused, his hand on the doorframe, and looked back at Alexander. "We will get her back, Lord Whitmore. I promise."

Then he was gone, his footsteps brisk down the corridor, already issuing orders to his staff.

Damien lowered himself carefully into the nearest chair, his hand pressed against his side. "I don't like this," he said. "The timing of it. Delacroix takes Isabel from the Crown Prince's own reception, under the noses of three hundred guests and a royal guard?"

"What are you saying?" Vera asked.

"I am saying that the marquis has been several steps ahead of us at every turn. The warehouse. The ball. Now this." Damien's blue eyes were troubled. "I have a feeling there is something we missed."

Alexander stared at the fire, his mind racing through scenarios and fears he could not voice.

"We will get her back," Vera said quietly. She moved to Alexander's side and took his hand. "You will find her, and you will bring her home."

They rode out at first light, and fate conspired against them from the start.

The December frost had turned the roads to ice, and the horses struggled for footing on the frozen ruts. Alexander rode at the head of the column, the Crown Prince beside him, thirty mounted guardsmen in royal blue strung out behind them in a double line.

The sky was low and grey, threatening snow, and the cold bit into every exposed inch of Alexander's skin, burning his face, his hands, the strip of throat between his collar and his jaw. He barely noticed. The cold inside him was worse.

They had been riding for twenty minutes when they reached the first obstacle.

A massive oak had fallen across the road, its trunk too wide to jump and its branches tangled into the hedgerows on both sides. The roots had torn free of the frozen earth, leaving a crater of dark soil and shattered ice.

"Bring axes," Finian ordered, and two of his men dismounted. It took fifteen minutes to hack through enough branches to create a passage. Fifteen minutes of standing still, of watching the grey sky lighten, of calculating how far ahead Delacroix was and what he might be doing to Isabel with every wasted second.

They pressed on.

A mile further, a second tree blocked the road. This one had been cut, not fallen. The saw marks were visible on the stump, pale and fresh against the dark wood.

"This was deliberate," Alexander said.

"Yes." Finian studied the obstruction, his expression grim. He turned to his captain. "Send two riders ahead to scout the road. I want to know what else is waiting for us before we ride into it."

The scouts returned ten minutes later, reporting a third blockage half a mile ahead and a washed-out section of road beyond that where someone had diverted a stream across the path. Finian ordered a detour through the fields, and the column picked its way across frozen pastureland, the horses' hooves breaking through the thin crust of ice into the mud beneath.

The journey that should have taken an hour took more than two.

When Darkwater Manor finally appeared on the horizon, Alexander understood why the marquis had chosen it as his home.

The estate sat atop a low rise, cutting a dark silhouette against the winter sky. It was less a manor and more a fortress. A medieval structure of blackened stone, its walls thick and high, buttressed at the corners with round towers capped in slate. A curtain wall enclosed the grounds, twelve feet tall and studded with iron brackets that had once held torches. The main gate was heavy oak, reinforced with iron bands, set into a stone archway and carved with the Darkwater family crest — a serpent coiled around a dagger.

No windows faced the approach. The walls presented nothing but blank, forbidding stone to anyone riding up the lane. The message was clear. This was a place built to keep people out.

Or to keep them in.

The column drew up before the gate. Alexander's horse stamped and blew, steam rising from its flanks.

"Open in the name of the Crown," Finian called, his voice carrying across the frozen air.

What followed was a long pause. Then the sound of bolts being drawn, and the gate swung inward. A man in butler's livery stood in the courtyard beyond, his expression one of polished bewilderment.

"Your Royal Highness." He bowed deeply. "What an unexpected honour. I fear you find us quite unprepared. His lordship is not at home."

"Where is he?" Alexander demanded, swinging down from his horse.

"Lord Darkwater has been at his townhouse in Greyport for the past week, my lord. Political engagements and social obligations. He is not expected back until the new year."

"That is a lie."

"Alexander." Finian dismounted and placed a hand on his arm. "Allow me." He turned to the butler. "We have reason to believe that persons are being held on these premises against their will. With your master absent, I trust you will have no objection to our conducting a search?"

The butler hesitated for the barest instant. "Of course not, Your Royal Highness. Darkwater Manor is at your disposal."

They spread out through the estate. Finian's men moved in pairs, searching methodically through every room. The manor's interior was cavernous and cold, furnished with the heavy, dark taste of old money. Faded hunting tapestries lined the walls, watched over by the hollow visors of armour standing sentinel in the shadows.

Alexander searched with a fury that soon turned into outright frenzy. He tore through drawing rooms, threw open wardrobe doors, descended into the wine cellar and overturned barrels. He checked the kitchens, the storerooms, the servants' quarters. He climbed to the towers and searched the upper floors, where unused bedchambers sat beneath dust sheets, their windows shuttered against the cold.

Nothing. No sign that anyone other than the skeleton staff of servants had occupied the manor in weeks.

An hour later, Finian found him in the great hall, standing before the enormous stone fireplace dominating the space, his hands braced against the mantel, his head bowed.

"Lord Whitmore." The prince's voice was gentle. "She is not here. My men have searched every inch of this place."

"She is here." Alexander's voice was raw. "He has hidden her. There must be cellars, underground passages, something we have not yet found."

"We asked the butler. The wine cellar is the only underground space, and we have already searched it."

"Then the butler is lying." Alexander turned to face the prince. "There must be more to this place. A structure this old, this fortified will have spaces that do not appear on any plan."

Finian studied him. "We have been here for hours. Every moment we spend searching empty rooms is a moment we could spend—"

"Give me five more minutes."

The prince hesitated, then nodded.

Alexander walked back through the corridors, forcing himself to slow down, to look with a strategist's eye instead of a desperate man's. He moved through the east wing, where the oldest part of the manor stood, its walls of rough-hewn stone predating the rest of the building by centuries. A long gallery connected the east tower to the main house, its walls hung with heavy tapestries depicting the Darkwater lineage.

He was halfway down the gallery when he stopped.

A large mirror hung at the far end, floor to ceiling, set in an ornate iron frame. It was a fine piece, clearly expensive, but it was wrong. Everything else in this part of the manor was medieval. The mirror was modern, its glass polished to a gleam, its frame worked in an elaborate pattern that did not match anything else in the room.

And there was a draught. The candle flames in the wall sconces on either side of the gallery leaned toward the mirror, drawn by a current of air that should not have been there.

Alexander crossed to the mirror and pressed his hand against the glass. Cold air seeped around the edges of the frame, a steady current that spoke of open space beyond.

"Lord Whitmore." Finian had followed him. "What is it? We should leave, there is no time to—"

Alexander gripped the iron frame and pulled.

The mirror swung outward on concealed hinges, revealing a narrow doorway cut into the stone wall. Beyond it, a spiral staircase descended into darkness, its steps worn smooth by years of use. Torches burned in brackets along the walls, recently lit, their flames flickering in the breeze.

"I knew she was here," Alexander said.

He did not wait. He plunged through the doorway and took the stairs three at a time, his boots ringing on the stone. Behind him he heard Finian call his name, heard the prince ordering his men forward, but the sounds were already fading as the staircase wound deeper beneath the manor.

The stairs ended in a corridor of rough stone walls with a low ceiling, the smell of damp earth and torch smoke filling the space. The passage split ahead of him. One branch led into unlit darkness, the other glowed faintly at its far end, and from that direction came sounds — the hum of machinery, a low metallic whine, and the muffled sounds of a voice he would have recognised anywhere.

Alexander broke into a sprint.

The heavy oak door burst inward when Alexander threw his shoulder against it.

The room beyond was large, circular, carved from the bedrock beneath the manor. Stone walls rose to a vaulted ceiling, and the space was lit by dozens of candles set into iron brackets. Shelves were lined with glass vessels, copper instruments, and leather-bound journals. Workbenches ran along the curved walls, cluttered with apparatus he did not recognise. He saw coils of wire, glass tubes filled with luminous liquid, and metallic devices that clicked and whirred.

And in the centre of the room stood a table. Iron. Bolted to the floor.

Isabel was strapped to it.

Leather restraints bound her wrists and ankles, and a device of metal and glass had been fitted over her head like a crown, its filaments pressing against her temples, connected by copper wires to a larger apparatus beside the table. Her eyes were open, wide with terror, and a strip of cloth had been forced between her teeth, gagging her.

Alexander shoved his pistol into the back of his waistband and ran to her, his hands reaching for the leather straps at her wrists.

The click of a hammer behind him made him freeze.

"I wouldn't do that, if I were you."

Alexander spun, reaching for the pistol at his back, but before he could draw and aim the marquis had already fired. The blast was deafening in the enclosed space, and the pistol was torn from his grip with a force that sent white-hot pain shrieking through his fingers. The gun clattered across the stone floor and disappeared beneath a workbench.

Delacroix stood ten paces away, his own pistol still smoking, his aim already adjusted to Alexander's chest.

"Well, well." The marquis's voice was smooth and unhurried. "It seems I have underestimated your determination, Lord Whitmore. Though I confess, I am not entirely surprised. A man in love is capable of extraordinary foolishness."

"Let her go."

"I think not. We were just about to begin." Delacroix turned to the apparatus and lifted the cane he held in his free hand. A circular socket sat fitted at the centre of the device, and Alexander recognised the shape of it at the same moment Delacroix lowered the crystal head into place. The cane locked into the socket with a soft click. The machine hummed to life, its pitch rising, and Isabel's body convulsed against the restraints. A muffled scream tore through the gag.

"No!" Alexander lunged forward.

Delacroix levelled the pistol at his head. "Another step and the next bullet finds you, Lord Whitmore."

Alexander stopped. His eyes moved from the pistol in Delacroix's hand, to Isabel, to the machine. The dark crystal head at its centre had begun to glow with a faint violet hue. The same colour as Isabel's eyes.

He reached for his shield. Felt it coil inside his chest, the same gathering pressure he had summoned at the warehouse. He hurled it outward in a burst, directing it at the marquis with every ounce of force he possessed.

Nothing happened.

Delacroix did not flinch. The crystal head in the machine flared briefly, and the marquis laughed.

"Did you think I would make the same mistake twice?" He gestured toward the apparatus, where the dark sphere pulsed with violet light. "After your little demonstration at the warehouse, I made certain improvements to my own shield, in both range and strength. Your parents' research once again proved most illuminating on that front. The very people who sought to protect magic users provided me with the tools to neutralise them." His pale eyes glittered. "There is a certain poetry in that, would you not agree?"

Alexander's stomach turned at the thought of his parents' life's work being twisted into a weapon.

Another muffled cry came from the table, and Alexander took a step toward Isabel. Delacroix's pistol barked again, the bullet striking the ground an inch from Alexander's boot, chips of stone spraying upward. Alexander threw himself behind the nearest workbench, glass shattering around him as he pressed his back against the wood.

"What are you doing to her?" he called out.

"What I have done to all of them." Delacroix's voice carried over the whine of the machine, tinged with ecstasy. "This machine extracts the magical ability from its host and stores it here." He pointed to the head of his cane. "Twenty years of work, Lord Whitmore. Twenty years of refining the procedure. And now it is finally complete. With Miss de Clare's projection I will at last be able to transfer every stored gift from this vessel into myself."

Another cry tore from the table, muffled by the gag, and Alexander slammed his fist against the workbench. "You are killing her!"

"A small sacrifice for the greater good." Delacroix did not even glance toward Isabel. "You see, a crystal can be taken, broken, or lost. It was always only meant as a temporary vessel. Miss de Clare's projection is the final key, the ability that will allow me to absorb what it holds. Not to wear these powers as a weapon, Lord Whitmore, but to become the weapon."

The man, it seemed, had lost his mind altogether.

Alexander's thoughts raced. He could not attack Delacroix directly, but perhaps he did not need to. Perhaps he could turn his shield to its true purpose, use it as a defence. Extend it to Isabel and use it to protect her from the machine.

He closed his eyes. Shut out the fear and the fury. Reached for the place inside his chest where his shield lived, coiled and waiting. This time he did not hurl it outward in a burst. He shaped it, slowly projecting it across the room toward Isabel in a sphere of protective energy, silent and invisible.

The moment it reached her, the connection blazed to life.

He felt her pain, sharp and blinding, and a fear that went beyond terror. But underneath he found the essence of her, that fierce and stubborn core that was Isabel de Clare.

I am here, he sent through the bond. *Hold on. I have you. You are going to be all right.*

The response came faint and trembling, but unmistakable. *Alexander.*

The shield wrapped around her, and through the connection he felt the machine's grip on her begin to weaken. The extraction was still running, but his shield was interfering with it, disrupting the flow between her mind and the device.

He needed to keep Delacroix talking. Needed time for the shield to do its work, time for Finian's men to reach them.

"Even if you succeed," Alexander called from behind the workbench, "even if you absorb every gift in that pendant, what then? You cannot hunt every magic user on earth alone."

"I will not be alone, Lord Whitmore. You would be surprised how many share my convictions. Men of influence who understand the threat and are willing to act. With the abilities I have gathered, I will be able to create others like me. Train them. Arm them. And together we will seek out every last carrier of the gift." He began to pace, the pistol still trained on Alexander's position. "With Miss de Clare's telepathy woven into me, I will be able to look into any mind and detect the dormant gift before it manifests. Your parents' research revealed a truth that no one wanted to face: the gift does not die. It sleeps in bloodlines for generations and resurfaces without warning. Eradicating the magic users who walk among us today is futile. Every family on this earth is a potential source. Every child born could carry the seed."

"Then you will never reach your goal," Alexander said. "You cannot eradicate what lives on in the blood of every person on earth."

"I can, if I live long enough." Delacroix's voice was calm, almost serene. "That is where individuals like your friend Dave and the healer Sarah prove so useful. With the ability to heal myself and an endless supply of life force at my disposal, I will never die. I will have centuries to finish what I started, and I will not rest until the gift is gone from this world forever."

"Why?" Alexander pressed. "Why this hatred? What did magic users ever do to you that could justify all of this?"

Delacroix's footsteps stopped, and when he spoke again, his voice had changed. The smooth, cultivated composure had cracked, and what remained was grief laid bare.

"I had a wife, Lord Whitmore. Catherine. And a daughter. Eloise. She was seven years old. She had her mother's eyes and her laugh, and she used to fall asleep with her hand in mine."

Alexander listened, his back pressed against the workbench, his shield still flowing silently toward Isabel.

"We were at the Midsummer Fair. There was a boy in the crowd. An elemental. Unregistered, unstable. A merchant at one of the stalls had refused to pay him for a day's work, and the boy lost control. The fire spread through the market in seconds." Delacroix drew a ragged breath. "Catherine shielded Eloise with her body. They found them together. The boy survived. My wife and daughter did not."

The laboratory fell silent except for the hum of the machine.

"I stood at their graves and I swore that no magic user would ever have the power to do that again. Not to another wife. Not to another daughter. Not to anyone."

"It was a tragedy," Alexander said. "A terrible, senseless tragedy. But what you are doing is worse. You are imprisoning people, stripping them of their very essence, probably killing them in the process. You have not prevented a single tragedy, Delacroix. You have manufactured dozens."

"Do not patronise me, Lord Whitmore." The pistol's hammer clicked as Delacroix cocked it.

A change in the hum of the machine made Delacroix turn his head. The violet glow of the crystal had faded to nothing. He strode toward the machine, checking the connections, then his gaze snapped back to Alexander.

"How fascinating," he murmured. "Your shield. You are interfering with the transfer." He raised the pistol and levelled it at the workbench.

"Then I will simply have to remove you from the equation. A shame. Your ability would have been a worthy addition."

He advanced. Alexander braced himself.

A shot rang out.

Delacroix staggered. His eyes went wide. He turned slowly toward the doorway, where Crown Prince Finian stood on the threshold, flanked by two of his guardsmen, a smoking pistol in his outstretched hand.

"You?" Delacroix whispered. His face was a mask of disbelief. "But you — I thought—"

A second bullet was fired and struck him between the eyes.

The Marquis of Darkwater swayed on his feet, the pistol slipping from his fingers, and crumpled to the stone floor.

Alexander stared at the body, then at the prince. Finian lowered his pistol and met his eyes.

"Lord Whitmore. Are you alright? I am sorry it took us so long. We encountered Delacroix's guards on the upper level and had to fight through them."

Alexander did not answer. He crossed the laboratory in three strides, seized the cane where it stood locked into the apparatus, and wrenched it free. The machine gave a dying whine as he swung the cane down against the stone floor. The crystal head shattered on impact, and a thin vapour curled up through the broken fragments and dissolved into the cold air.

He dropped the ruined cane and turned to Isabel. Finian appeared at his side as he unbuckled the restraints around her feet and wrists with shaking hands. He pulled the gag from her mouth, eased the metal device from her head with trembling fingers, and gathered her into his arms.

She was limp, her skin ashen, her breathing shallow. But she was alive. He could feel her heartbeat against his chest, faint and rapid, and through the bond that he had been holding open, he felt the dim flicker of her consciousness.

Her eyes opened. The violet glow in them was barely there, a thin ring of colour in eyes that were mostly dark.

"Alexander...?" Her voice was so faint he could barely hear it.

"I am here. You are safe." He pressed his lips to her forehead. "It is over."

Her eyes closed, and she went still in his arms.

"Bring her upstairs," Finian said beside him. "Lord Daventry should be arriving with the carriage any moment. Take her back to Greyport. Go see a physician immediately."

"What about the others?" Alexander asked, his voice hoarse.

"We found them. There are cells down here. My men are working on the doors as we speak." Finian's expression was sombre. "We will get them out, Lord Whitmore. Every last one of them. I will see to it personally. Now go. Take care of her."

Alexander carried Isabel through the laboratory, past the body of the marquis, past the work benches and journals. He climbed the spiral staircase, his lungs burning, his legs unsteady, and emerged into the grey December light of the gallery above.

In the great hall, Finian's guardsmen held Delacroix's staff at gunpoint. The butler, two footmen, a handful of maids and a dozen armed guards who had been subdued in the fighting. The front doors burst open and Damien rushed through the entrance, his face white as he saw Alexander with Isabel limp in his arms.

"Is she alive?"

"Yes."

"And Delacroix?"

"He will not be a problem any longer."

Damien searched Alexander's face, then nodded once. He helped his friend carry Isabel down the steps to the carriage that waited outside.

They lifted her inside together. Alexander settled her across his lap, her head cradled against his shoulder, his arms wrapped around her. Damien swung up opposite and rapped on the ceiling.

"Go," he told the driver. "Greyport. As fast as you can."

The carriage jerked into motion, and behind them, the dark walls of the manor began to fade in the winter mist.

The first days of January brought snow to Greyport, a soft, persistent fall that blanketed the rooftops and quieted the streets. Isabel watched it from the window of the grand salon.

She was still recovering. Her body had not yet forgiven what Delacroix's machine had done to it, and there were mornings when the ache behind her eyes was so fierce she could barely open them. Her telepathy had returned in full. The destruction of the crystal head had released whatever energy had been bound within it, and the abilities of every magic user the marquis had taken had flooded back to their rightful owners. But the process of extraction had left bruises on her mind that would take time to heal.

Alexander had not left her side. He had carried her from Darkwater Manor to the carriage, had held her through the ride to Greyport, had sat beside her bed while the physician examined her and declared her battered but whole. He had been there every morning when she woke and every evening when she fell asleep, and the steadiness of his presence was as much a part of her recovery as the medicine and all the rest.

Now she sat in the armchair nearest the fire, a blanket across her lap despite her protests that she was perfectly well. The salon was bright with winter light and the scent of the pine boughs Vera had arranged along the mantelpiece for the season.

Alexander stood beside her chair, his hand resting on its back. Vera occupied the settee, her pose impeccable as always. Damien sat beside her, his posture much improved, looking almost like himself again.

They were expecting the Crown Prince.

Finian arrived at half past ten, as announced, dressed in travelling clothes. He would be departing for the capital today, and this was his final visit before the journey.

Hartley showed him in, and the prince greeted each of them in turn.

"Miss de Clare. You look considerably better than when I last saw you," he said.

"I feel considerably better, Your Royal Highness. Thank you."

"I am glad to hear it." He settled into the chair Hartley had positioned for him and accepted a cup of tea. "Now then. Lord Whitmore. Tell me how things stand."

Alexander stepped forward, his hands clasped behind his back. "The shelter in the Warrens has been restored and expanded. All magic users recovered from Darkwater are being housed and cared for there. We have a physician in residence, and those who were in the worst condition are being monitored around the clock."

"Excellent." Finian set down his teacup. "My men completed their search of Darkwater Manor last week. The marquis's records have been seized and catalogued. There is more than enough evidence to confirm the full scope of his activities. The documentation will be archived and presented to the council in due course." He turned to Isabel. "And Miss de Clare, have your abilities returned?"

"In full, Your Royal Highness. The destruction of the crystal seems to have released them. All of us have our gifts back."

"How fascinating," the prince said.

Isabel frowned, but before she could say why, Finian was already moving on.

"Well," he said, rising from his chair, "I must take my leave. The road to the capital is long, and I have a mountain of paperwork waiting for me that will not sort itself. This entire affair has generated more administrative correspondence than a minor war."

Alexander stepped forward. "Your Royal Highness. I cannot thank you enough for everything you have done. Without your support, without your presence at Darkwater—"

"You would have found a way, Lord Whitmore. Of that I have no doubt." Finian clasped his hand. "But I am glad I could be of service." He held Alexander's gaze for a moment. "There is one more thing I wish to say before I go." His tone shifted. "I understand that you and Miss de Clare care for each other. I would have to be blind to miss it, and I am many things, but blind is not among them."

Isabel felt heat rise to her cheeks.

"I want you both to know," Finian continued in Isabel's direction, "that while the current law does not yet grant magic users full equality of status, I am working to change that. In the meantime, the rights of freed magic users are clear. They are no longer property, they may live freely, and they may marry whomever they choose. The rest is a matter of societal opinion." He paused and met Alexander's eyes. "And in my experience, societal opinion tends to fall in line when the Crown makes its position known. There will always be those who condemn. But if we want this world to change, someone has to take the first step. And I can think of no better man to take it."

Alexander drew a breath. "Thank you, Your Royal Highness. That means more than I can express."

Finian placed his hand on Alexander's shoulder and gripped it firmly. "Goodbye for now, my friend. You will have to pay me a visit at the capital soon. I expect a full account of how things progress in Greyport." He released Alexander's shoulder and turned. "Lady Vera. Lord Daventry. It has been a pleasure."

Vera rose and curtsied, her grey eyes bright with emotion. "Your Royal Highness. We are so grateful."

"The gratitude is mine, Lady Vera."

The prince bowed, collected his coat from Hartley, and walked to the door. He paused on the threshold, looked back at Isabel one last time, and gave her a nod that was equal parts farewell and acknowledgement.

Then he was gone.

The front door closed, and soon after, the sound of his departing carriage faded into the snow-muffled streets.

Vera sank back onto the settee, her composure dissolving into sadness as she watched the prince ride away through the window. "Well, that is that," she said softly. "I think he scarcely even noticed the new gown I had made to match his colours."

"You look lovely today, Vera," Damien said quietly. "Every bit worthy of receiving royalty."

She glanced up at him, surprised. "Are you feeling quite well, Damien? That sounded dangerously close to a genuine compliment."

"A momentary lapse. It won't happen again."

"I thought so."

She turned back to the window, missing entirely the look on Damien's face.

Alexander came to stand beside Isabel's chair.

"Now," he said. "There is only one thing left to do."

He moved to stand before her. From the inside pocket of his coat, he withdrew a folded document, its edges crisp, a wax seal pressed into the lower corner. He held it out to her.

Isabel looked at the document. She knew what it was without opening it. She had dreamed about this moment, longed for it for over twelve years.

She took the papers and opened the seal.

Be it known that the magic user identified as Isabel de Clare, designated as Telepath, is hereby released from bondage under the Protection of the Realm Act, Section 7, Clause 3: Voluntary Manumission by Master. Said individual is granted permission to exist freely within the kingdom's borders, subject to all restrictions and limitations prescribed by law for persons of magical designation.

Her vision blurred. She blinked hard, pressing her lips together, and the words swam back into focus.

"You are free, Isabel," Alexander said, and she could hear the tremor in his voice. "Free to go wherever you please. Though I hope..." He paused and sank to one knee.

Behind them, Vera gasped, and Damien went still.

"I hope you will choose to stay. Because I love you, Isabel. I will love you until the end of my days."

He reached into his pocket and drew out a small velvet box to reveal a ring of filigree gold, its sapphire the exact shade of the pendant he had given her the night of the autumn ball.

"Isabel de Clare, will you marry me?"

The tears she had been fighting back for so long finally spilled over and ran down her cheeks. The first tears she had shed in twelve years, and she did not even try to stop them.

"Yes," she said. "Yes, a thousand times yes."

Alexander's face broke into a smile so wide that it wholly transformed him. He rose, pulled her from the chair, and kissed her. She wrapped her arms around his neck and kissed him back, and through the bond she felt his joy crash into hers, vast and overwhelming.

Behind them, Vera let out a sound that was half laugh and half sob. She seized Damien's hand, pulling him toward her in her excitement, and kissed him on the cheek. Damien froze, his blue eyes wide, one hand raised halfway to his face where her lips had been.

Vera, oblivious, had already released him and was rushing toward Isabel with her arms outstretched.

"I knew it!" she cried, pulling Isabel into a fierce embrace. "Oh, Isabel. I am going to have a sister."

Then Alexander drew her gently back into his arms, and Vera stepped aside, wiping her eyes.

Isabel pressed her face against Alexander's chest and held on.

She was free. She was home. And for the first time in twelve years, belonging to someone was exactly what she wanted.

Epilogue

The wedding was held on the first day of spring, when the gardens of Whitmore Hall were flush with snowdrops and the air carried the faint, green promise of warmer days ahead.

Isabel wore white silk and a crown of fresh violets that Vera had woven for her that morning, and Alexander wore an expression that Damien later described as "utterly besotted and making no effort whatsoever to hide it."

The ceremony was small. Vera had wanted grand. Alexander had wanted private. Isabel had wanted both of them to stop arguing about it. They compromised on forty guests, an afternoon reception in the gardens, and a string quartet that Vera had hired over Alexander's protests and which, he admitted afterward, had been an excellent decision.

Dave and Lena stood together near the rose arbour, his arm around her shoulders, her head tilted against his chest. They looked well. Dave had filled out again, the gaunt hollows of the dungeon replaced by steady meals and fresh air and the particular nourishment of having the woman he loved back at his side. Alexander had sent for Lena at his first opportunity after Delacroix was defeated and Dave freed, and when she had stepped off the ship at Greyport harbour three weeks later, Dave had been waiting on the quay. With Delacroix's involvement in the harbour fire exposed and the gunpowder traced back to his operation, all charges against Lena had been dropped. She was the only guest without a coat, Isabel noticed, standing in the crisp spring air in nothing but her dress, perfectly comfortable.

Isabel and Alexander found them between dances.

"Lady Whitmore," Dave said, and bowed with a formality that was instantly ruined by his grin. "Congratulations."

"Thank you, Dave. It's good to see you on your feet."

Lena embraced her, fierce and brief. "Thank you," she said. "For what you did. For all of them. For Dave."

"You should thank my husband for that," Isabel said, glancing at Alexander. "He was devoted to our cause long before I arrived."

"And I intend to continue," Alexander said. "The shelter has resumed its operations and expanded its capacity. Dave, if you are willing, I would like you to keep running it."

Dave's eyes brightened. "It would be my honour, my lord."

Lena turned to Alexander. "There is one more person I owe my thanks to. If not for Captain Raines, I would never have made it out of that prison. Is he here?"

Alexander shook his head. "We have not heard from him since he sailed for the Serpent's Passage. But Dominic Raines is not a man who disappears quietly. When he surfaces, I will make sure to pass on your gratitude."

The quartet struck up a waltz, and the guests drifted toward the lawn where a wooden floor had been laid between the hedgerows. Vera appeared at the edge of the crowd, radiant in pale green, and seized Damien's hand before he could protest.

"You owe me a dance, Lord Daventry. You have been avoiding me all afternoon."

"I have been recovering from your last assault on my feet."

"Your feet are fine. Come."

She pulled him onto the floor, and he went, grumbling, his hand finding her waist with an ease that suggested his reluctance was purely performed. They moved together well, and as the music carried them across the floor, Isabel watched Damien's expression shift from theatrical suffering to something quieter and far more honest.

A wisp of his thoughts drifted toward her as he leaned down to whisper something in Vera's ear, and Isabel caught just enough to make her smile before she turned her attention away and let the moment belong to them. Vera laughed, bright and genuine, as she looked up at him.

"Shall we?" Alexander's voice came from beside her, his hand extended, his grey eyes warm.

She took it. The connection opened, and the silence wrapped around her, vast and familiar and full of him.

He led her onto the dance floor, and as they moved together in the spring sunlight, he sent a word through their bond.

Safe.

She smiled, leaned into him, and sent one back.

Home.

— THE END —

Enjoyed Silent Heart?

Thank you so much for reading. As an independent author, I don't have a big marketing machine behind me—I have you.

If you enjoyed this story, please consider leaving a short review. It takes only a minute, but it makes a huge difference in helping other readers find this world.

Thank you for your support! ♥

Leave a review on Amazon:

Leave a review on Goodreads:

A Brief History of Elthera

Long ago, magic flowed freely through the Kingdom of Elthera. Those born with gifts—fire starters, healers, storm callers, and others—were valued members of society, serving as advisors, protectors, and pillars of their communities.

But magic does not breed true. Over generations, the gifts became rarer, skipping bloodlines, appearing unpredictably. What was once common became exceptional, and what was exceptional became envied. Fear followed envy, as it so often does.

The Church spoke first against the gifted, declaring their abilities unholy. The common people, already uneasy, found permission for their fear in holy doctrine. The witch hunts began.

It was a dark time. Magic users were burned, drowned, hanged. Entire families fled to the wild Northern Reaches or sought refuge in the Western Planes, where the Fae held sway. Those who remained in the Eastern Territories lived in hiding or died in flames.

In 1742, King Edmund IV faced a choice: allow the extermination to continue, or find another way. His solution pleased no one and satisfied no one. The Containment Decree declared magic users less than human—property to be owned, controlled, and contained. They would not be killed, but neither would they be free. Assigned to noble families as servants and slaves, they became assets to be registered, traded, and inherited—their abilities monitored, their powers used only at their master's command.

For over a century, this was the law of the land.

Then came the Protection of the Realm Act of 1847. King Eldric VII, the present monarch, found the old ways barbaric. Under his reform, magic users were recognized as human once more. Masters could grant freedom. Harassment of the freed became punishable by law.

But freedom, as many discovered, is not the same as equality.

Freed magic users, by law, can neither own property, nor run businesses, nor testify against their betters in court. They are human in name, but not in right. Many choose to remain in service—at least a noble household offers food and shelter, a measure of protection. Those who venture out alone often struggle to survive.

The faint glow in their eyes marks them—an ethereal shimmer that brightens when their power stirs. The slurs follow: Demons. Cursed. Devil-touched.

Twelve years after the Reform, tensions simmer beneath Elthera's polished surface. There are whispers of magic users disappearing without explanation. The old envy stirs once more, and there are those who seek to claim by force what nature did not grant them. And in the shadows of Greyport's Warrens, small acts of resistance flicker like candle flames against the dark.

The law may have changed.

The hatred has not.

Magic Users of Elthera

Elementalists
Those who manipulate matter

Fire Starter — Wields flame, immune to burning and cold
Storm Caller — Controls weather, wind, and lightning
Stone Shaper — Mends and manipulates stone and crystal
Tide Weaver — Commands water in all its forms

Mentalists
Those who manipulate mind and energy

Telepath — Reads thoughts and emotions
Shield — Immune against magical interference
Life Force Enhancer — Transfers vital life force energy
Healer — Mends wounds and cures ailments

And others, rarer still

About the Author

Kaelis Knight's love affair with romance began at thirteen, when she discovered her mother's collection of paperbacks and devoured them in secret. That summer ignited a passion that never faded — guiding her first to a career translating romance novels for a major publisher, and eventually to writing stories of her own.

After years of carefully shaping other authors' words into new languages, Kaelis found that her own characters had begun to whisper. Her own worlds demanded to be built. Her own love stories refused to stay quiet.

Now she writes gaslamp fantasy romance — stories set in worlds of Victorian elegance and forbidden magic, where love builds slowly and burns bright. She writes for readers who stay up too late turning pages, and for everyone who believes that love is the most powerful magic of all.

When she isn't writing, Kaelis enjoys playing guitar, painting, and losing herself in a good book.

Visit **kaelisknight.com** for more.

www.ingramcontent.com/pod-product-compliance
Lightning Source LLC
LaVergne TN
LVHW091039080826
845145LV00002B/550

* 9 7 8 1 7 6 4 4 6 9 4 3 2 *